TURNER PICTURES PRESENTS

A JOHN FRANKENHEIMER/DAVID W. RINTELS FILM

"ANDERSONVILLE"

JARROD EMICK FREDERIC FORREST TED MARCOUX

CLIFF DE YOUNG JAN TRISKA

CASTING BY MARSHA KLEINMAN, C.S.A. MUSIC BY GARY CHANG

COSUTME DESIGNER MAY ROUTH EDITED BY PAUL RUBELL, A.C.E.

PRODUCTION DESIGNER MICHAEL Z. HANAN

DIRECTOR OF PHOTOGRAPHY RIC WAITE, A.S.C.

CO-PRODUCER DIANE SMITH

EXECUTIVE PRODUCERS ETHEL WINANT JOHN FRANKENHEIMER

WRITTEN AND PRODUCED BY DAVID W. RINTELS

DIRECTED BY JOHN FRANKENHEIMER

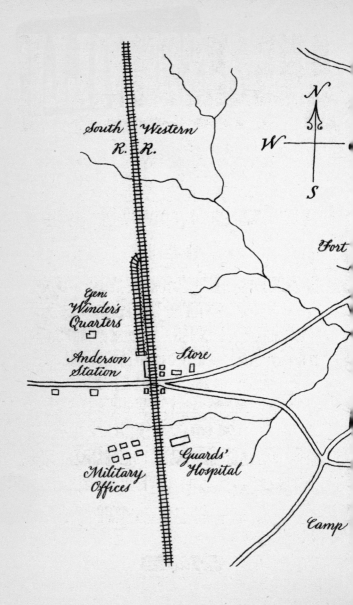

Fort

Stockade

Dead line

North
Gate

Main Street

Bakery

Creek

Sinks

Swamp

Dead
House

Gallows

South
Gate

Dead line

Stockade

Outer Stockade

Fort

Hospital

ANDERSONVILLE

ROBERT VAUGHAN
based on the screenplay by David W. Rintels

BOULEVARD BOOKS, NEW YORK

ANDERSONVILLE

A Boulevard Book / published by arrangement with
Turner Pictures

PRINTING HISTORY
Boulevard edition / March 1996

The Putnam Berkley World Wide Web site address is
http://www.berkley.com

ISBN: 1-57297-147-9

BOULEVARD
Boulevard Books are published by The Berkley Publishing Group,
200 Madison Avenue, New York, New York 10016.
BOULEVARD and its logo are trademarks
belonging to Berkley Publishing Corporation

PRINTED IN THE UNITED STATES OF AMERICA

10 9 8 7 6 5 4 3 2 1

Chapter 1

The red and white signal flag atop the signal tower fluttered brightly against a clear blue sky. A cannon shell, launched by a Confederate Napoleon gun some three thousand yards distant, rushed in, sounding like a disconnected freight car rolling rapidly down the track. The twelve-pound missile burst in an explosion of flame and smoke, just in front of a ragged line of Union foot soldiers. The men of I Company of the 19th Massachusetts Volunteers had already experienced three years of war, and by now were quite expert at gauging the danger. They perfunctorily ducked the shrapnel that whistled and snapped through the limbs and leaves of the trees.

Methodically, Corporal Josiah Day, a young man lean

and tough as rawhide, rammed home a paper cartridge, wad, and bullet as he recharged his muzzle-loading musket. They were firing into trees on the other side of the field. Flashes of light and drifting clouds of smoke gave evidence that the Confederate soldiers were returning fire.

Called Josie by his friends, the young man, who before the war had been a printer by trade, was a good soldier. Like many in his company, he had come into the war at its very beginning, and by now had been under fire so many times that it took more than a small skirmish and a few random artillery bursts to get him excited.

One of the other men in the skirmish line fired, and Josie saw a puff of dirt where the bullet struck. It had fallen far short of its intended target.

"Thomas, make sure you have your sights adjusted for the distance," Josie cautioned. "This far away, you've got to get 'em with plunging fire."

"Hell, you think we don't know that, Josie?" Bob Reese said with a chuckle. "We didn't come into this fracas yesterday, you know." Though Josie was a corporal and Bob a private, Bob could be familiar with him not only because they had been through the entire war together, but also because he was Josie's first cousin and best friend.

Another artillery shell exploded, this one a little closer, but still far enough away so as not to pose any immediate danger.

His musket reloaded now, Josie turned back toward the far trees, raised the fifty-six-inch rifle to his shoulder, elevated the rear sight, and fired. The heavy .58 caliber bullet caused the weapon to kick hard against his shoulder, but he was so used to the sensation that he barely noticed it.

He brought the rifle down and began reloading.

"Josie, lad," Sergeant McSpadden said, just as Josie finished reloading. McSpadden had been walking back and forth behind his men, supervising the action. "Go tell the captain there's only a few of 'em. We can swing around"—he motioned with his hand—"and drive 'em right into his arms. In five minutes, unless he tells us no."

"All right, Sergeant," Josie answered. Finished with the reload, he fitted the ramrod back into its holder, then got to his feet. Bending over into a crouch, Josie moved to his right, passing behind some of the men in the skirmish line: Tucker, a young Boston tailor; Thomas Sweet, a huge but gentle, baby-faced farm boy; and his cousin, Bob.

Lifting his musket to high port, Josie started through the forest, leaping over fallen logs, ducking under low branches, and splashing through streams. He frightened a deer getting a drink, and it bounded off. Its sudden movement startled Josie, who stopped and brought his rifle into the ready position until, with a relieved smile, he saw what it was.

The sound of his footsteps and his ragged breathing formed a counterpoint to the sharp bark of musketry and the heavy boom of distant cannonade. When he reached an open space on the other side of the wood line, Josie paused for a moment. All appeared clear, so he dashed across, then leaped over a knee-high stone wall, landing in the midst of several Union soldiers who were waiting to be called upon. The uniforms of these soldiers, like Josie's, were long on use and short on niceties. A couple of them, surprised by Josie's sudden appearance, raised their weapons, then relaxed when they recognized him as one of their own.

"Where the hell did you come from?" one of them asked.

"I'm on the other side of the thicket with Sergeant McSpadden. Where's Captain Russell?"

"Over there," a soldier replied, nodding toward a tree stump about twenty yards behind the stone wall.

Josie saw the fifty-year-old bearded commanding officer standing with his second in command, Lieutenant Oliver. Josie hurried to him and saluted.

"Corporal Day, how's it going on your side of the woods?" asked Captain Russell.

"Sergeant McSpadden says there's just a few of 'em, sir. We can swing around"—Josie made the same sweeping motion that McSpadden had made—"and drive 'em into you. Five minutes, 'less you tell him not to."

At that moment a sharp rattle of musket fire erupted from the other side of the clearing. The three men looked in that direction, but saw nothing.

"I don't know there's any such a few of them," Captain Russell said. He stroked his beard. "See any more of 'em on your way over?"

"No, sir. The thicket's clear."

"How about cavalry? See any cavalry?"

"No cavalry, sir."

"You know McSpadden, sir," Lieutenant Oliver said. "He'll say he'll drive 'em, he'll drive 'em." Oliver, younger and clean-shaven, had been a lawyer before the war. He made no bones about the fact that he intended to enter politics someday, and he was counting on a good war record to help him win votes.

Another sharp round of shooting caused Captain Russell to look across the clearing again. "That sounds close." He turned to Oliver. "Doesn't that sound close?"

"It may just be an echo from the woods. That would make it sound close," Oliver suggested. He pointed to the little stone wall. "And we do have a perfect spot here to wait for 'em, if McSpadden and his boys can flush 'em out, sir."

Captain Russell stroked his beard again, studying the trees on the other side of the clearing. His expression indicated that he didn't think things were quite right, though there was nothing he could put his finger on. Finally he sighed.

"All right, Corporal, maybe you're right. Go back to your sergeant. Tell him to drive away."

"Yes, sir." Turning, Josie started back across the field.

Russell and Oliver watched him move quickly across the clearing, then disappear into the woods.

"As long as there's no cavalry," Russell said. He was still uneasy about the situation, but he couldn't come to a standstill because of it. "Better get 'em ready, Lieutenant."

4

"Yes, sir." Oliver started toward the long, low stone wall where the men of the company were waiting the call to action. "Get ready, boys." Oliver pointed toward the trees. "Sergeant McSpadden is going to be driving them toward us, and they'll be comin' in from over there."

Josie was loping through the woods, retracing his path, jumping over logs and splashing through streams. Suddenly there was a loud popping in his ear, and a minié ball knocked off his cap and spun him around. Josie hit the ground hard, his face bleeding from splinters thrown into his cheek when the ball smashed into the tree beside him. He dropped his rifle; it slid across the ground and came to rest several feet in front of him.

Stunned, Josie got to his hands and knees, then started crawling toward his musket. Suddenly a pair of gray-clad legs appeared in front of him. Then another pair, and another. Josie looked up and saw six Confederate infantrymen staring down their rifle barrels at him.

"We got us a Yank over here, Major Sowell," one of the soldiers called.

Still dazed, Josie picked up his rifle. He heard the metallic click of a revolver being cocked.

"Better leave it there, boy," Major Sowell said. The mounted Confederate officer was holding his pistol on Josie.

Josie's heart was pounding, and he took several deep breaths, fighting the fear that was building up. Where did all these people come from? He looked around, trying to find an escape route. Two more mounted Confederates disabused him of that notion when they galloped onto the scene with carbines at the ready.

Major Sowell made a motion with his pistol, signaling Josie to lay down his rifle. Josie leaned over to put it down, then straightened up.

"What do I do now?"

"Son, you won't be doing anything anymore unless we

5

tell you to," Sowell said. He looked toward the Confederate infantrymen and picked out a corporal. "Take him over and put him with the others."

"Yes, sir."

Sowell and the other two cavalrymen galloped off as the Rebel soldiers marched Josie away.

When Josie reached the place where he had left McSpadden and the others no more than fifteen minutes earlier, he saw that they, too, were prisoners. Sergeant McSpadden had a wound in his shoulder that was being bandaged by Bob Reese. Seven or eight others from Josie's company, as well as several more from other companies, were sitting on the ground, weaponless, guarded by half a dozen Confederate infantrymen.

In addition to McSpadden, Reese, Sweet, and Tucker, there was Billy Gates, who, having just turned eighteen, was the youngest soldier in the platoon.

Looking at the battlefield, Josie saw several Union dead who had not been there when he left. One of the Confederates who had been escorting Josie jabbed the business end of his rifle roughly into Josie's back.

"Sit down!" he barked.

Josie sat on the ground next to his cousin and Sergeant McSpadden.

"Cousin," Josie said, "you hurt?"

"No. Are you?"

"No." Josie looked toward McSpadden. "How are you, Sergeant?"

"Just a scratch."

Behind McSpadden, Bob shook his head slowly, letting Josie know that the wound was considerably more than a scratch.

"Not such a few as I thought, eh, lads?" McSpadden said. "Sorry excuse for a sergeant, I am, not even knowing there was horses in the neighborhood. Deaf and blind . . . deaf and blind."

6

Josie looked at the dead, then let out a sorrowful sigh as he recognized one of them. "Oh, damn, they got Peter." Yesterday he had written a letter home for Peter, a very special letter in which Peter had asked his girl to marry him when next he came home. This morning, as a way of saying thank you, Peter brought over a freshly killed rabbit that he spitted over a fire and shared with Josie for breakfast.

Bob nodded, then cocked it to his left. "And Benjamin, over there."

Josie looked at the others in his company. Sweet and Tucker were depressed. Billy smiled wanly. "We've had better days than this one, hey, Josie?"

"That we have, Billy, that we have."

More men were arriving. Captain Russell, Lieutenant Oliver, and some of the men who had been with them were escorted by a group of Confederate infantrymen. Among them was Private Tyce.

Josie didn't know Tyce all that well—nobody did. He was a brooding young man who stayed to himself most of the time, but always did his duty without complaint. At first, Josie thought he had a special hatred for Southerners, but he had come to believe that Tyce's hatred was not based on prejudice. He seemed to hate everyone.

"Sit there, you Yankee bastards," one of the Rebels said, jabbing them with his rifle.

"Those men are officers!" Sergeant McSpadden said, his jaws clenched tightly in pain and rage. "And by God, you'll treat 'em as such!"

"Not to me, they ain't officers," a Confederate private said. "To me they're just damn Yankees, no different from the rest of you."

"Private, treat these officers with the respect due their rank!" a stern voice snapped. Major Sowell rode onto the scene.

"Yes, sir," the private replied sullenly.

Major Sowell rode over to Captain Russell and saluted. "My respects, Captain. I know you'll want to bury your dead. If you'll detail two of your men, I will allow you to do so."

"We do, sir. Thank you." Russell returned the salute.

Captain Russell looked over toward his men, but he said nothing. He didn't have to, because Josie and Bob had already gotten up, unbidden.

"We'll do it, Cap'n," Josie said. He and Bob walked off with a couple of the Confederate guards.

"Captain, you'll be staying here tonight," Major Sowell continued. "You and the other prisoners will move on in the morning. I take it, sir, that you have rations and blankets for your men?"

"Our haversacks are over there, sir," McSpadden said, pointing them out.

"Corporal, have them brought over," Major Sowell said. He saluted Captain Russell again before leading the other cavalrymen away at the gallop. With Sowell gone, the cold-eyed Confederate corporal who had captured Josie was left in charge of the prisoners.

"Y'all lay flat on the ground," he ordered. "Don't nobody stand, don't nobody move till mornin'."

"What about them fellas, Corporal?" one of the guards called, indicating Josie and Bob, who were digging graves just a few feet away. "Want 'em to lay down, too?"

"'Ceptin' them," the corporal said. "They can go about their business for now. When they're finished, bring 'em back here with the rest."

Once the dead had been buried, Josie and Bob returned to the others. They could still hear the sound of fighting, but any hopes they might have had of the Union Army rescuing them quickly faded as the sound of musket and cannon fire grew more and more distant.

Josie looked around at the men who had been taken prisoner with him. Their faces reflected disbelief, disgust, and fear—mirroring, he was certain, the expression in his own.

Captain Russell seemed to be most affected by what had

happened. He took his responsibility very seriously, felt deeply the loss of each man, and was devastated that he had allowed so many of his men to fall into Rebel hands.

Sergeant McSpadden was suffering greatly, though he bore the pain in silence.

From his cousin, Josie sensed determination. Even now, he knew, Bob would be working on a way out of here. Bob had never given in to any problem.

Tucker and Sweet seemed confused by what was happening to them. Several times during the afternoon, they glanced toward Josie, as if asking what they should do. For three years they had been good soldiers, obeying orders without question in the innocent faith that, no matter the circumstances, their leaders would get them through. They did everything that was expected of them, yet here they were, prisoners of the Rebels.

It's up to you, Corporal, Sergeant, Lieutenant, Captain, they seemed to be saying. *It's your job to tell us what to do to get out of here.*

Tyce was brooding more than usual. Josie could read nothing but anger and hate in his expression.

But of them all, Billy Gates was the one Josie was most concerned for. Billy was hanging on the edge of panic, and Josie was afraid that at any moment, he might get up and start running. If he did, the guards would shoot him without hesitation.

The hours dragged on, and the sun slowly sank behind the wooded hills. Darkness crept in from the draws and notches, came down from the hills, and moved out of the woods. The stars popped out, one by one at first, then in clusters, then in great clouds. Finally, the night sky was filled with them.

"Brubaker," the Rebel corporal said, "get a fire goin'."

"Why don't you have 'em do it?" Brubaker nodded toward the prisoners.

"Because, goddamn it, I told you to do it! Besides, I don't want 'em movin' aroun' out there in the dark."

"A'right, a'right," Brubaker said with the air of one who

was being put upon. He laid his musket down and went to gather wood.

Tyce was looking at the rifle, and Josie knew exactly what the young man was thinking. He stared hard, until Tyce looked over at him, then slowly shook his head.

"You want to try an' pick up that gun, Yank, why you jus' go right ahead," the corporal said matter-of-factly. "Onliest thang, by the time you touch it, I'll done have your brains splattered all over the place."

Tyce glared at the corporal.

"What you starin' at, you Yankee son of a bitch?"

Tyce looked away.

"Coley, you're not really that bad of a boy," Father Bonnington had told him. "Why do you want to make everyone think you are?"

Ten-year-old Coley Tyce glared at the director of the orphanage. "I want ever'one to be a-scared of me."

"But that's no way to make friends."

"Don't need no friends."

"Oh, sure you do. Everyone needs friends."

"Don't need nobody."

Father Bonnington reached into the voluminous sleeves of his cassock and withdrew a small sack. Opening it, he took out two pieces of horehound candy and put one piece in his mouth.

"Well, let's just talk about that, shall we?" He saw Tyce looking hungrily at the other piece of candy. "Oh," he said, as if it were an afterthought, "would you like a piece of candy?"

Tyce said nothing.

"I guess not," Father Bonnington said. He started to put the candy away.

"Yes," Tyce said.

"Well, I don't know, Coley. I mean, if we were friends, I'd share with you. But you said you didn't need any friends. . . ."

"Keep your goddamn candy!" Tyce shouted, turning on his heel and running back into the orphanage.

"Here's the wood," Brubaker said, coming back with an armload. Within a short time they had a fire going. A gleaming bubble of light pushed out from the fire, and, inside that bubble, their forms painted orange by the flickering flames, the Rebel guards maintained their watch while the Union soldiers waited.

Tiny glowing sparks, riding vertical columns of heat, drifted high into the night sky to join the winking stars. In the adjacent woods, insects screeched, frogs thrummed, and whippoorwills called. Gradually the prisoners began to fall asleep, but Josie, Bob, and Billy lay awake. Billy was on his stomach, feeding twigs into the fire.

"Cousin?" Josie whispered to Bob.

"What?"

"Did you ever think we'd wind up caught like this?"

"I never did. Did you?"

"No, never. Thought I might get wounded, maybe even killed. Never thought I'd wind up as a prisoner."

"I want you to know, Josie, I wouldn't have given up, but there was too many of 'em."

"I know."

"So what do we do now?"

"Pick our time and make a run for it."

"Yeah, that's what I was thinkin'. How about now?"

Josie looked into the sullen faces of the Confederate guards, then shook his head. "They're all watching."

"But it's night, and if we can get out of the firelight, we got a good chance. Besides, once they get you in their prison camps, they got you good."

"Yeah, I know."

"How 'bout this?" Bob suggested. "I'm going to stand up slow, say I have to take a piss. They'll send a guard with me. I've got a knife in my pocket. When they hear it and come after me, you run for it. Run like the devil. You know the farm with the smokehouse we passed this morning? Looks like Uncle John's?"

"Yeah, I saw it."

"I'll meet you there."

"Who'll look after McSpadden?" Josie asked.

"Give 'em my love in Boston," McSpadden said quietly.

"We will, Sergeant," Josie promised.

"Ready?" Bob asked.

Josie looked around, then nodded.

Slowly, unthreateningly, Bob started to get up. "Gotta take a—"

The dark was suddenly broken by a muzzle flash. The loud bang that followed startled everyone awake. Even before he was halfway up, Bob was dead, pitching forward with a bullet hole between his eyes. He fell on Billy, who shouted in horror and rolled over into the fire. Billy rolled out of the fire just as quickly, slapping at the burning embers in his hair and on his arms.

"Bob!" Josie shouted, starting to stand.

"No, lad! Sit! Sit!" McSpadden grabbed Josie's arm with some effort and pulled him down.

"Told you. Nobody stands, nobody moves around," the Confederate corporal said quietly. He spoke the words as simply and easily as if he had just swatted a mosquito. He was reloading his musket.

Josie looked around at the other guards, who now had their rifles pointed toward the prisoners. The horror was all the greater because of the little import the corporal gave to the fact that he had just blasted a man into eternity.

Tyce, still sitting apart from the others, glared at the corporal with intense hatred. The corporal looked at Tyce, who stared him down.

"And don't you give me no trouble, neither," the corporal said.

Tyce said nothing, and his expression remained the same.

Late afternoon of the following day:

Josie and eight others from I Company of the 19th Massachusetts, plus twelve prisoners from other Union units, were being marched down a long, empty dirt road. They were heading south, away from the battlefield, the sounds of which were now a distant whisper. Deeper and deeper into Confederate territory they marched. Guarding them were the same six infantrymen who had been with them from the beginning, including the murderous corporal.

McSpadden's condition had worsened, so Josie was walking alongside him, supporting him. Tucker was behind Josie, then came Sweet, who was carrying someone on his back. Billy was next, his head down and shaking, then Captain Russell, who was supporting Lieutenant Oliver much as Josie was supporting McSpadden. All were carrying their haversacks.

They had come a long way today, and Josie was hot and tired, and his throat was choked with thirst. He had been thirsty for some time, but there wasn't much water left in his canteen, and he was rationing the little he had. Earlier they had passed a stream, but their guards didn't let them fill their canteens, or even stop to get a drink. Now, he could hold off drinking no longer.

Josie took one swallow, then handed his canteen to McSpadden. McSpadden took one swallow, then passed it to Sweet, who also took one swallow.

Captain Russell and Lieutenant Oliver watched eagerly, almost covetously. Involuntarily, Oliver let his tongue slide out, raking across dry, cracked lips.

Josie got the canteen back from Sweet, then looked at his two officers. He wasn't sure of the etiquette. Would officers drink after an enlisted man? He extended the canteen toward Captain Russell. Russell looked at it for just a moment.

"I shouldn't be taking your water, lad. You've barely

enough for yourself, and you're sharing it with everyone else."

Josie continued to offer the canteen, and Captain Russell's reserve broke down. "Thank you, Corporal Day. I lost mine back there someplace." Russell was very careful to take but one swallow, then handed the canteen to Oliver.

"Very kind of you, Corporal Day," Lieutenant Oliver said.

"The young man the guard shot last night, your cousin. I believe he had a wife back in New Bedford?" Russell asked as he capped the canteen and handed it back to Josie.

"Yes, sir. And a little boy."

"Give me their address, so I can write them."

"Yes, sir, I know they'll appreciate it."

Leaving the two officers, Josie moved back to walk alongside Sergeant McSpadden once again.

"Better keep an eye on Billy, lad," McSpadden suggested quietly. "I think he's havin' a real hard time of it."

Josie looked back over his shoulder at Billy, who was stumbling blindly along by himself, shaking his head from side to side.

"Yeah," Josie said. "I see what you mean."

They continued to walk, and Josie's mind slipped back to the last time he had seen Bob's wife.

"Sarah, what is it about women, that they want to get every single man they know married?" Sarah had invited Josie to have supper with them, enticing him with the promise of her special apple dumpling for dessert. But he wasn't the only guest. Sarah's cousin, an attractive young woman from Boston, was also there. A few minutes ago, Sarah had asked Josie if he would help her bring the dessert out, and now they were alone in the kitchen.

Sarah smiled at him. "It's just that we know how much happier men are when they're married. Look at Bob. Don't you think he's much happier now than he ever was?"

"Bob's happy."

"And, be honest with me, Josie. Don't you think Elaine's beautiful?"

Josie looked into the dining room. Bob was holding little Matthew; Elaine was smiling at the baby and tickling him under the chin. The baby was smiling back at her.

"Yes, she is pretty."

"She's going to be here for two weeks," Sarah said. She looked into the dining room, then said in a low voice, "At the picnic, Sunday, her basket will be the one with the red and white handle. Make certain you're the high bidder."

Josie shook his head. "Sarah, what are you trying to get me into?"

"Hey, look up there," someone called. The shout brought Josie out of his reverie, and he looked around, surprised to find himself still marching down the road, under guard, as a prisoner of the Confederate Army.

"What is it?" Captain Russell asked.

"They's a whole bunch more folks up there, Cap'n."

"Reckon that's where we're goin'," someone else said.

"Y'all just keep it quiet, now," the Confederate corporal ordered.

What had aroused everyone's attention was a much larger group of Union soldiers, also under guard.

"Must be nearly two hundred of them," Josie said quietly.

The men were dirtier and more haggard-looking than Josie's little group. As the newcomers arrived, some of them looked up, but most were barely aware of the arrival of more of their own. They sat unmoving, their heads hung in defeat and their eyes glazed over as they lost themselves in whatever thoughts and prayers they could call upon to sustain themselves.

"We must be goin' to get on a train," Sweet said. "There's a track."

"Get over there, men," the Confederate corporal ordered. "Take your seats on the ground 'longside them other Yankee sons of bitches."

As Josie and the others found a place to sit, two of the prisoners already there scooted over to greet them. One, a young storekeeper type, wore wire-rimmed glasses. His cap pin identified him as a member of the 2nd Wisconsin. The other soldier was bearded, older. According to his cap badge, he belonged to the 60th Ohio.

"Nineteenth Massachusetts? Second Wisconsin. You were on our left, second day at Gettysburg."

"I remember you boys," Tucker said. "They couldn't move you."

"Tried hard enough though, didn't they?" 2nd Wisconsin said. He nodded toward some nearby prisoners. "They were on Cemetery Ridge. Gave that place its rightful name."

"When'd they get you boys?" 60th Ohio asked.

"Yesterday afternoon," Sweet answered. "Back there. One minute we thought we were whippin' them, the next minute they were all around us."

"Know what you mean," 60th Ohio said. "'Twas like that with us, too."

"Know where they're takin' us?" 2nd Wisconsin asked. "Won't tell us a thing."

"They can take me anyplace they want," McSpadden said. He tried to laugh, but the laughter was hollow. "Promised my mother nothing'd happen to me till I saw home one more time."

Josie sat quietly, trying to appraise the situation. By now, most of the prisoners were quiet, though some began exchanging small talk: where they were captured, who they were with, where they were from.

"You boys wouldn't have any water with you, would you?" 2nd Wisconsin asked. He pointed to the water tower alongside the track. "There's prob'ly a thousand gallons of water in that tank there, but we haven't had a drop all day."

Josie passed over his canteen.

Second Wisconsin shook it. "It's nearly empty. Wouldn't want to take your last drop."

"Drink it," Josie said, shrugging his shoulders. "They're bound to give us some water soon."

"Thanks."

As 2nd Wisconsin, and then 60th Ohio, finished the water, Josie tried to make McSpadden comfortable. McSpadden's wound was now causing him to wince, but he didn't cry out. Josie glanced toward Billy and saw the young man sitting away from the others. His head was down, and his body was shaking. Josie moved over to sit next to Billy.

"How you farin', Billy?"

Billy shook his head. "Last night," he said. "Last night, last night." His lips began to tremble, and he bit them. Tears began to slide out of his eyes.

"You're just goin' to have to put it out of your mind, Billy. Things like that happen in war." Even as he was talking, however, Josie realized that he wasn't talking about something in the abstract. He was talking about his own cousin.

"All right, men, listen to me!" someone shouted.

A Confederate captain was approaching them.

"I'm Captain Sills. You new men," he said, looking toward Josie and his companions, "I know some of you haven't eaten anything today. We're sorry, but we don't have anything here for you . . . or for us either. But we've sent to town for a wagonful, so please be patient. All right?"

"You folks catched us! Now, 'cordin' to the rules, you gotta feed us!" one of the prisoners shouted.

"Yeah, and get us some water!" another called.

Josie looked toward Tyce. He had said nothing, but he was glaring at Captain Sills with the same hatred he had shown the Confederate corporal who had been in charge of them.

"Sure hope they're quick about gettin' that food here," 60th Ohio said. "I ain't et since yesterday. My belly button's rubbin' up 'gainst my backbone."

Josie turned to Billy. "Tell you what, Billy, why don't you come over here with me and the sergeant? I'm going to need you to help me with him."

Josie moved back, and without a word, Billy got up to follow him. They sat down next to McSpadden.

The sun beat down upon them mercilessly, and some of the men began moaning for water.

Sweat poured from Josie's back, and he opened his tunic to let the air get inside.

Some of the men slept.

The day wore on.

After a few hours, Josie reached into his haversack. Some of those nearby, thinking he might be going for food, sat up and watched him closely. When they saw him take out a tablet and a pencil, they lay down, disappointed, or looked away.

Josie poised the pencil over the tablet for a moment, but he couldn't think of anything to write.

"Here she comes!" 2nd Wisconsin said. "Wagon coming!"

It wasn't a wagon, but was a carriage driven by a black coachman in full livery. Its passengers were four very pretty, very well-dressed young women.

When the men saw that it wasn't the wagon of food, they grumbled in disappointment.

"Nothin' for us," Tyce said. He spit on the ground.

"Not a goddamn thing," another added.

Captain Sills walked to the road to meet the carriage. When it stopped, he swept off his hat, then bowed low.

"Good afternoon, ladies."

"Good afternoon to you, Captain," one of the women replied.

"Fine day for a ride in the country."

"Yes, it certainly is."

One of the women, looking toward the prisoners, suddenly realized who and what they were.

"Oh, my," she said, her eyes opening wide. "Why, Captain, I do believe these men are Yankee soldiers!"

Captain Sills nodded toward the seated, sullen men.

"They *were* Yankee soldiers, ma'am. Now they're prisoners of the Confederacy. But not to worry. We're escortin' these uninvited visitors out of your neighborhood."

"Very thoughtful of you, Captain."

"Hey, Captain! Maybe the ladies'd like to inspect the prisoners. Prob'ly never seen a Yank close up before," one of the guards suggested.

Josie looked at the expressions of his fellow prisoners. It was obvious they weren't pleased by the prospect of being put on exhibition. Then he looked toward the carriage. It was equally obvious that the young women found the suggestion intriguing, perhaps even titillating. Covering their mouths with their fans, they conferred, giggling often. Finally one of them spoke for all.

"Thank you very much for your kind invitation, Captain. But we think we will decline."

"Hey, Yankees, get on your feet," one of the guards said. "You're in the presence of fine Southern ladies here."

None of the prisoners made any effort to stand.

"Say, maybe the ladies'd like to hear 'em sing a song," the corporal suggested.

"A song? Oh, well," one of the ladies said. "I don't know . . . I've never been serenaded by a Yankee."

Captain Sills made a small bow, then turned toward the prisoners. "Will you favor the ladies with a song, gentlemen?"

"Make 'em sing 'Dixie,' Cap'n!" one of the guards shouted.

"Yeah, you boys can't carry rifles no more. Maybe one of you can carry a tune."

A civilian, who had been standing on the far side of the troop, came up behind the prisoners and quietly started kicking them in the back. "Git up!" he said. "Git up and sing 'Dixie' for the ladies. You all come down here, think you can shoot us, burn us out. Git up, damn you!"

Neither Captain Sills nor the ladies could see what he was doing as the civilian moved down the line, his kicks becoming harder, and more vicious.

"Get up, damn you! Get up and sing 'Dixie'!"

The situation was becoming dangerously tense. Some of the prisoners, including Tyce and 60th Ohio, were enraged. Josie began to worry about what Tyce might do.

"Son of a bitch kicks me, I'll kill him," Tyce said under his breath.

McSpadden, attempting to defuse the situation, struggled to his feet. He turned to the ladies. "'Dixie,' you say? I don't believe I know any such song as that. But would you ladies let me sing 'Kathleen Mavourneen'?"

McSpadden's offer stilled the kicking civilian and silenced the group.

"Very well, Sergeant, sing," Captain Sills invited.

McSpadden cleared his throat and started to sing in a beautiful tenor voice. And as the poignant tune and deeply moving words seeped into the souls of all who were present, guard and prisoner alike, the mocking of the guards and the grumbling of the prisoners stopped. The four women were entranced by the singing, and at least two of them were moved to tears.

When the song was over, there was an extended period of silence as, for all too brief a moment, everyone realized that the things that united them—love, homesickness, compassion for a friend—were much stronger than the politics that separated them.

"Thank you, Captain," one of the women said. "It was . . . quite moving." She nodded to the driver; he slapped the reins against the horses, and the carriage started forward. As the carriage drove past Sergeant McSpadden, one of the women who had been moved to tears looked over at him, then nodded her head ever so slightly. McSpadden nodded back, and in that instant, across the gap of a cruel war, their souls touched.

Chapter 2

It was dark; the only light came from smoking torches placed strategically around the group of prisoners. The wagonload of food promised by Captain Sills had arrived, and it and water had been distributed. Those who had been the last served were still eating, wolfing their food down.

Having been served earlier, Josie and those captured with him were now busy with other things. Tucker, the tailor, was expertly sewing a rip in his shirt. Josie was sitting in the dim light of a flickering torch, staring at the paper and holding a pencil that still had not produced any words for him. McSpadden was lying nearby. He pulled himself up, wincing, as a wave of pain swept over him.

"You all right, Sergeant?" Josie asked.

McSpadden nodded, but the beads of sweat on his

forehead revealed that he was suffering a great deal more than he was letting on.

"Bob's wife?" McSpadden nodded toward the letter Josie was attempting to write.

"Yeah."

"I always see you readin' and writin'."

"Letters home, so the folks won't worry."

"When you finish that, would you write one for me?"

"Course I will."

"I never did learn my letters." McSpadden was silent for a moment, then added, "What's it like, being so educated?"

Josie shrugged. "The more education you get, the more you realize how much you don't know."

"You go ahead and write your latter, lad. I don't want to bother you."

"You're not bothering me, Sergeant." Josie wanted to explain, feeling a need to communicate on a deeper plane with this man who had become so much a part of his life. "My father's a printer, you see, and he taught me. And my mother always read to me while I was growing up."

McSpadden chortled. "Any letters as I might write to my mother would have to go to the priest, so's he can read them to her. She's never got a letter in her life, you know." Seeing that Josie was poised to write, McSpadden nodded. "You go ahead. Write your letter."

Josie held the pencil over the page for a long moment, then, with difficulty, began to write.

Dear Sarah,

> *This is the letter I never wanted to write.*
> *Bob was killed last night.*
> *He died in my arms with all our friends around and did not suffer, even for a moment. No man was ever braver or a better companion. Everyone in our Regiment says so.*
> *His love for you and Matthew was. . . .*

Josie was interrupted by the whistle of an approaching train. As he looked down the track, he saw the soft yellow gleam of a distant headlight.

"Here comes the train, boys," someone said.

"Ever'body get up," one of the guards called. "Ever'body get up and get ready. You boys are goin' for a train ride."

The train was closer now. Sparks leaped from the smokestack and burning embers spilled onto the track from the firebox. It was chugging mightily, and white steam billowed from the escape valves of the piston-rod cylinders. The engine, apparently smaller than standard, was pulling two slat-sided cattle cars and a caboose. Josie turned his attention back to his letter.

"We are being taken south, to where, only the Lord knows. Please tell my father and mother I am content to leave it in His hands. I will write them when I get to wherever we are going.

Your loving cousin-in-law,
Josiah Day

Hastily, Josie addressed the envelope, then asked Billy to help him get McSpadden to his feet.

"Enlisted men only," Captain Sills called when he saw Captain Russell and Lieutenant Oliver starting toward the train. "All officers over here, please. This train is not for you."

"I would like to stay with my men," Captain Russell called.

"Over here, please, Captain," Captain Sills said again. "There will be another train for the officers."

"What do you think that's all about, dividin' us up like that?" McSpadden asked.

"I don't know," Josie answered. "Here comes the captain now."

"Sergeant McSpadden! Corporal Day!" Captain Russell

called, pushing his way through the crowd of milling men.

"Help me get to him," McSpadden said.

Pushing men out of the way, Josie led McSpadden through the crowd until they reached Captain Russell. The captain was clearly upset at being separated from his men.

"They aren't going to let us. . . ."

"Yes, sir, I know," McSpadden said.

Captain Russell, silent for a moment, looked at the throng of soldiers, moving toward the train.

"Hurry up, men. Let's get on the train!" Captain Sills called.

"Quit shovin'!"

"Can't help it. Someone's shovin' me."

Captain Russell licked his lips, then looked at McSpadden. "So, uh, how are you, Sergeant?" He nodded toward the wound. "I mean, how's the . . . ?"

"Never better, sir."

"I just want to say . . . you've both always been good soldiers." Captain Russell paused, finding this moment difficult. "Always did what had to be done." He looked at Josie. "You don't say much, Day, but I never heard you complain, and I could always count on you to do the hard jobs."

"No more than anyone else, sir."

"Pleasure was ours, Captain," McSpadden added.

There was another awkward silence, then Josie spoke.

"Captain . . . Bob's wife's address is on this letter I just wrote. You may have an easier time getting it sent than I would."

"All right," Captain Russell said, taking the letter. "I'll get it mailed, I promise. You two, you're noncommissioned officers. When you get where you're going . . . I'm counting on you to take care of the boys."

"Don't you worry none, Captain," McSpadden said. "The boys can take care of themselves just fine."

"I know. I know they can. It's just that . . . I hate like

the devil having to leave them. We've been through a lot together, haven't we?"

"Yes, sir, we have," McSpadden agreed.

"Well, Sergeant, you're in charge now. Do what you can for them." Captain Russell turned to Josie. "Corporal Day, if something happens to the sergeant, you'll be in command."

"I'll do my best, sir."

"I know you will. I know you both will." Captain Russell looked at the others, those who had been in his company and those who had not. "God bless you, boys!" he called, raising his arm. "Go along with 'em, now." Then, more quietly, he said to Josie, "Don't worry about your letter. I promise you, I'll mail it."

"Thank you, sir."

Sergeant McSpadden pulled himself painfully to attention, then saluted. "See you back in Boston on a sunshiny day, Captain."

Captain Russell returned the salute, then turned away quickly, not realizing that it was too late . . . the men had already seen the tears in his eyes.

"All right, let's go, we don't have all night! Let's get on the cars!" one of the Confederate guards bellowed. "Get in there, now!"

"Let's go, let's go!" the other guards took up the shout.

Grumbling, the prisoners began to move toward the inclined ramps that led into the open cattle cars.

"Get in there!"

"Holy shit, they expect to get all of us in those two little cars?"

"Pack it in close! Pack it in!"

"Hey, Johnny Reb, you want to tell us where you're taking us?" Tyce called.

"You'll find out soon enough, Yank. Get in there."

"Help me with the Sergeant, Billy," Josie said as they started up the ramp.

Inside the car, they were pushed hard to make room for

more coming in behind them. There was no room to lie down, sit, or turn around.

"Watch my arm, you fool!" someone said, angrily.

"No more! You can't put no more in here!"

"Get on in there! There's plenty of room."

"There's no more room in here, you dumb Rebel son of a bitch!" Tyce shouted angrily. "We can't even breathe."

"Then hold your breath till you get there, Yank." The rest of the guards laughed.

Despite the protests, the guards continued to push the prisoners up the ramps and into the cars. At last, when not one more person could be shoved inside, the doors were slammed and bolted shut.

Josie, Billy, and Sergeant McSpadden were roughly shoved into the side of the car. It was painful, but in the long run, they would be better off. At least they would be able to get a little air. Also, Josie could see outside.

One of the train crewmen waved toward the front of the train. That was answered with two long whistles, signaling the brakemen to release the brakes. There was the squeal of metal against metal, followed by the explosive venting of pent-up steam. Then, with bone-rattling jerks, the train began moving.

Josie looked back toward the open space where, just moments before, more than two hundred prisoners had been waiting for the train. Now there were only six or seven Union officers remaining; still under guard, they were standing alongside the track, watching the train leave. Captain Russell was in the middle of the group, and Josie's last glimpse of him was of the bearded commander pinching the bridge of his nose between his thumb and forefinger, as if that would hold back the tears.

Someone in the car began singing "Battle Hymn of the Republic." At first he was the only singer, then another joined in, then another, until, by the time the train was a mile down the track, the entire car was singing—including, Josie noticed with some surprise, Tyce.

On board the train:

In the seventy-two hours that followed, Josie tried hard to make his mind and body numb. He willed himself to dissociate from reality so that he could observe, rather than physically experience, the sights, sounds, smells, tastes, and tactile sensations of the crowded car.

The train passed farmland where black field hands looked up from chopping cotton, moved through woods, crossed slow-moving rivers, and ran alongside swiftly flowing streams. It rolled through small towns untouched by war, where children and old people came to stand at trackside and gape at the train carrying these men who had invaded their soil.

The train stopped to take on water for the engine, and to allow a few cups to be passed inside to the prisoners, who received only enough to wet the lips and tongue.

Through it all the men stood jammed together, no room to sit or even turn, constantly moaning in their thirst and misery.

Josie looked at Sergeant McSpadden, who, through his pain and discomfort, somehow managed to grin and shrug back at him.

"Get us some more water down here, you Rebel sons of bitches!"

Was it Tyce who called out? And if so, when? Did he do that before they left, in the middle of the trip, or was it more toward the end? Did Tyce shout at all? Josie could no longer be sure. It might have been his own burning need for water, manifesting itself by his imagining the shout as coming from Tyce's lips. This was borne out by the fact that when Josie looked over at him, Tyce seemed to be lost in his own thoughts.

• • •

"And why do you want to be priest, my son?" Father Bonnington asked. Coley Tyce, now eighteen, had just come into his office with the announcement that it was his intention to enter the priesthood.

"Because you're a priest, Father."

"I see. And you think that by entering the priesthood, you would please me?"

"Yes, Father."

Father Bonnington leaned over to the table and opened a jar, then took out two pieces of horehound candy. He gave one to Tyce, and popped the other piece into his own mouth.

"I believe you like that candy more than any of the boys do," Tyce said.

Father Bonnington chuckled, and held up his finger. "Ah, my boy, how long did it take you to figure that out?"

"Not too long, Father."

"Good. Then we know you're at least astute enough to enter the priesthood. The question that remains is, do you have the proper motivation?"

"Yes, Father."

"And what is your motivation?"

"I want to please you."

"I see."

"And to honor you.

"Why would you want to do that?"

"Because you're my . . . friend," Tyce said, unable to find the proper word that carried the love he felt for this man who had been the only mother and father he had ever known.

"I'm flattered, my son. I truly am. But don't you see that that isn't enough?"

"Why isn't it?"

"Coley, the priesthood isn't something you enter into lightly. It's a lifetime commitment. You can't make such a commitment to a mere mortal, no matter how you feel *about that person. I would be the only purpose for your being a priest, but I'm going to die someday. And after I'm dead, you'd still be a priest, but you'd be a priest without purpose."*

"Then after you die, my purpose will be to serve God."

"After I die?"

"Yes, Father."

Father Bonnington shook his head. "No, my son, for that would put God in second place, don't you see? And it would neither please nor honor me to be placed above God."

The train jerked around a sharp curve, and inside the cars the men were thrown against each other. Tyce was pushed hard against the side of the car, and a sharp pain brought his thoughts back to the present. Angrily, he pushed back against the man who had pushed him, even though he knew it wasn't the man's fault.

The men in the car twisted and turned to get near the slats so they could breathe good air. Josie and Billy, now so tired as to be unaware of it, automatically positioned their bodies to keep the others from leaning against McSpadden's wound.

Sometimes, someone from in the middle of the crowded car would say he had traveled through this part of the country, and would assure the others that he could tell them where they were if someone would just give him a boost over to the side. Three or four times the others fell for the ploy, and with painful effort the would-be guide was passed across the shoulders of the others so he could look out, only to admit he didn't know where they were.

Next to Josie, a parched man tried to find one more drop of water in a dry canteen; he turned to his friend, who just shrugged. The friend's canteen was bone-dry, too.

Then, just before dawn of the second day, Josie seemed to free his mind from his body. His body was still trapped inside the crowded car, helping Billy to support McSpadden, aching, hungry, and burning with thirst. But his spirit was floating alongside the train, looking at the guards on the roof of the caboose. Josie's mind moved forward with the train, peering into the engine cab, where he could see the fireman throwing on more wood as clearly as if Josie were there in person.

But when Josie tried to really break away, to send his mind flying back to his father's print shop in Massachusetts, he couldn't do it, and body and soul were jarringly rejoined. Once more he was inside the car, watching Tucker and Sweet twisting and turning to peer through the slats to see where they were going.

It was day again, and the train continued to roll through the Rebel countryside. Josie wondered how many state lines they had crossed.

The train passed more fields and through more woods and over more bridges as it made its way south. Then, in the middle of the afternoon of the third day, the train stopped.

"What is it?" someone asked in a weak voice. "What's going on?"

This stop was different from the earlier fuel and water stops. This stop had a feel of permanence to it, and everyone in the car sensed it.

"Hey, look," someone said. "Look at all them guards out there. Them guards wasn't on the train."

"Boys, we must be here."

"Yeah, but where is *here*?"

"I don't know where *here* is, but it's got to be better than the hell we've just been through." That observation was seconded by a chorus of amens.

The door to the car was thrown open and Confederate guards, standing on the ground just outside, started yelling. "Let's go, Yanks! Ever'one out of the car!"

This time there was no ramp, and the men, weakened and dispirited, had to jump down as best they could. Josie and Billy helped McSpadden down. The sergeant, now nearly delirious with fever, walked to the platform and held up his arm.

32

"Nineteenth Massachusetts, I Company, form up," he called in his best military voice.

Tucker, Sweet, and Tyce tried to fight their way through the milling prisoners to respond to McSpadden's command, but the Confederate guards stepped in and roughly pushed them aside.

"Don't you be listenin' to that fool! Ain't nobody goin' be givin' you folks orders anymore but us!" one of the guards said. "Now you boys want to form up, you just form up right here."

Totally dispirited, the prisoners obeyed weakly. Even Tyce could manage no more than a dull glance toward the guards.

With pushing, shoving, and a few blows from their rifle butts, the guards managed to get the prisoners into the kind of formation they wanted. Then a Confederate sergeant took charge and started the group moving down a dusty road.

"Anybody don't keep up, gets shot," one of the guards said matter-of-factly. "So don't none o' you boys lollygag."

The road they were on ran east by northeast from Andersonville Station. They passed over one stream, then marched alongside another.

"Lookit that, Josie," Billy said in awe, pointing ahead of them. The object of his wonder was a massive palisade of huge timbers, set upright in the ground, watched over by a star fort and a redoubt. The star fort bristled with five cannons, and the redoubt had three. All around the wall, about 150 feet apart, were elevated sentry boxes with a guard in each of them. From here, the guards were black silhouettes against the bright sky. A few of the guards were watching the new prisoners march up the road, but most were looking inside the prison.

The prisoners were halted just in front of two massive wooden gates. They looked at the gates, the cannons, and the towers with increasing trepidation.

"Hey, Johnny Reb," 60th Ohio shouted. "Where are we?"

The Rebel guard, a scarecrow of an old man, spit a stream

of tobacco juice between a gap in his teeth. Some of the juice ran down his chin, and when he raked the back of his hand across it, he managed only to smear the brown stain, not eliminate it.

"Georgia."

The newly arrived prisoners' attention was arrested by a commotion on the road to their right. Two Union prisoners were being herded at a fast pace by bayonet-wielding guards and snarling bloodhounds on leashes.

The thin guard cackled.

"You Yankee boys don't never learn. Them two boys got outta here yestiday, thought they was goin' to make it all the way back to Ohier or some such damn place. 'Stead, Cap'n Wirz is goin' to see to it that they'll be spendin' some time in the stocks."

Captain Wirz, mounted on a prancing white horse, was riding alongside the would-be escapees. They were brought to the stocks, then forced into a position that would allow the restraints to be clamped shut.

"Teach you to run!" Wirz said.

The dogs continued to snap at the immobile men even after the stocks were shut on them.

"What the hell is this?" one of the newly arrived prisoners asked. "Dogs? Stocks? Bayonets?"

Wirz remained until the escapees were securely clamped into the stocks, then angrily wheeled his horse around and rode up to the newly arrived men. Since this man figured to play a prominent role in Josie's life for an undetermined period of time, Josie studied him closely.

Henry Wirz wasn't a big man, nor imposing in any way. He was of average size, with a small, pointed moustache and a full beard. He had a wounded right arm that he favored. But if he wasn't imposing in physical stature, there was something about his eyes that was arresting. At first Josie was puzzled, but, then, as he studied the man more closely, he realized what it was. Wirz's eyes had a serpentine quality, like those of a snake studying its prey. Here was a man, those eyes said, who could kill without the slightest compunction. He was, Josie decided, a man to fear.

"Open the gate," Wirz called.

Josie and the others waited as the crossbar was moved on the gate. Then McSpadden turned to the tobacco-chewing guard who had answered 60th Ohio's question.

"And what do you call this little piece of heaven?"

"This?" The guard squirted another stream of tobacco juice. "Why, boys, this here is Andersonville."

Once the gate was swung open, the Confederate sergeant who had marched them from the train gave the order, "Forward, march."

The prisoners moved through the gate, past the dogs and the guards, past the cannons and the stocks and the towers, and past the dead, flat, but watchful eyes of Captain Henry Wirz.

As soon as they got through the big gate, they were stopped. They were now in a sally port between two walls, one that kept out the outside, and another that closed in the inside. The gate through which they had just come was closed and barred behind them, and the one leading into the prison compound was not yet open.

"Let me have your attention, men," someone called. The new prisoners looked up toward one of the guard towers. A red-headed Confederate lieutenant was standing on the platform at the back of the tower, looking down at them.

"My name is Lieutenant Barrett. I'm about to give you the rules of this place. Pay very close attention to what I have to say, because if you violate the rules, you will be shot. It's as simple as that."

The men became very attentive.

Barrett chuckled. "Thought that might get your attention. Now, first off, you may think you're in a giant toilet once you get inside, but you aren't. There's rules and regulations as to where you can do certain things, like relieving yourselves. Don't relieve yourselves anywhere but at the sinks. The surgeons have orders that anyone 'committing a nuisance' "—he paused and looked at the men—"and I think you know what that means . . . will be shot.

"Trading with the guards is strictly forbidden. Anyone we catch trading with the guards will be severely punished.

"And finally, but most important, once you get inside, you'll see a knee-high rail fence, set back about twenty feet inside the wall. This is 'the Deadline.' Do not"—Barrett paused a moment for effect—"do not, under any circumstances, or for any reason, cross that Deadline. If you do, the guards have orders to shoot."

Barrett let his words sink in.

"Open the gates," he said to the guards, "and pass 'em through."

The second set of gates swung open, and Josie, McSpadden, Billy, Sweet, Tucker, Tyce, 2nd Wisconsin, 60th Ohio, and all the others who had been captured during the fight at Cold Harbor crossed into the stockade.

They were stunned by the sights, sounds, and smells that assailed them. It was like a huge, sprawling city of derelicts . . . emaciated scarecrows dressed in rags, or not dressed at all, milling around like maggots on a dung heap. The shelters, if they could be called that, were a collection of tents, pits, and grass-and-twig huts. The area was divided by a road that ran from east to west, and by the stream they had seen outside. In here, however, the steam was cesspool slime and filth.

"Josie, lad!" McSpadden gasped, looking at the sight that greeted them. He reached over to squeeze Josie's arm. "Would you look at this?"

"My God!" Josie said. He didn't know if he was saying a prayer or swearing an oath.

Chapter 3

The moment the gates closed behind them, they were swarmed over by dozens of the emaciated creatures.

"You boys got 'ny food with you?"

"You was with Grant in Virginia, wasn't you? How we doin' up there?"

"Any you fellas from New Jersey?"

"You boys hear anythin' 'bout us gettin' exchanged?"

"Got anything you want to trade? What'll you take for that coat?" Then, whispering, "I got eight dollars in greenbacks."

"Hey, don't push!" one of the old prisoners suddenly yelled at another.

"You were standing on my damn foot!" the second replied.

The first prisoner pushed back, then the second prisoner knocked the first down with a single punch to the jaw. None of the old prisoners seemed to notice the outburst of violence.

• • •

On a small rise a few dozen yards from the newly arrived group, Dick Potter stood looking down at them. He was staring particularly hard at Josie and a few of those closest to him, because he was sure he recognized them. He lifted his hand to shield his eyes from the sun's glare, balancing himself as he did so, because the hand he lifted was holding one of his crutches.

Then he saw a path opening up in the crowd of old prisoners as a cheerful little ferret of a man began pushing his way through the group to get to the newcomers.

"Munn, you bastard," Potter muttered. "No you don't. Not if I can help it." Shifting his crutches under his arm, he started toward them.

"Hey!" Munn shouted, greeting the new arrivals. "Fresh fish! Welcome to Andersonville, boys!"

The old prisoners fell quiet as Munn reached the group.

"Fine-looking place, don'tcha think?" he asked, a broad wave of his hand encompassing the compound. "For a hog pen, maybe," he added with a chuckle. He stuck his hand out. "The name's Munn. So tell me, where'd you boys get caught at?" Seeing the unit pins on their caps, he added, "Virginia, from the looks of things. Well, that's good, that's good. Means Grant's going forward, Bobby Lee's going back, just the way us good Union men like it."

Munn grabbed the arm of one of the men nearest him, then motioned to the others. "Come on, boys, let me show you around your new home, get you a good place to stay. You want to be up near the wall, you do, away from the Swamp. Don't stink so bad over there, and there ain't so many bugs. Nor people, neither."

Several of the new men had started to go with Munn when, suddenly, he was jabbed very hard in the chest with a crutch. Surprised, he was knocked back by the force of the blow.

"You get away from them, you sorry bastard!" Potter

said. "I know what you're about, Munn. You just get the hell away from them!"

Josie watched in shock as the rail-thin, shirtless man with gleaming eyes, wild hair, and flaring beard attacked Munn. He looked at the older prisoners to gauge their reaction. Though they weren't physically taking sides, it was obvious by their expressions that there was an unspoken approval of Potter's attack on Munn.

One of the prisoners, a rag-clad young man, began dancing around, laughing and teasing Munn.

"I'm Mad Matthew, Mad Matthew," he shouted. He put his thumbs in his ears, then waved his fingers at Munn. "Can't get me, don't you see. Can't get me!"

"You better watch yourself, mister," Munn said, ignoring Mad Matthew and pointing at Potter.

"Uh-uh, you shit-breath bastard," Potter said. "You'd better watch yourself. Look around you, Munn. There's no one here to help you."

Like a cornered rat, Munn looked around furtively, suddenly realizing the truth of what Potter said.

Fifty yards up a nearby hill a dozen or so prisoners had been watching events unfold. These prisoners were sleeker, better fed, better dressed, and considerably healthier than the others.

"What do you think, Collins? Looks like Munn's got himself a mite of trouble," one of them said.

Collins was big and rough, little changed from the saloon keeper, bouncer, and brawler he had been before the war. He was brilliantly and outlandishly dressed in a long green coat and waistcoat. He stood out like a peacock in a flock of pigeons.

"Yeah," Collins grumbled. "We'd better get him back here." He cupped his hands to his mouth and called loudly to Munn, "Let the fish go! We'll roast 'em another time!" Then, lowering his hands, he said quietly, "You give 'im a yell, too, Curtis."

Curtis, not as big as Collins, was a humorless, cold man of purpose.

"Munn, don't waste your time with that bunch," he called. "Come on back up here with your pards."

"And you know who they are, don'tcha, Mick?" one of the others added.

Down at the site of the confrontation, Munn had already backed off. Again he raised his hand and pointed at Potter. "I'll be takin' care of you, later," he snarled.

Potter raised his crutch and took a quick step toward Munn, as if to swing at him, but Munn retreated at a trot as those who had gathered around laughed. Seeing that the move with the crutch was a feint only, Munn stopped running, mustering as much bluff as he could, and sauntered up the hill to join Collins, Curtis, and the others.

Potter brought his crutch back down. He leaned on both crutches, giving his legs a rest, as he watched Munn retreat up the hill.

"Call 'em Raiders," Potter said. Then, turning to face the group of new prisoners, he added, "But hyenas is more like it. One of 'em steers the new boys over to the rest, where they hit 'em over the head. They'll kill you even, so they can steal your goods for themselves."

Josie, unable to believe what he was hearing, looked incredulously at the other old prisoners. They nodded, confirming Potter's claim.

"Why the hell doesn't someone stop 'em?" McSpadden asked.

Some of the nearby prisoners stared at the ground in humiliation.

"You don't understand," one of them said. "They run the place."

"*They?* What do you mean, *they* run the place?" McSpadden asked. He pointed to the towers. "What do the Reb guards do? Why don't they stop 'em?"

"Stop 'em? Hell, Sergeant, they *trade* with 'em. Give 'em food, whiskey, anything they want."

"Took 7th Vermont's coats," another prisoner said. "Blankets, rations, shoes. Cold nights, then. Them Vermont boys never had a chance. Didn't last a week."

"You ask me, I think the Rebs are glad they're in here. In their own way, they help the Rebs keep things under control."

McSpadden shook his head. "And these men were on our side, you say? They were soldiers, just like us?"

"Not soldiers," one of the old prisoners said contemptuously. "Mostly they're bounty jumpers. They're no better'n vermin that crawl out of the sewers of New York."

"They're rats who signed on for the joining-up money," another prisoner added. "All they meant to do was run away 'fore they saw any fighting, but they wound up gettin' catched, same as us."

Josie's eyes followed Munn up the hill until he rejoined Curtis and Collins. Collins said something. Whatever it was, the others seemed to agree with it, because they all nodded, and one of them even laughed. Josie turned to Potter.

"Well, we're very much obliged to you, friend."

"Friend?" Potter replied in a hurt tone. "You call me friend?" He looked crestfallen. "Josie, Sergeant McSpadden, do you not know me, then?"

Josie looked at the others who had been in his company, but none of them showed the slightest recognition of their benefactor.

"Boys, it's me, old Dick!" Potter said earnestly. "I only joined up with you, is all. It's old Dick, who fit with you at Seven Pines and the Chickahominy, at Antietam and—"

"Dick . . . Potter? Is that you?" Josie cried.

Pleased that he had been remembered, even if not immediately recognized, Potter smiled broadly. "Yeah, it's me. Well, it's no wonder you didn't recognize me. No food to eat, no clothes to wear, no way to see how bad I look."

Smiling broadly, Josie took Dick's hand and began shaking it. "But we thought you were killed two years ago!"

The others gathered around.

"Yeah, at Antietam!" Billy added.

"Lord, Dick, we'd give up on you!" Tucker said.

"You look fine, Dick," Sweet put in. "Handsome as you ever were."

Potter, cheered by their outpouring of affection, laughed.

"Why, shucks, warn't killed at all. Shot in both legs is all. Surprised to see me, Josie?"

"Surprised and happy. When're we going fishing again?" Josie looked at the other prisoners. "Dick and his father are the best fishermen in New Bedford."

"And that's saying a lot," Potter added.

"Say, how 'bout tellin' us what sort of place we're in here, Dick?" Tucker said.

Tucker had just put into words what was on everyone's mind, and they all gathered around to hear his answer.

Inside Captain Henry Wirz's quarters:

Wirz had taken off his shirt and was holding his injured arm over a washbasin. With his left hand, he poured water onto the wounds in his arm, and watched it cascade off each side, then splash into the basin. For a moment Wirz was able to feel some relief . . . but it was only for a moment. After that, he knew, the pain would return, a constant reminder of his participation in the Battle of Seven Pines.

Someone knocked on the door.

"*Ja*, in come." Wirz had refilled the pitcher and was again pouring water over his arm. Lieutenant Barrett entered. "Something?" Wirz asked.

"Thought you might want to know, we just got a new batch of prisoners."

"*Ja*, I saw them when I was bringing in the escapees." Wirz picked up a towel and began, very gingerly, to pat his arm dry. "How many this time?"

"Two hundred and twelve, sir."

Wirz put the towel down and slipped into his tunic.

"Did they see the men in the stocks?"

"Yes, sir, I'm sure they did."

"*Gut.* If they see how swift and certain is the punishment, perhaps more will not be foolish enough to try and escape. Anything else?"

"What about the food? Withhold rations again today?"

Wirz nodded. "*Ja.* No rations until the one who stole the bridle and halter confesses."

"Yes, sir. Captain, did you intend to cut the rations from one cup to three-quarters of a cup per day?"

"*Ja*, Lieutenant. I do not do things I do not intend to do."

"Yes, sir. Well, the only thing is, that's not hardly enough to keep a man alive. 'Specially seein' as that three-quarters of a cup contains ground-up cob as well as corn."

"It is to General Winder you should talk, not to me. I have asked for more food, many times." Wirz pointed to his desk. "I have copies of the requests I have made, but always General Winder says no, there is no more food. I get more prisoners, but I do not get more food. What should I do, Lieutenant? You tell me. I think General Winder and his family are selling the prisoners' rations."

"You could write a letter to Richmond."

Wirz shook his head. "No. This I will not do. I am a soldier, and I have been given orders. It is my duty to carry out these orders, and I will carry them out."

"Yes, sir. Captain, what about the lumber? Do we give it to the prisoners to build barracks?"

"The prisoners' hospital we are building, and outside where the air is more healthy. But now, there are too many prisoners for the lumber we have, and we cannot build shelter for everyone. So, who shall we tell can have shelter, and who cannot?"

"I see what you mean, sir. Something like that could cause trouble."

"*Ja*, and above all else, trouble we do not need." Wirz pointed to the stockade. "There are more than thirty thousand men here. That is more soldiers than the Yankees had at Seven Pines. And what do I have to keep them here? A few hundred soldiers only. Soldiers?" Wirz snorted. "They are not soldiers, they are old men and young boys, unfit for service in any army in the world. But they are all that stand between an enemy army of thirty thousand and our nation's backside."

"Yes, sir, we do have quite a responsibility. It's no wonder conditions here are so harsh."

"If the conditions here are harsh, Lieutenant, it is the Yankee bastards' fault. If the rules the prisoners would obey, we could have a clean and orderly camp. But they do not have discipline. And with no discipline, there is only chaos. And that chaos has created the misery in which these men must live."

"Yes, sir, that's very true, sir."

"Is the new guard relief ready to go on parapet?"

"In about five minutes, sir."

"*Gut*. I will have a surprise inspection and see if they are ready. Perhaps I cannot have discipline among the prisoners, but I will have it with the guards, even if they are young boys and old men."

"I will fall out the guard, sir," Barrett said, leaving quickly.

Private Mike Allen was oiling his musket before going on guard. The rifle didn't really need his attention; it was, without doubt, the best-maintained weapon in the entire platoon. But Private Allen welcomed the task because it occupied his time, and helped take his mind off the letter he had received three days ago.

"Mike," his mother had written, "we have sum bad news to tell you wich is that yur brother Jubal was shot and kilt by Yankee soldiers someplace up in Tennese. Please be careful and come home to us is our prayer."

Immediately after receiving that letter, Private Allen had gone to Lieutenant Barrett, requesting that he be sent somewhere to fight against the Yankees. "I'd like to kill ever' Yankee bastard in the whole Yankee army," he said.

"Your request for transfer is denied," Barrett told him. "Your duty is here, guarding Yankee prisoners."

"What good am I doin' here? They prisoners, they ain't soldiers."

"Look at it this way, Private. The thirty thousand men we're keeping prisoner here aren't out killing our men . . . men like your brother. Besides, who knows? Could be that the soldier who killed your brother is one of these prisoners."

Lieutenant Barrett had made the suggestion to keep Private Allen satisfied with the task at hand. He had no idea that Allen's frame of mind, coupled with his naïveté and limited intelligence, would convert the suggestion that his brother's killer *might* be one of the prisoners into his conviction that his brother's killer *was* one of the prisoners.

"Second relief! Form up!" someone shouted. Rising from the blanket on the ground that was his bed, Allen started toward the sally port, where the second relief of guards would be formed up before climbing the towers to relieve the previous shift.

"Damn, lookit that," one of the guards said to Allen as they were moving into position. "That damn Wirz is out here. Prob'ly goin' to inspect us or something, the foreign bastard."

"Captain Wirz is all right," Allen said. "He's a good soldier. We had more officers like him, more Yankees'd be dead."

"Guard relief, attention!" Lieutenant Barrett called. The new guards came to attention.

Captain Wirz walked up and down the line of guards, inspecting them closely. Although very few had full uniforms, Wirz inspected them as if they were going on parade. He made corrections here, assessed punishment there, until, finally, he was standing in front of Private Allen. Allen raised his rifle to inspection arms.

"Have you ever had to use your musket, Private?"

45

"Use it, sir?" Allen replied, not quite sure what Captain Wirz meant.

"Have you ever had to kill a Yankee?"

"No, sir."

"Could you kill one if you had to?"

"Yes, sir!" Allen said loudly.

"What makes you think you could?"

"Because one of them Yankee sons of bitches kilt my brother, that's why."

Wirz looked surprised. "One of our prisoners?"

"Yes, sir, it was," Allen said, totally convinced of it.

Wirz reached out to put his good hand on Private Allen's shoulder, and Allen could see a profound sadness in Wirz's eyes.

"War is a bad thing," Wirz said. "Especially when good men like your brother must be killed. But perhaps the time will come when you will have the opportunity to avenge your brother, *ja*?"

In that moment Private Allen knew that he loved his commanding officer with all his heart and all his soul, and he would do anything for him.

The inspection completed, the new guards started to their posts.

"Hey, Mike, watch me when I get up there," Private Wiggins called over.

"What you goin' to do?"

Wiggins held up an ear of corn. "I'm goin' to have some fun with the Yankees." He smiled broadly. "Goin' to ask 'em if they want 'ny of this corn."

"Hell, don't give it to the damn Yankees. If'n you're goin' to give that corn away, give it to me."

"I ain't givin' it to no one, you danged fool. Told you, I'm just goin' to fun with the Yanks a little."

"Oh." Allen laughed weakly. He wasn't in the mood to fun with any Yankees. He was in the mood to kill them.

As soon as Allen got into position on his guard tower, he primed and loaded his weapon. Then, holding it just below the stacking swivel, and with the butt on the ground, he started looking out over the prison compound.

"I know you're out there, you cowardly bastard," he said, gazing over the sea of filth and squalor that stretched for a quarter of a mile in every direction. "Wish I knew which one of you it was."

Allen lifted his rifle to his shoulder and pointed it toward the prison. A few of the close-in prisoners saw him, then looked around to see what he was aiming at. Wiggins, in the post next to him, also saw Allen raise his musket.

"Mike, what're you doin'?"

"It coulda been him," Allen said, lining his sights up on one of the prisoners. "Or him. Or him." Each time, he picked out a new man and aimed at him.

"Don't you go shootin' no Yankees 'less'n you got a reason to. Otherwise, you'll get yourself in a heap o' trouble, and next thing you know, you'll wind up on the inside with 'em."

"I don't think so."

"You two guards up there!" Lieutenant Barrett called.

"Yes, sir?"

"Quit blathering and pay attention to what you're about. Captain Wirz is going inside."

Chapter 4

Inside the compound:

"Hey, Wirz is comin' in," someone shouted. Wirz, mounted on a white horse, was accompanied by Barrett and surrounded by a dozen armed guards. He rode to the edge of the Deadline, then looked out over the prisoners, many of whom had gathered closer to hear what he had to say. As he spoke, Wirz continually flexed his right hand.

"So, I ask again, you Yankee sons of bitches. Where is my bridle and halter?"

No one answered.

"So, you don't care? Well, then, for you today is no rations. And no rations it will be, unless to me the thief returns what he stole."

"Why you punishing us, you goddamned Dutchman?" someone deep in the crowd shouted.

"Yeah, Wirz, we didn't do it. You goin' to starve us all to death over a stinking bridle?" another yelled.

Ignoring the comments, Wirz looked toward some men who were digging wells. "If for drinking water you are digging wells, then is all right. But if for tunnels the holes are dug, then you will suffer the consequences." Wirz looked at those who had just arrived. "So you should know, tunnels are useless. Even if you are outside. I will give any two men a twelve-hour start, and then I can track you with dogs." Wirz held up his good hand to make his point. "And this I tell you. When I catch you, you will suffer the consequences!"

Then, unexpectedly, Wirz smiled. "But why bother? I know absolutely that there are talks going on for exchange this moment. Any day you will all be paroled, and in quick order."

The smile left his face as quickly as it had arrived. "So, to see that we understand each other? No bridle . . . no halter . . . no rations."

Several of the prisoners swore aloud and started toward him. "Damn you, Wirz, you sorry bastard!" one of them shouted.

Though the prisoners never got close enough to be a threat, Wirz was frightened, and he started to back up. Pulling his pistol, he waved it back and forth as he moved quickly out of danger.

Lieutenant Barrett put himself between Wirz and the advancing prisoners. Like Wirz, he raised his pistol, but his face showed no fear.

"Go on about your own business now," he said in a calm, cold voice.

Muttering, the crowd began to disperse.

"Where's he from?" Sweet asked. "Why does he talk like that?"

"I don't know. Switzerland, or some such place in Europe," Potter answered.

"Why's he over here, fighting in our war?"

"He's not fighting anymore," 60th Ohio said. "Do you see how he favors that arm?"

"Yeah, he got it shot up pretty good at Seven Pines," one of the old prisoners put in.

"Wirz is nothing but a damn liar, anyway," Potter said. "You fellas been outside, hearin' the news. You hear anything about any exchange for us?"

"No," Josie said.

"Didn't think so. He always tells new men there's about to be an exchange, so they won't try to run off. The rest of us know better."

"What was this other business? The part about no rations? You haven't eaten today?" Josie asked.

"Nope. Nor yesterday neither. Somebody stole a bridle off a cart horse, so Wirz's punishing the whole camp."

"Here, take this," Josie said. He reached into his pocket and pulled something out.

"What's that?" Potter started to say, then his eyes grew wide. "Salt pork? That's really salt pork? My God, I ain't seen salt pork ever since I been here."

"Rebs gave it to us 'fore they put us on the train," Josie said.

"Rebs?" Dick snorted in disbelief.

"Yeah. Here, you can have it." Again, Josie offered the pork. Potter looked at it hungrily, but he made one last attempt to dissuade Josie.

"You really sure 'bout this? You may want it yourself."

When Josie motioned again for him to go ahead, Potter grabbed the pork and began tearing the raw fat with his teeth.

"Ain't you gonna fry it up, Dick?" Tucker asked, surprised.

"No wood," Potter mumbled, his mouth full. "Got no wood for a fire."

"I got a onion you might want," Sweet offered, holding out the vegetable.

51

"An onion! Damn me if I ain't forgot what a onion tastes like."

As Potter chewed ravenously, several of the other old prisoners gathered around to watch enviously. Josie felt a great pity for them. That pity was followed almost immediately by a sense of fear for himself and his friends. What on God's earth had they gotten into?

Finished now, Potter belched and sucked the fat off his fingers. "Now there was a meal fit for a king." He smiled at his new friends. "Well, boys, would you care to look around now, see your new home? Let's see, what would you want to see first?"

"Is there a surgeon here, Dick?" Josie asked.

"A surgeon?"

"I want him to look at the sergeant. Got a bullet in his shoulder."

Potter gave a contemptuous snort, then pointed toward a long line of men.

"See that?"

The men in the line looked in worse condition than McSpadden. Most of them were lying in the dirt.

Josie nodded.

"That's sick call. Do nothin' for you.

"Hell, I'm fine," McSpadden said, injecting an artificial bravado into his voice. "Show us around, Dick."

"All right. Let's see, we'll start over there." Potter pointed to half a dozen men, chained together around a thirty-six-pound ball.

"The Rebs caught those boys trying to escape."

"How long they been hooked up to that thing?"

Potter shrugged. "Don't rightly know. Forever, I guess. Leastwise, since the day they was caught. Let's see, what else can I show you? Oh, I know." He looked at Josie and smiled. "I'll show you where we *ain't* goin' fishin'. Come on."

Potter led the little group through the crowded camp until

they reached a slow-moving stream. A cloud of flies and other insects hung just over the water.

"This here, we call the Swamp. As you can see, it just about cuts the prison in half. This is the north half. Cross the bridge over there"—he pointed to a little footbridge near the wall—"and you'll get to the south side. There's two streets run across, Main Street, right behind us, and South Street, way down to the other end of the compound. Tell me, what do you think about our water supply?"

"My God!" Josie said, turning his head away in disgust.

"Should a warned you, I guess. It's a little fragrant if you catch it just right."

The stench was overwhelming, and the incessant buzzing of the flies was even louder than the constant chatter of the hundreds upon hundreds of men who were gathered around the stream. Some were bathing in it, others were doing their laundry, and a few were using it as a latrine. Despite all that, some people were drinking from it.

Before they reached the edge of the water, the flies attacked them in droves. Josie and the other new men began waving their arms madly to drive them away; Potter and the older prisoners made only a few halfhearted swipes at them.

"What the damn Rebels did," Potter said, as if unaware of the swarming insects, "was build this whole place downstream from their own tents and horses and dogs and everything. So they do whatever they do into the water 'fore it even comes here. And, believe me, you're not seeing the tenth of what *we* do to it."

"But men are actually *drinking* that water," 2nd Wisconsin said.

"Yep," Potter answered. "But them as do has already gone crazy. A man with any sense'd die rather'n drink from it."

"Is that the only water there is?" 2nd Wisconsin asked.

Potter scratched at his beard, pulling out some lice. He examined them for a moment, then tossed them aside. "Some boys and I are planning on digging a well up there."

He looked around, then continued, in a quieter voice, "Two, really. One for drinking and one for getting away. Want to see?"

"Yeah, we want to see it," Josie said.

Sweet was still looking at the Swamp. "You mean to tell me they do . . . *everything* in there?"

Potter nodded.

"Then that's why this whole place has such a stink to it," Sweet said.

"You'll get used to it. You'll get to where you don't even notice it so much after a couple months. C'mon, got some pards I want you to meet."

"Won't notice it?" Sweet said quietly to Josie. "My pigsty back home don't smell as bad as that."

"Now, this here road is Main Street I was tellin' you about," Potter continued, pointing to a dirt road that ran east and west through the middle of the camp, parallel to, and just north of, the Swamp. "My shebang is just about a hundred yards north of here."

As if conducting a tour, Potter led the little group away from the Swamp, and toward the north end of the open field.

Josie looked around the camp as they followed Potter. It was teeming with people, some moving about animatedly, others sitting lethargically, and still others lying down, in the last stages of a lingering death. They passed a sign advertising a laundry and tailor shop. This place was like a community. A community from hell, perhaps, but a community nevertheless.

"Hey, Tuck, you got all your tailorin' things with you?" McSpadden asked. "Shears and thread and such?"

"Yes."

"Well, then, one of us is goin' to be all right in here. One of us is goin' to be rich."

Tucker and the others laughed.

"And we'll enter old Sweet here in the prizefights," Potter suggested. "He's a big boy, 'spect he'll do pretty well."

"What are these things?" Josie asked, sweeping his hand out.

"What things?"

"These . . . these shelters. I see them on both sides of the Swamp. They're everywhere, but they're not tents."

"We call 'em shebangs."

"Shebangs?"

"Don't know who come up with the name, but it seems to fit. When we first got here, we didn't have no shelter of any kind. The Rebs hadn't built no barracks, 'cause what wood they was able to come up with, they used for the stockade walls an' such. What tents they had, they give to the Rebel guards. Us, they just turned loose here in the open field and said this was goin' to be our home."

"What did you do?"

Potter sighed. "What *could* we do? We began putting tents together out of whatever we had . . . blankets, shirts, extra pants, haversacks. Went up pretty quick, but some of 'em has got downright comfortable . . . what with diggin' a hole and buildin' up walls and coverin' it with a roof of sod, and all."

"Hey, look over there," Tucker said, pointing toward the Deadline. "What's goin' on?"

A prisoner was calling up to one of the guards in the tower.

"Look at that guard," Josie said. "Why, he can't be more than . . ."

"Twelve, thirteen, more'n likely," Potter said.

"I've seen youngsters as drummer boys," Josie said. "But that's a little young to be guarding a bunch of prisoners, isn't it?"

"It's all the Rebs got left," Potter explained. "The real young ones and the real old ones, that's who guards the prisoners. Their fightin'-age men is off in the war."

"Hey, sonny!" the prisoner at the Deadline called up to the guard tower. "Sonny, you got somethin' to eat?"

"Yeah," the young guard answered. "I got something to eat."

"What you got?"

"Got me two ears of corn."

"Give you a dollar for 'em." He held up the bill. "A Yankee greenback for both ears."

"What you think, Mike?" Wiggins called over to Allen's guard station. "Should I give the Yankee this here corn?"

"Done told you, Wiggins. You plannin' on givin' any food away, you give it to me."

"Watch this," Wiggins said, grinning. "Hey, you, Yankee. Whyn't you come over here?"

The prisoner shook his head. "Not me, I ain't comin' over there."

"Ethan, best you stay where you're at," one of the other prisoners called out.

"Don't worry none about me," Ethan called back. "I know what I'm doin'."

Josie felt Potter tense up. "What is it? What's going on?"

"I don't like the looks of this," Potter said. "Look over into that other turkey roost, there."

"Turkey roost?"

"That's what we call the guard towers. You see what I see?"

Josie saw Lieutenant Barrett calmly watching the exchange between the prisoner and the guard.

"That there is one of the most evil sons of bitches you'll ever run across," Potter said. "If he's got 'nything to do with it, even just a-watchin' it, it can't come to no good."

"You comin' over here to get your corn, or ain't you?" the young guard called.

"I told you, I'm not comin' across the line," Ethan replied.

"Why not?"

"'Cause it's the Deadline. You'll shoot me if I do."

"Who says I will? Now, you want something or not?"

"Yeah, I want them two ears of corn."

"All right, then, step across." The guard held up one of the ears of corn, and took a tiny nibble. "Won't last long."

Ethan turned to several of his friends, grinning broadly. "What do you think? Should I do it?"

"He's a Reb, Ethan. Don't trust him," one of the prisoners called back.

"Don't go, fella," Potter said under his breath. "If you do, he'll shoot you, sure as a gun's iron."

"Fellas, that's just a little boy up there," Ethan said. "Why, I've spanked pups older'n him. He ain't goin' to do nothin' to me."

"I think he's right," McSpadden said. "I can't see a boy that young doin' anything. Don't know what he's doin' up there in the first place."

"Told you, he's up there 'cause the Rebs done run out of men."

"Clearly, the boy's just playin'," McSpadden said. "Look at him. He's just havin' a good time, that's all."

Potter shook his head. "These kiddies scare me worse'n the soldiers. Folks say they get a thiry-day furlough ever' time they shoot one of us."

"I can't believe he'd really shoot," Josie said. "He and the prisoner are teasing each other, that's all."

"Yeah, and that just proves how new this here Ethan fella must be," Potter said. "I'm tellin' you boys right now, and I want you to listen to me. The Deadline is somethin' you don't ever want to tease about."

"But the lieutenant, he's watchin' it all." McSpadden pointed to Barrett, who hadn't taken his eyes off the developing drama. "Surely he'll stop it before it gets out of hand."

"Huh," Potter grunted. "He's probably the one that'll sign the furlough."

"Come on, Ethan, get away from there!" one of Ethan's friends shouted.

"Ah," Ethan said, "he ain't goin' to shoot me. He wants the dollar. Probably never had one before."

"Don't do it, Ethan."

"I sure do want that corn." Ethan turned toward his friends. "Can't you just taste it?"

The young guard took another nibble of the corn. "Better hurry!"

Ethan hesitated for a moment, then stuck his toe right up to the Deadline.

"Watch it, Ethan," some of his friends called to him.

"Damn, there's Mad Matthew!" Potter said, pointing out a young man who was dancing, clapping his hands, and making faces at the guards.

"Mad Matthew? That what you call him? I saw him right after we got here."

"His mind's gone," Potter said. He sighed. "Truth is, it's a wonder ever'body's mind ain't gone, with what we've had to go through here."

"The corn's goin' fast!" the guard warned. "You want it, you better come get it." He took another bite, bigger this time, and made a great show of enjoying it.

Ethan looked at his friends once again. "What the hell? I'm goin' to do it, fellas. You watch me if I don't." He called to the guard, "All right, here I come."

Private Allen had been watching the interplay between Wiggins and the prisoner, and he looked at the expression on the face of the prisoner. It was laughing, even mocking. Allen could feel hate for the prisoner filling his gut. He raised his rifle and sighted down the barrel, putting the bead sight right over the center of the prisoner's chest. The prisoner, keeping a wary eye on Wiggins, was unaware that Allen had just aimed his rifle at him. Trying to keep Wiggins calm, the prisoner fixed a smile on his face.

"Was you grinnin' like that just afore you kilt my brother, Yankee?" Allen asked under his breath. He thumbed back the hammer.

"Ethan, no!" someone yelled, just as Ethan stepped over the Deadline rail and started toward the turkey roost.

Private Allen didn't see a prisoner making a benign move across the Deadline. What he saw was a murderous Yankee coming toward his brother. He pulled the trigger.

The hammer snapped down, the cap popped, then the musket boomed and kicked back against his shoulder.

The report of the rifle startled Josie and the others. They looked on in shock as Ethan staggered backward, his hands clutching his throat, blood spilling through his fingers. His eyes were open wide, more in disbelief than anything else. He fell back, his body half on one side of the Deadline and half on the other. He flopped once, then died.

"You runty little son of a bitch!" one of the prisoners shouted, and several of the others began yelling and gesturing toward the young guard with the ear of corn.

"Weren't him! 'Twas the other un!" someone shouted, pointing toward Private Allen.

Allen brought his rifle back down while smoke was still coming from the barrel. With hands shaking so hard that he could barely control them, he started reloading.

Several prisoners, including Mad Matthew, reached across the Deadline to grab Ethan and drag him back.

"Don't nobody cross the line! Don't nobody else cross it!" Potter shouted, then pointed to the other towers. All the guards were holding their muskets at the ready.

"Hey, Barrett, you bastard! Give the little son of a bitch his thirty-day furlough . . . the dirty little coward."

"You fellas all know the rules," Barrett called down to them. "You all know the rules."

Josie saw the prisoners who had been most vocal turn and walk away, shaking their heads in anger and disbelief.

"Thirty-day furlough," one of the oldtimers shouted. "What a Reb won't do!"

"My God," Billy said. He hadn't been able to take his

eyes off Ethan's body. "These aren't people. These are animals."

"What do they do, Dick? Shoot you for fun in here?"

Allen had just finished reloading when a guard climbed the ladder to his post.

"The sergeant wants to see you, Allen," he said.

"Can't. My time ain't up yet."

"He sent me to do the rest of your time for you. He wants to see you now."

Allen swung his musket around.

"Hold it!" the new guard said, holding up his hand. "Unload that piece afore you climb down. Don't want you shootin' me like you did that poor dumb Yankee."

"Yeah, all right. Forgot." Allen used the ramrod to take out the wad and ball.

A few moments later, Private Allen reported to Sergeant Martindale, the sergeant of the guard. Martindale was sitting at a field table just inside the tent where the next relief guards were waiting to be posted.

"What'd you shoot the Yankee for, Private Allen?"

"He . . . he put his foot over the line. You can ask anyone that was out there. He come across the Deadline."

"I don't deny that. Half a dozen other men saw him come across."

"Well, then, see? I'm tellin' the truth."

"Half a dozen other men saw him come across," Sergeant Martindale repeated. "But none of them shot him. You're the only one who did."

"Lieutenant Barrett was there," Allen said. "Ask him. Did he say I done wrong?"

Martindale stroked his beard, then sighed and shook his head.

"No, he didn't say you did wrong."

"Then why you gettin' on to me? Warn't doin' no more'n my duty."

"I'm not getting on to you, Allen. I just wanted to know

why you saw fit to shoot the prisoner when no one else did. Was he a real threat? From what I understand, he was just comin' after the corn Wiggins was goin' to give him."

Allen snorted. "Wiggins warn't goin' to give him no corn. Don't you know that, Sergeant? He was just funnin' with him."

"Funning with him? You mean Wiggins was trying to draw the prisoner across the line?"

"Yes."

"So you could shoot him?"

"Yes."

"That's not much less than murder."

"No such thing. This here's war, ain't it? Soldiers get kilt in war."

"No, this isn't war. The war's over for them. They aren't soldiers anymore, they're prisoners. And you don't bait and kill prisoners like they're wild animals. We're responsible for their care and keeping, same as if they were our own."

"That ain't what Cap'n Wirz says. He asked me if I'd ever used my gun."

"When?"

"He asked me that today, just afore I went on guard. I told 'im I ain't, but he said maybe someday I'd get to avenge my brother. And that's what I done today."

"You think that what you did out there today avenged your brother?"

"I know it did, Sergeant. Hell, I kilt the son of a bitch that kilt my brother."

"I thought you shot someone because he came across the Deadline."

"I did. I shot 'im 'cause he come across the Deadline, and because he was the one kilt my brother."

"The same one?"

"Only kilt one today, Sergeant." Allen chuckled. "Kilt 'im deader'n shit, too. You shoulda seen the blood come flyin' outta his neck."

"Private Allen, what in God's name makes you think the

man you killed today is the same one who killed your brother?"

"Oh, I don't just think he is, I know he is. Cap'n Wirz tole me."

"Captain Wirz told you that?"

"That's exactly what he tole me. Sergeant Martindale? You know that thirty-day furlough you s'posed to get for killin' a Yankee?"

"That's just something the prisoners say. I know of no such policy."

"Well, it don't make no difference, 'cause I don't want no furlough. What I want is a chance to kill me some more Yankees."

Captain Wirz's headquarters:

Captain Wirz was having his lunch when Sergeant Martindale came in.

"May I speak with you for a few moments, Captain?"

"If you wish." Wirz pointed to the black-eyed peas on his plate. "When first I come to this country and this vegetable I see, I ask myself, what is it? It is not like any beans I have seen in Europe. It is not like any peas I have seen. It is most unusual."

"It's just plain ole black-eyed peas, Captain."

Wirz raked a piece of cornbread through the juice, then popped it into his mouth, sucking the juice from the end of his fingers. "Ah, but I have grown quite fond of them. Now, what brings you here?"

"Did you read my report on Private Allen?"

Wirz transferred a forkful of peas to his mouth. "*Ja*, I read your report. What about it?"

"Well, sir, I was wondering about your response to my suggestion that Private Allen be taken off parapet and given other duties."

"Nonsense, why would I want to do a thing like that? I know Private Allen. He is *gut* soldier."

"He's the one who shot the prisoner today."

"*Ja*, this I know. But the prisoner crossed the Deadline."

"Yes, sir, and several other guards saw him as well, but Private Allen was the only one who took it upon himself to shoot."

"Then punish the others, those who did not shoot . . . not the one who did. Private Allen was only following my orders."

"I don't believe your orders are what Private Allen was thinking about when he shot the prisoner. Private Allen tole me that he actually believes the prisoner he shot is the one who killed his brother. What's more, Captain, he told me he got that idea from you."

"*Ja*, so, what is wrong with that? Nothing, I think, if the job it makes easier."

A knock on the door interrupted their conversation.

"*Ja*, in come," Wirz called.

Lieutenant Barrett stuck his head into the room.

"Excuse me, Captain Wirz, but I thought you'd like to know there are a couple of officers coming up the road."

"Who are they?"

Lieutenant Barrett shook his head. "Don't know, Captain. I do know that one of 'em is a colonel, though."

"A colonel? Coming here?" Wirz got up and quickly cleared the dishes from his table. "I wonder what they want."

Barrett heard one of the guards greet the arriving officers. "I don't know," he replied. "But they're here. I guess we're about to find out."

"*Ja*, we will find out. Sergeant Martindale, return to your duties."

"Yes, sir."

"And Sergeant Martindale," Wirz called. Martindale paused.

"Yes, sir?"

"For Private Allen, make no trouble. He is *gut* soldier. For him, make no trouble. *Verstehen sie?*"

"Yes, sir."

After Martindale left, Wirz nodded to Barrett to show the visiting officers into his quarters.

"Gentlemen, I extend the welcome of my command."

"Captain Wirz? I'm Colonel Chandler, and this is my aide, Lieutenant Dahlgren."

"So, Colonel, to what do I owe the honor of this unexpected visit?"

"The Department of War has detailed me to inspect all our prison camps." Colonel Chandler showed Wirz his credentials. "We'll try not to create any fuss, though we may be here for a while."

"Yes, of course. If there is anyth—"

"No," Chandler said, cutting him off. "Just proceed with your duties. If I need to speak with you, I'm sure I'll be able to find you. Thank you, Captain."

Wirz and Chandler exchanged salutes, then Chandler and his aide left. Wirz turned back to Barrett.

"Lieutenant Barrett, what do you suppose brought them here? Why has Richmond suddenly become concerned with what goes on among the prisoners?"

"I have no idea, sir. But I'm not concerned. We're doing the best we can do, under the circumstances."

"*Ja, unter* the circumstances," Wirz said, almost as if talking to himself.

Inside the prison compound, near Dick Potter's shebang, Tucker was cutting Potter's hair. The others had made themselves as comfortable as they could. A few feet away, near another shebang, a sergeant stood quietly, almost as if he were on guard.

"That's John Gleason," Potter said of the quiet, watchful man. "Good man. He's the leader of the group from the 184th Pennsylvania."

"Hold still," Tucker said.

Potter chuckled. "You're taking five pounds of hair and ten pounds of bugs off me."

"Dick, what're those men doing over there?" Josie asked. Three soldiers and seven slaves, carrying long sticks and ax handles, were poking into the ground around the shebangs.

"Oh," Potter said, nonchalantly. "That there's a tunnel gang."

"A tunnel gang?"

"They're lookin' for tunnels."

Suddenly the ground outside one of the shebangs gave way, and the man who found it called to the leader of the group.

"Tunnel! Tunnel!"

"What do you mean, tunnel?" a prisoner protested. "Ain't no such thing!"

"Looks like they found the Iowa tunnel," Potter said, as the guards grabbed the protesting prisoner.

"It's not a tunnel, it's a well!" he yelled as they dragged him off.

One of the prisoners, who had been watching the tunnel gang at work, started moving toward the Pennsylvania shebang.

"Who's that fella in such a hurry?" McSpadden asked.

"That'll be Martin Blackburn. He's one of the Pennsylvania men."

"Found the Iowa tunnel," Blackburn said to Gleason. "They're headin' this way."

Gleason immediately ducked into the Pennsylvania shebang. McSpadden turned again to Potter.

"Dick, these Pennsylvania boys. Do you think they're diggin' a tunnel?"

"What makes you ask that?"

"I've got a hunch. How about it? Are they?"

Potter hesitated for a moment. "You're my sergeant, but . . . some questions it's hard to ask in here."

McSpadden thought for a moment, then nodded. "I can

understand that. I'd like you to go tell that sergeant I'd be grateful for a private word with him."

Potter, his hair freshly cut, stood up.

"Tell him we mean no harm, and he can trust us."

"I'll do what I can."

Josie, McSpadden, and the other Massachusetts men watched as Potter disappeared inside the Pennsylvania shebang. A moment later he came back outside, accompanied by Sergeant Gleason. Gleason looked at McSpadden skeptically, then motioned to him.

"Follow me, over here." McSpadden and Josie started toward him, but Gleason held up his hand to stop them. "Just you," he said, pointing to McSpadden. "Alone."

Gleason waited until they were out of earshot of anyone else, then he turned to McSpadden. "What do you want?" he asked.

"I don't want to do anything against the grain here, Sergeant. We mean you no harm. Dick Potter will vouch for us. I've got some good men with me who'll do anything they can to get out of this place. If there's a way, could you use some help?"

Just out of earshot of the two sergeants' conversation, Josie waited quietly.

"What's goin' on, Josie?" Sweet asked. "You think they're makin' some kind of a deal?"

"I think they're at least talking about it."

The Massachusetts men studied the two negotiators, trying to tell from the expressions on their faces, and the way they held their heads, hands, and bodies, whether the deal was being made.

At the Pennsylvania shebang, another group of men was watching just as intently, for their own fate depended upon how good a judge of character their sergeant would be. If his trust was misplaced, it would affect them all.

A hard, wiry man, who had obviously been digging, came out of the Pennsylvania tent.

"What's going on?" he asked.

"Hello, Wisnovsky," one of the other Pennsylvania men said. "Sergeant Gleason's working a deal."

"What kind of a deal?"

"We don't know yet."

A barely perceptible nod passed between McSpadden and Gleason, then they shook hands.

"We're in, boys," Josie said, smiling broadly.

McSpadden took half a dozen steps toward his men, then stopped. "You men follow me."

Josie and the others followed their sergeant into the Pennsylvania shebang. There, in addition to Gleason, Blackburn, and Wisnovsky, they also met a young man, not yet twenty, named Tobias.

"I told him, course we'll help with the digging," McSpadden said, shifting his position to ease the pain in his shoulder. "And glad for the chance."

"You men got 'ny tools?" Gleason asked.

"Boys?" McSpadden asked.

The Massachusetts group looked at each other dejectedly. Had they been included, only now to be excluded because they had no tools?

"Spoons, pans, canteens, nearly anything will do," Potter told them.

The mood lightened and the men smiled.

"Sure, we've got things," Tucker said. "If things like that are all it takes, then we've got 'em." Eagerly the men began sorting through the contents of their haversacks, coming up with an assortment of items they could use as implements.

"Sergeant Gleason, we appreciate you including us. But we don't want to do anything that would hurt your chances. So, if you think we'd be a problem to you . . ." Josie let the rest of the sentence go unstated.

Gleason shook his head. "No, this is good. More of us

they have to follow, the better the chances some of us will make it."

"What's the chances of getting outside the walls?" McSpadden asked.

"Actually, that'll be the easiest part," Gleason answered.

"The easiest?" McSpadden was surprised.

"Don't mind tellin' you, Sergeant, we know a thing or two about tunnelin'," Blackburn said proudly.

"These boys," Potter said, indicating Gleason, Blackburn, and Wisnovsky, "are coal miners from west Pennsylvania."

"And once we get outside?" Tucker asked. "What are our chances then?"

Potter snorted. "They heard Wirz talkin' 'bout his dogs."

"We didn't just hear about 'em, Dick. We saw 'em," McSpadden said.

"We got a nice surprise for old Wirz," young Tobias said. "Can we tell?" he asked Gleason.

"What the boy is talkin' about," Gleason explained, "is that one of the slaves the Rebs have got working on the wall for 'em brung us a map. We can go creek and river the whole way . . . swim and float on logs—creeks to Flint River, Flint to Apalachicola, Apalachicola to the Gulf of Mexico."

"Ain't a dog alive can follow us if we never touch land," Tobias said proudly.

Tucker, Sweet, and Billy looked at each other, then smiled. Gleason chuckled.

"You boys been frettin' 'bout them dogs?" Gleason asked.

"We sure have," Josie said. "This is good news."

"When can we start digging?" McSpadden asked.

"Soon as we eat in the morning," Gleason answered.

"That is, *if* we eat," Wisnovsky added.

"It's hard work," Blackburn said. "Need to keep your strength up." He looked at McSpadden, obviously concerned about his wound. "You might want to wait a few days, Sergeant. Seems like they took a piece out of your arm, there. We should take a look at it."

"I'll be fine," McSpadden said. "How long will the diggin' take?"

Gleason shrugged. "Month. Maybe more, maybe less."

Josie dumped his haversack on the ground, emptying it of rations. "All we have is a little hardtack," he said. "But you're welcome to half of it."

Josie and the others began passing out bits of food to their new friends, who took it gratefully and divided it into equal shares before they started to eat. Only Potter declined.

"I already had mine," he said, belching.

McSpadden's condition was growing worse. Even though he was sitting down, he was having trouble keeping his balance. Suddenly he fell to one side.

"Let's give him some room," Josie said, quickly taking charge of the situation. "Massachusetts men, you wait outside."

"Pennsylvania men, too," Gleason put in. "All except Blackburn. You stay."

The men left as directed, shuffling past the now unconscious McSpadden.

"Josie, you think . . . ?" Billy asked.

Josie put his hands on Billy's shoulder. "Go on, Billy. We'll do what we can."

After everyone was gone, Josie and those who remained looked down at McSpadden.

"All we got's a pocket knife," Gleason said.

Josie looked at him. "You ever do anything like that?"

"No. You?"

Josie shook his head, then looked at Blackburn, who also shook his head. Josie took a deep breath. "Yeah, well, the thing is, I don't see as we have much choice."

Gleason looked down at McSpadden. "Wish I had some whiskey for you, friend," he said quietly.

McSpadden opened his eyes. "Hell, I always wish I had some whiskey."

"This is the best we can do, Sergeant," Josie said, handing a dirty rag to McSpadden. McSpadden took the rag, then jammed it into his mouth. Biting down hard, he looked at the others and nodded.

Gleason wiped the knife blade on his pants a few times while Blackburn washed McSpadden's shoulder.

"The water's clean, Sergeant," Blackburn reassured him. "Come from a well, not from the Swamp."

"You two fellers better hold him down," Gleason said, getting the knife into position.

"Got 'im?" Josie asked, taking hold on one side.

"Got 'im," Blackburn answered.

Gleason began to cut.

"Mmmmmmmmmh!" McSpadden moaned as the knife cut into his flesh.

"You're goin' to have to hold 'im still!"

"We're tryin' but he's a strong man," Blackburn explained.

Gleason pushed the knife in deeper, twisting and cutting.

McSpadden's eyes were open wide, and his muscles were taut in his neck and shoulders as he bit down hard, fighting against the pain.

"I found the bullet. If I can get the son of a bitch out . . . ," Gleason said. By now his hands and McSpadden's shoulder were covered with blood. "Hang on just a little longer. I've got ahold of it."

McSpadden arched his back, strained against Josie and Blackburn, then suddenly relaxed and fell back, his head lolling to one side.

"Dead?" Gleason asked, looking up from his work.

"No, passed out," Josie said. "Probably a good thing. Keep going."

Gleason returned to the task at hand.

Chapter 5

It was night. The turkey roosts thrust darkly into the star-dusted sky. Leaning over the railing of the towers, the guards, shadows upon shadows, kept a close watch on the prisoners below. Here and there, like winking fireflies, tiny candles flickered in the void, but they did little to push away the darkness.

This was the time for sleeping, but even when sleep did come, it provided little rest, for the prisoners were sleeping the slumber of the exhausted. Now, as during the day, they fought hunger, thirst, pain, insects, stench, and the numbing closeness of each other. Only the merciless heat of the sun was missing.

One part of the camp, however, stood out from the rest. A group of men gathered in the glare of a dozen or more torches. This was the area where the Raiders congregated; here, well-fed and better-clothed men wee singing bawdy songs, drinking whiskey, and having a party. Their raucous behavior was presided over by a large man in a gaudy green coat.

Collins, the man in the green coat, watched as one of his lieutenants prepared a hotfoot for one of the more recent recruits. Unaware of what was happening until the burning punk reached his foot, the recruit jumped up and let out a howl of pain.

"Ouch! Who did that? What'd you go and do that for?"

The protest was met with an outburst of laughter.

"Peters, way you was hoppin' aroun' there, folks'd think you was doin' a dance!" Curtis teased. Again, the others laughed.

"Gimme some more that whiskey," Collins demanded. In the gleam of the torchlight, the bottle changed hands. Collins took several hefty swallows.

"Collins, you think we'll ever get outta here?" Peters asked, gingerly putting weight on his foot.

"Hell, boy, what you want to get outta here for?" Collins took another drink of whiskey. "You know, gents, we got it good here, better'n before we was captured, even. I say, let those other fools stay out there on the battlefield and get themselves shot. Long as you fellas stick by me, you'll have all the food, water"—he held up the whiskey bottle—"and whiskey you need. Now, you tell me. What more could a body want?"

"Maybe a pretty woman," Munn suggested.

"Hell, Munn, you never had no pretty woman before you was catched. What makes you think you ought to have one now?" Curtis said.

"Pretty woman? Hell, somebody's ugly as you prob'ly never had no woman," Collins added, passing the whiskey bottle around.

The Raiders laughed uproariously at their leader's joke.

"Jamie, m'lad," Collins said.

"Yes, sir, Mr. Collins?"

"I've a taste for some cheese with my breakfast eggs.

Take a stroll over to see our man Mason, see if he can come up with any."

"What we got to trade?"

"Take a couple dollars in Yankee greenbacks. That'll satisfy 'im."

"Yes, sir, Mr. Collins."

Collins reached into his pocket and pulled out a roll of money. He had nearly a thousand dollars stuffed into the various pockets of his jacket, shirt, and trousers. All the money they had taken from the new prisoners, from the time they hit upon the scheme, had gone directly to Collins. Ostensibly he was the treasurer of the Raiders, so this wasn't his money, it was "their" money. But only he had the right to decide when, and for what, the money was to be spent. And if he spent some on himself, for the cheese, eggs, pork, flour, peas, and other food for his private mess, he also spent a lot on the rest of the Raiders. He bought all of their liquor and their food . . . and if it wasn't quite as good as his private mess, it was still many times better than anything the rest of the prisoners had.

"Munn," Collins called.

"Yes?"

"The new fish arrived today. Know where they went?"

Munn smiled. "Sure do. Went over there with that Pennsylvania bunch."

Collins took another swallow of whiskey, then passed the bottle to Munn.

"Why don't you get a few of the boys together?" he suggested.

Munn drank deeply, then handed the bottle back. "I'll choose them as may be lookin' for a little excitement."

Some distance from the Raiders' area, Billy and Potter were walking through the darkness. Billy was holding a spare shirt Josie had given him. They picked their way carefully through the shebangs, stepping over and around sleeping and quietly talking men.

"Need some whiskey! Got a shirt here to trade. Need some whiskey for a sergeant!" Potter called.

"You know, Dick, Josie said it don't have to be whiskey," Billy said quietly. "Says he'd rather have medicine."

"Wouldn't trust any medicine as we might get in here," Potter replied.

"Hi, fellas, what's up?" asked a young boy, not quite sixteen, as he joined them.

"We're tryin' to get some whiskey to use as medicine for our sergeant," Potter answered. "Billy, I'd like to introduce you to Patrick Shay. He was a New York drummer boy that got catched at Culpepper."

"You're kind of young for a place like this, aren't you?" Billy asked, secretly pleased to see someone younger than he.

"Young?" Potter laughed bitterly. "Hell, this boy ain't young, Billy. He's been right here in this prison ever since they built the damn place. So when you get to thinkin' about it, I reckon that makes him about the oldest man here. Now he's sort of the camp's good luck piece."

"I do bring folks good luck," Patrick said. "Maybe I can bring your sergeant some." He began calling out with the others. "Got a good shirt here . . . need some good whiskey for a good sergeant . . . good shirt, good man, need some whiskey."

"Whiskey," Potter called.

"Need some whiskey," Billy added, holding up the shirt to advertise what they had to trade.

Inside the Pennsylvania shebang, Josie was sitting on the ground beside the prostrate form of his feverish sergeant. Josie's knees were drawn up in front of him, and he was writing a letter by the flickering light of a small candle.

Dear Mother and Father,

I'm writing you from my new home, in Andersonville Prison, in Georgia. We arrived today after a long, and

not very comfortable, ride by railroad. I'm with my
Sergeant and Thomas Sweet and Elijah Tucker and some
of the others, and we are most all well.

We did find the most wonderful thing when we got here.
Dick Potter is alive, and was not killed as we all thought.
He has been here a long time, and is "showing us the
ropes," as we say. He was wounded in both legs but is
better now. We're going fishing with his father as soon as
we come home, and then I want him to visit with us,
mother, so you can fatten him up with your butter biscuits
and mince pie.

McSpadden groaned and moved. Josie looked up from
his letter to see if there was anything he could do. Putting
his hand on McSpadden's forehead, he felt the heat of the
fever, then remoistened the cloth and placed it again on his
sergeant's forehead.

Josie could hear someone singing "Kathleen Mavourneen." The singing was accompanied by a banjo.

"You hear that, Sergeant? That's Martin Blackburn singing. He's not doing as good a job as you did for those
beautiful Southern ladies, but you have to admit, he's not
half bad."

Outside the shebang the Massachusetts and Pennsylvania
men were listening appreciatively to the concert. Blackburn
noticed that one man in his audience, Thomas Sweet,
seemed particularly attentive.

Blackburn leaned toward Sweet. "You like music, I can
tell. You play anything?"

Sweet shook his head. "Wish I did, though."

"C'mere," Blackburn invited. "Sit by me, and I'll teach
you."

"You will?"

"Sure I will. Now, the first thing you got to learn is the
fingering," Blackburn explained, beginning his lesson.

• • •

Inside the Pennsylvania shebang, McSpadden's fever broke, and he started shivering in his uncomfortable sleep. Josie took off his shirt and wrapped it around McSpadden to help ward off the chill.

Billy and Potter came back into the shebang.

"How's he doing?" Potter asked.

"Not very well."

"That your shirt around him?" Billy asked.

Josie nodded.

"Here," Billy said. "We didn't find no whiskey, so you might as well put this on."

"Thanks," Josie said, taking the shirt. He looked at Billy as he slipped the shirt on. "You all right, Billy?"

"Yeah, I'm fine, now. I mean, just knowing we're going to get out of here." He looked at Potter. "You know, with the coal miners. That makes it a lot easier."

"It makes it easier for all of us," Josie agreed.

"Would you like me to sit with him for a while?" Billy asked.

"Sure." Josie stood up.

"I'll watch him good, Josie, I promise."

"I know you will, Billy." Josie put his hand on Billy's shoulder and gave it a squeeze. Then he and Potter left.

Josie and Potter found a place to sit down outside, and Josie, having finished his letter, fished out an envelope.

"Writing home, Josie?"

"Yes."

"Give 'em my respects, will you?"

"I already did that." Josie cocked his head to one side, then smiled. "You know, Dick, that was some haircut Tucker gave you. Now you're bald as a new-hatched egg."

"Egg? Egg? Give you ten dollar for it," a distant voice called.

From somewhere in the darkness, another man laughed.

Dick ran his hand across the top of his newly shorn head.

"Must've had a thousand chiggers in my hair. Itched like the devil."

From a few yards away, Josie heard Tucker's voice. "Friend, when they *do* feed you around here, what do they feed you?"

"Mush," someone answered.

"Mush?" Tucker asked.

"Mush!" half a dozen voices said as one.

"Rotten cornmeal mush," the first voice reiterated.

Tucker gave what might have been a laugh.

"Josie? Tell me about the boys," Potter said. "How's the old company doin'?"

"We're way down, Dick. From a hundred to forty-two, last I knew."

"Your cousin Bob? How's he farin'?"

"Killed at Cold Harbor," Josie answered bitterly. "Benjamin and James, too." He paused for a moment. "Listen, Dick, is there any way I can get a letter out of here?"

"Yes, if you give a guard two dollars. You got two dollars?"

Josie shook his head.

"Well, I got one squirreled away, but one ain't enough. You'll have to come up with another one." Potter looked directly at Josie. "Josie, you think my father knows I'm a prisoner? I mean, if you all thought I was killed. . . ."

"I don't know, Dick."

"I would-a wrote him, but I didn't have the money either." Dick was silent for a moment. "Be terrible, he thinks I'm dead."

Josie smiled. "Yes, but just think how it'll be when you show up alive and kicking."

Potter chuckled. "Well, I don't know about the kicking." He lifted his crutch.

A few yards away, Blackburn was still showing Sweet the fingering for the banjo. "Tomorrow, if you like, we'll go greyback racing," he said.

"Greyback racing?"

"That's what we call the lice. We race 'em, and we bet on 'em."

"We call Johnny Reb 'greyback,'" Sweet said.

Blackburn grunted. "Well, in here, we call lice 'greybacks,' and Johnny Reb, 'lice.'"

"Well, I'm glad those other fellas have quit their caterwaulering," Tucker said.

"What caterwaulering?" Wisnovsky asked.

"The singing and shouting over there."

"Oh, you mean the Raiders. Well, you get to where you pay no attention to 'em. There's no tellin' what they'll be up to next," Wisnovsky said.

"Wonder why they quit." Gleason looked toward the Raiders.

"Who cares, long as they did. Why don't you two fellas play some more?" Tucker asked. "That was real nice."

Blackburn and Sweet went back to their music.

Potter and Josie were still talking, quietly enough not to disturb anyone who wanted to listen to Blackburn's banjo playing.

"The way you kill the lice in here, Josie," Potter began, "is to get some wood, hold your clothes close as you can to the fire without them catching, and they'll go pop-pop-pop . . . flies and chiggers and gnats and things. Truth is, though, you can't do anything about it. They get you even at night."

"Dick?"

"Yeah?"

"Why do they keep the officers separate from the men? Is it like they say? That they don't want the men to have their own leaders?"

Potter nodded. "Yes. Well, actually we do have a couple officers in here with us. Got two captains from the 54th Massachusetts. They led colored troops, so they're being punished by gettin' put in here." He picked up some loose stones and began playing with them. "Anyhow, we don't really need officers. Never saw the day a plain New Bedford fisherman couldn't outfight, outthink, outanything a Johnny Reb might do."

"What do you do when it rains?" Josie recognized the voice as that of 60th Ohio.

"Get wet, you dern fool!" another voice answered.

There was more laughter in the distance, and Josie wondered how that could be . . . how there could be laughter in hell.

"It's good for us when we get rain," Potter said, loudly enough that 60th Ohio could hear him. "'Cause what you do is, you catch it."

"Huh?"

"You catch the rain in your clothes," Potter explained. "Catch it in your clothes, then wring the clothes out and drink the water. That's the best place to get water, 'cause you sure don't want to drink it from the Swamp. Do that and you'll get sick, and you'll die."

"What do you do when it doesn't rain?" Josie asked.

"We do without."

"How do you do that?"

"Well, you gotta teach yourself. And I get a swallow from a well every now and then. You can do it, Josie. Lotta the boys can't, but you can."

"Hi, fellas," someone said.

Potter and Josie looked up, and Dick smiled. "Why, Patrick Shay, what are you doing here?"

Patrick held out a bottle of whiskey. "Brought this for your sergeant."

Josie gasped in surprise. Quickly he reached up to take the bottle. He held it under his nose and smelled it.

"I figured we could count on you, Patrick," Dick said. "You're a good man, probably the best man in this whole prison."

Patrick beamed under the praise.

"Damn! This is good whiskey!" Josie said after taking a sniff. He held the bottle out and looked at it. "I don't know where you got this. Wait a minute. Let me give you the shirt."

Josie started to get up, but before he was on his feet, Patrick was gone.

"Why did he leave like that?" Josie asked.

Smiling, Potter shrugged. "That's Patrick for you. He did it 'cause he wanted to, not to get paid."

Josie held the whiskey bottle out to study it for a moment, then he sighed. "I'm going to take this in to Sergeant McSpadden."

Inside the shebang, Billy was trying to keep McSpadden comfortable.

"Any change?"

"No."

Josie handed Billy the bottle. "Give him this when he wakes up."

"All right."

"You sure you don't want to be relieved?"

"No, Josie, I'm fine."

Josie nodded, then stepped outside.

"Give it to him?" Potter asked.

"He's still asleep."

"I don't know, Josie," Potter said, chuckling. "Ol' McSpadden goin' to taste that, he's goin' to think he's died and gone to heaven."

Josie sat on the ground beside Potter, then looked around at this new world into which he had been suddenly and cruelly thrust.

"Will you tell me what else I have to do, Dick, to stay alive in this place?"

"Yes," Potter promised. "And, Josie, we really will go fishing together, won't we? Soon as we get back?"

"Get outta here. I've been looking forward to that more'n anything."

"It'll be somethin', won't it?" Potter said. "You know, of all my friends, my father always liked you and Bob best." He paused for a moment, then added, "Me, too."

"Well, Dick, I'm truly honored that—"

Josie's reply was cut off by a loud shout of alarm.

"Raiders! Raiders!"

Martin Blackburn's banjo music stopped in mid-chord.

"What the hell?" a muffled voice called from outside.

Quickly Josie and Potter got to their feet, as did everyone around the Pennsylvania and Massachusetts areas. "What is it?" Josie asked.

"It's Collins and his boys. Sounds like they're pullin' a raid on us."

The Massachusetts and Pennsylvania men were alert, on their feet, and ready to meet the invaders. But they were overwhelmed by more than fifty of the Raiders, armed with clubs, knives, and rocks. Collins and Curtis, carrying heavy clubs, were leading the assault.

"Get 'em, boys!" Collins shouted. "Get 'em good, then take everything they've got!"

Collins began swinging the club left and right, crashing onto the startled and unarmed men. Josie avoided the first swing at him, then managed to catch the club wielder with a hard punch in the nose. Before he could follow through, another club wielder took a swing at Josie. Josie ducked; the club missed his head but caught him on the shoulder, sending pain radiating throughout his body.

Inside the shebang, Sergeant McSpadden's sleep was broken by the commotion. "Billy, what is it?" he asked.

When the fighting started, Billy didn't know whether he should go outside to help his friends or stay to protect Sergeant McSpadden. He decided that McSpadden was his responsibility, so he stayed.

Suddenly the shebang came down around them as the Raiders jerked the bits of cloth and canvas off the frame Potter had built. Billy threw himself over McSpadden, but despite his best efforts, a dozen feet kicked and stamped on his sergeant even as he was feeling the blows himself.

Outside, Munn was dancing around, waving his knife while shouting directions to the others—and being careful to stay out of danger. Josie, Dick, Tyce, and Sweet moved closer together, putting their backs against each other to form a tight little circle that would prevent anyone from getting behind any of them. Though they were badly outnumbered, their defensive posture was such that the Raiders who did get in paid a price for their effort. Tyce managed to grab one of their attackers and bite off half his ear, spitting out the piece of flesh, then grinning with blood-stained teeth as the Raider retreated, screaming in pain.

One among the defenders was at a distinct disadvantage. Potter's leg wounds prevented him from standing without the crutches. Seeing that, Curtis snatched one of his crutches while another Raider grabbed the other one. Potter was now barely able to stand, and weaponless, as two Raiders moved in to take advantage of the situation. They pulled him out of the defensive circle the others had formed.

"Dick!" Josie called out in alarm.

Laughing, Munn danced around the group, waving his knife. When he saw that Potter had been pulled away, he shouted, "That's him! That's him! Get him! Get the son of a bitch!"

Collins swung his club at Potter, who, twisting to avoid it, presented his back to Munn. That was all the opening Munn needed.

By now Gleason and Wisnovsky had joined the fray. They were strong, capable fighters, and though their presence didn't bring a victory, it did allow Josie and the others to survive.

Inside what had been the shebang, the attacking Raiders continued to kick and pummel the two men on the ground. Billy managed to inflict some damage. A hard thrust with the heel of his boot smashed the kneecap of one, a toe in the groin brought down another.

"Clean 'em out!" Collins yelled. "Clean 'em out! Take what you can, and let's get out of here!"

Though he was fighting desperately, Josie was unable to hold off the attack any longer. Three of the Raiders grabbed him, and a fourth began smashing his fist into Josie's face. His mouth tasted of blood, and one of his eyes swelled shut. He felt his knees buckle, then he went down.

"Let's go, men! Let's get out of here!" Collins ordered. Almost as quickly as the attack began, it was broken off as the Raiders obeyed Collins' order to withdraw.

"My shears!" Tucker shouted. "My thread!"

"Anyone hurt?" Gleason asked, assessing his casualties now that the immediate battle was over.

"My coat, my blanket," 2nd Wisconsin mourned. "They got my coat and my blanket."

Slowly, Josie got to his hands and knees. The Raiders were moving back into their own area. They were well armed and formed a powerful attack group. They feared no one.

Shaking his head to clear it, Josie saw that one of the Raiders was carrying his haversack. Another had Blackburn's banjo. Then he saw Collins—almost marching, not running away. Laughing, he was holding up a coat and a blanket, waving them over his head like trophies.

"Yes, sir, boys, stick with ol' Collins!" he shouted. "You'll live like kings!"

Curtis, with Munn at his side, was carrying two haversacks. Munn was holding Blackburn's banjo, looking defiantly over his shoulder, daring anyone to come after him.

At the scene of the battle, McSpadden, blood streaming into his eyes, managed to pull himself up. Out of instinct, he spoke the words he had spoken many times. "Massachusetts men! Give me a report! Everybody all right?"

The Massachusetts men were stunned by what had just happened to them, too stunned to notice that Sergeant McSpadden had managed to pull himself up.

With no small effort, Josie stood up. He looked at the

remains of Potter's shebang. Nothing was left except a few broken sticks scattered about, and the bruised and bleeding men who had fought so gallantly in its defense.

"Don't worry about your shebang, Dick. We'll help put it together again," Josie said. When he didn't get an answer, he looked around. "Dick? Dick, where are you? You all right?"

"Josie," Tucker said, pointing.

Josie looked to where Tucker was pointing, then felt a wave of grief and anger as he saw Potter's body. Its contorted position was stark evidence that his friend was dead.

"Dick! No!" Quickly Josie knelt beside his friend's body.

"The bastards," Blackburn said. "They took my music. . . ."

Sweet put his hand on Blackburn's shoulder. "We'll get it back. I promise."

McSpadden, blood streaming down his face, was still on his feet. "Josie, lad, where are you?"

"I'm here, Sergeant," Josie replied quietly. He picked up Potter's crumpled form, then cradled him in his arms.

"Are you all right, lad?" McSpadden asked. "Are you all right?"

"He's dead, Sergeant. Dick is dead."

Chapter 6

The next morning:

Sometimes, in Andersonville, death was a welcome visitor to men who had been suffering for a long and agonizing time. At other times its arrival was swift and unexpected, as with Dick Potter. Regardless of the circumstances, they all wound up at the Deadhouse.

The Deadhouse was just outside the south gate, inside the sally port between the stockade and the outside wall. It was here that carts, filled with bodies of men who had died during the night or the previous day, were brought.

When Josie and Tobias came out of the Deadhouse after having delivered Potter's body, a guard was watching them as he casually ate a buttered biscuit.

"Look at the little son of a bitch," Tobias said. "I'd like to shove that biscuit down his throat."

Josie chuckled. "No, I'd rather shove the biscuit down *our* throats, then shove his teeth down *his* throat."

They laughed out loud.

"What you Yankee bastards laughin' at?" Private Allen asked.

"Nothing you'd understand, Reb," Josie answered.

Allen picked up his rifle. "You two get on back in there, now. I done kilt me one Yankee son of a bitch for crossin' the Deadline. Wouldn't bother me none to kill the two of you."

"You can't do it, you little shit," Josie said. He nodded toward the rifle. "You've only got one load. You could get one of us, and the other one would kill you before anyone else could get here."

A line of perspiration broke out on Allen's upper lip, and he licked at it. He motioned toward the gate with his rifle. "Go on," he said, his voice cracking nervously. "Git back in there."

Allen watched as the inner gate was opened and the two Yankee prisoners went back inside. He didn't like guard duty when he was on the ground with them. He much preferred being on the turkey roosts. There, he was fifteen feet high. Couldn't nobody get to him up there.

As Josie and Tobias started back to the stockade, a wagon creaked slowly by. This was one of the wagons that picked up those who had died during the night. The driver had a handkerchief tied across his nose to blot out the stench of his cargo.

Josie stopped and stared at it. He was no stranger to death, having seen bodies on the battlefield. But this type of slow, lingering, and senseless death was beyond him.

"Look at that," he said.

"It's like that purt' near ever' mornin'," Tobias replied.

"It doesn't have to be this way. With just the slightest bit of humane treatment, the same kind you'd give to farm animals, all these men wouldn't have to die."

"We ain't equal to the farm animals, far as the Rebs are concerned," Tobias said matter-of-factly. "We're more like the barnyard shit on their shoes." Tobias saw some heavy pieces of wood on the ground. He called to the closest guard, "Hey, Reb, all right for me to get those?"

The guard shrugged. "Sure, go ahead, you can have it."

"Thanks."

Tobias picked up the wood and put it on his shoulder.

Just inside the south gate stood another wagon, pulled by a team of mules. This was the rations wagon, and prisoners, mostly sergeants, were beginning to gather around, waiting for the distribution of food that they would take back to their individual groups. Gleason was among them.

"Wait a minute," Gleason called to them. "When I get the sack of food, you can go back with me."

Josie and Tobias walked over to stand beside him. The sorrow of the task he had just completed was still evident in Josie's face. Noticing it, Gleason asked, "You fellas just take Dick to the Deadhouse?"

Josie nodded.

"It's a bad thing," Gleason said.

"What makes it real hard is, we all thought he was dead. Then we came here and found him alive. And now . . . ." Josie shrugged.

Tobias was younger than Josie, but he had been in the prison much longer, and had long ago hardened himself to the loss of friends. Dick's death was already behind him. He was staring at two Confederate officers he had never seen before. One was a colonel, the other a lieutenant.

"Who's that?" he asked, pointing toward them.

"Heard the colonel's name is Chandler," Gleason said. "The lieutenant's Dahlgren. The Reb government sent 'em to inspect us." Gleason spit on the ground. "Nice to know they care."

"Sergeant, if you don't mind, I'm going on back, check in

on McSpadden," Josie said. He looked at the two Confederate inspectors. "You think there's any chance their being here might actually improve our conditions?"

Gleason shook his head. "Don't see how it could. Hell, it wouldn't take more'n a minute to look at this place for a person to know what's wrong. The fact that they're still hangin' around tells me their bein' here don't mean a damn thing."

"Yeah, maybe you're right."

"See you later, Josie. I'm going to stay with Sergeant Gleason," Tobias said. He showed Gleason the two pieces of wood. "Look what I found on the way back from the Deadhouse, Sergeant."

Gleason looked at them without comment, then picked up the small burlap sack of meal that was to be their food ration. When they started back, he said, "You did good, Tobias. We'll use 'em for a tunnel brace."

Tobias beamed under the praise.

When Josie returned to the area, he saw Wisnovsky and Benton rebuilding the Pennsylvania shebang. Tyce was there, too.

"Did you get Dick delivered all right?" Wisnovsky asked.

"Yeah." Josie looked at the wrecked shebangs and at the bloodied men of the Massachusetts and Pennsylvania groups. "It didn't seem right, just taking him in there and leaving him like that. No funeral, no one to say any words, no prayers."

"That's all right," Wisnovsky said. "God'll know he's there. He doesn't have to be reminded."

"There is no God," Tyce said. His voice was flat, expressionless.

The others looked at him in surprise.

"Now, how can you say a damn fool thing like that?" Benton asked.

"I guess he just doesn't believe," Josie said.

"Not a matter of believing or not believing. I *know* there is no God," Tyce said resolutely.

"You're full of shit, Tyce," Wisnovsky said.

Tyce didn't hear Wisnovsky's comment. As so often happened, he was already in his own world, recalling the incident that had brought him to this conclusion.

Novitiate Coley Tyce, of the Order of St. Timothy, had already walked three miles to call on Father Bonnington, but when the good father asked if Tyce would go to the docks with him to see a former inmate of the orphanage, Tyce didn't hesitate for a moment.

"His name is Asa Murphy," Father Bonnington said as they started down a long, dark alley. "Don't know if you remember him, Coley. I think he left a little before you arrived."

"And he lives down here?"

"He works on the docks, and he has a room at the rear of one of the warehouses. But he has a bit of a problem with 'the creature,' so sometimes he misses several days of work. When that happens, he forgets to take care of himself. I like to drop in from time to time, just to see that he has a bite to eat."

"Father, you can't be responsible for every drunk in Boston."

"I know I can't, lad. But I can be responsible for those who were once my boys. As I'm sure you will be, once you take your vows."

"If I take the vows, Father. There's still that unresolved question of whether I seek to serve you or God."

Father Bonnington chuckled. "You've come a long way, my boy. If you can recognize that, and if you're now questioning whether or not you should even be a priest, then you're halfway home."

"And what will home be, Father? Will I be a priest, or not?"

Father Bonnington shook his head and raised his finger. "Oh, no, my boy. You don't get off that easily. It's your decision to make, yours and no one else's. Neither I, nor anyone, will attempt to influence you in any way. But when you finally do make the decision, I have no doubt it will be the right one."

At that moment, Tyce noticed three men at the far end of the alley. At first, he wasn't sure what they were doing, then he saw that they were beating a fourth man. He put his hand out to stop Father Bonnington, but the priest had seen them at the same time.

"Coley, come quickly! That's Asa! Those men are attacking Asa!" Father Bonnington shouted at the top of his lungs. He started running toward them. "You men! Stop that!"

"Father, stay back here!" Tyce shouted, starting after Father Bonnington.

"What the hell?" one of the three shouted when he saw two cassocked men coming at him. He laughed out loud. "Why, would you look at this, Johnny? We got us a couple o' men in women's clothes."

Moving quickly for an older man, Father Bonnington was on the three before Tyce could get there. Father Bonnington reached down toward Asa, who lay, bloodied, on the ground. Before he could touch Asa, however, one of the three men stepped in and made a great slashing motion. Tyce saw something silver flash in his hand as it moved toward Father Bonnington's abdomen. As the hand swung up, it was red. Father Bonnington spun around as blood gushed, fountainlike, from a long slice across his belly.

"No!" Tyce shouted. "No, please, God, no!"

"Come on, preacher man," the assassin taunted, standing spraddle-legged, his bloody knife pointing toward Tyce's belly.

With a shout of grief and rage, Tyce launched himself with a long leap.

"What the hell?" the knife wielder shouted. Jumping back to avoid Tyce, he stumbled into one of his friends. While he was trying to get disentangled, Tyce caught the knife arm and bent it back at the wrist, twisting it until the bone snapped.

The man shrieked with pain as he dropped the knife. Quickly, Tyce reached down and picked it up, then whipped it up in a wicked thrust, stabbing into the man's side just below his rib cage. Tyce turned the knife blade-edge up, letting the man's own weight tear open his gut as he fell, spilling blood and intestines onto Tyce's hand.

Stepping away from the mortally wounded man, Tyce turned to face the other two. He wiped his right hand across his forehead, leaving a bloody smear. With his eyes blazing with rage, his jaw clenched, and his face smeared with blood, he was a terrifying apparition. The expressions of the other two assailants turned from contempt and easy confidence to fear.

One of them had a knife, and he lunged toward Tyce. Tyce turned his body to one side, and the knife missed. The lunge left the man off balance, and Tyce rammed his fist into his stomach. The man doubled over, but before he fell, he managed to grab Tyce around the waist, pulling him down.

The third man, taking advantage of the situation, punched Tyce in the side of the head powerfully enough to separate the two men. A second punch sent Tyce onto his back. Grinning, the man charged him, trying to finish him off. As he closed in, Tyce kicked him in the groin. He went down with a mighty oath of pain. Tyce rolled quickly onto the man's prostrate form and slammed his knee, hard, into his chest. Then he grabbed the man by his hair and began smashing his head against the cobblestones, once, twice, three times. By the third time, the back of the man's head was pulp, and the cobblestones were spattered with blood and brain tissue. The man's eyes were open and sightless.

Tyce stood up and faced the third attacker. His eyes now wide with fright, he hesitated only a moment before he turned and started running. Tyce took half a dozen running steps in pursuit, then stopped. He turned around and went back to Father Bonnington.

"Father! Father!"

"My boy," Bonnington said, laying his hand on Tyce's face. His hand, covered with his own blood, added to the gore that was already on Tyce's face. "I'm dying. Give me extreme unction."

"No!" Tyce said. "No, I won't let you die!"

"It's not your will, my son! It's God's will. Give me last rites before it's too late."

Tyce held Bonnington's head in his lap. "God, don't let him die, don't let him die!" he begged.

Bonnington's breath began coming in shallower gasps. "Unction," he begged. "Please, extreme unction."

Tyce crossed himself, then made the sign of the cross on Bonnington's forehead. He opened his mouth to speak, but nothing came out—not the first word, not even the first syllable.

What a mockery extreme unction was. What cold comfort.

Tyce heard a death rattle in Bonnington's throat, then the priest stopped breathing.

Tyce was still sitting there, holding the dead priest's head in his lap, half an hour later when the police arrived. The police were shocked by the carange. There was blood everywhere . . . a significant amount of it on Tyce—his hands, his face, his cassock.

"What in the name of the Almighty happened here?" one of the policemen asked.

"These two men, and a third, killed Father Bonnington. And they hurt that man." He pointed to Asa, who was barely alive.

"You said these two men and another. Where's the third?"

Tyce shook his head. "I don't know. He ran."

"The people who did this go after him?" the policeman asked.

Tyce didn't answer.

"Who killed these men?"

"I killed them," Tyce answered matter-of-factly.

"You? You did this?"

"Yes."

"But how could you? You're a man of God."

Tyce looked at the policeman with dead, flat eyes. "There is no God," he said, dully.

"Tyce? Tyce, you all right?" Josie asked.

Tyce nodded. "Bring any grub?"

"No, but Gleason's up there now. He'll be bringing some."

"Know why I joined this army, Corporal?" Tyce asked. "I joined it 'cause I'm not like one of your farm boys. Days I didn't work, I didn't eat. I figured I'd at least get three meals a day." He gave what might have been a laugh.

Josie laughed, too, not because it was funny but because it was the first time Tyce had made any attempt at humor.

Leaving the Pennsylvania shebang, Josie moved to the ruins of Potter's shebang. McSpadden, still covered in blood, and Billy, badly bruised, were sitting on the ground inside the circle of what had been the shebang.

"How's it going?" Josie asked more brightly than he felt. When he got no reply, he sat down next to the two men and looked at them. He thought about his relationship with them—Billy, who had always been so eager to please, and McSpadden, the man who had exercised so much control over his life for the last three years. Now both had withdrawn into their own world.

"How's the shoulder? How's the eye?" Josie asked.

McSpadden just nodded.

Josie sat quietly for a moment longer, then looked over at the Pennsylvania men. They had been here a lot longer than

Josie and his group, yet they seemed to be doing fairly well. What was keeping them going?

Then, in a sudden, brilliant insight, Josie realized what it must be. These men were surviving because of Sergeant Gleason. They had someone to lead them. He looked at McSpadden. Reluctantly, Josie had to admit that this man who had been his leader for so long, who had brought him and so many others safely through the war, was no longer capable of leading. And, remembering the promise he had made to Captain Russell to take over if something happened to McSpadden, he realized that the leadership of I Company of the 19th Massachusetts had, for all intents and purposes, fallen to him.

"All right," he said aloud. "If I have to do it, I'll do it."

McSpadden looked at him. "Beg pardon?"

Josie took a deep breath. "Billy, go find some clean water. Clean the sergeant up. Trade for it if you have to." It wasn't a request, it was an order, and Billy immediately caught the change in Josie's voice.

"Yes, sir," Billy said, reacting much more positively, now that someone seemed to be exercising some direction.

Josie waited until Billy was gone, then spoke quietly to McSpadden. "Know how many they've got lying over there in the Deadhouse just from today? Forty-six."

That got McSpadden's attention, and he looked over at Josie, eyes wide in awe. "God in heaven. Forty-six?"

"Two by the Raiders, one shot at the Deadline. The rest starved, or . . . I don't know. They looked to me like they were water-bloated."

Josie looked away for a moment, then continued. "I went into the Deadhouse and looked at the bodies. They've tied name tags around the big toes of most of 'em. I guess that's so when they bury 'em, there'll be some kind of record."

McSpadden waited a long time before he spoke. "You do that for Dick? Identify him, I mean? His folks will want to know."

"Yeah. You know, Sergeant, last night Dick was telling

me about the water here. We can't drink from the Swamp. It'll kill you."

"We have to tell the boys that," McSpadden said. "Tuck! Thomas! Wisconsin!"

Tucker got up, but Sweet stayed where he was, sitting with his new best friend, Blackburn, and looking, with barely repressed anger, toward the area where the Raiders were. The object of their intense scrutiny was Blackburn's banjo, which was being played, slowly and very badly, by Munn.

There were nearly two hundred men in the Raiders' camp, sitting in front of shebangs that were noticeably better constructed than those of the other prisoners. These men were also better dressed and better fed, and while the rest of the camp was beginning to prepare its lunch of mush from the cornmeal that had just been issued, Curtis was gnawing on a chicken bone. Another was sopping up gravy from his tin plate with a large hunk of bread, and a third was eating an apple.

Collins, the undisputed leader of the Raiders, his belly warm with the roast pork dinner he had just eaten, was sitting on his chair as if it were a throne. Indeed, only he was authorized to use the chair. He was being shaved by one flunky while another was on his knees, greasing his boots. Growing irritated by the sound of the banjo, Collins turned to Munn.

"You call that music? I've heard better noise come out of dried chicken guts. Give us something a man can dance to!"

That was all the invitation another Raider needed, and he reached over to pluck the banjo out of Munn's hands.

"Hey, what the hell?" Munn said, reaching for it.

"If he can play it, let 'im," Collins said. He looked at the new man. "But if you can't, I'm goin' to bust it over your head."

The second man smiled ingratiatingly at Collins, then

began strumming a series of fast chords. It was quickly obvious that he knew what he was doing.

The Raiders, cheered by the music, began to clap their hands.

"Hey, everybody," one of them shouted. "Hey, look at me! I'm doin' the fandango!" He got up and started dancing.

"How 'bout you, Collins? Why don't you dance?" Curtis shouted.

"All right. Boys, you get that clumsy cow outta the way, and I'll show you some real dancing." Collins got up and started dancing a jig. Quickly he became the center of attention as his group cheered him on, clapping their hands in time to the music.

At the Pennsylvania shebang, Sweet and Blackburn continued to watch. "That's your banjo they're using," Sweet said.

"You mean it was my banjo."

Munn, safe in the middle of the Raiders, saw Sweet and Blackburn staring at them. He smiled broadly, then began waving at them and making motions with his hands as if he were playing the banjo.

"The bastard," Blackburn said quietly.

Tucker, 2nd Wisconsin, Tyce, Gleason, Tobias, and Benton were gathered around Josie and McSpadden.

"How's your sergeant?" 2nd Wisconsin asked.

"He doesn't look so good," Tyce replied. "Took a crack in the eye."

McSpadden managed to open one eye. "I can see well enough to know that we're none of us no better-lookin' today than we were yesterday."

"Tuck," Josie said, "we're going to need some shelter here. You'll have to sew us up something."

Tucker nodded toward the Raiders. "Don't know how I'm goin' to do that, Josie. They got my kit last night. My needles, thread, scissors."

"Somebody'll have some," Benton suggested. "Got some

buttons? Brass buttons? Everybody wants 'em. They trade 'em to the Rebs for stuff."

"We'll get you needle and thread," Josie said to Tucker. "Everyone who still has haversacks, give 'em to Tuck. He'll cut 'em up, make us a shebang. We'll stay right here."

Tucker nodded. "Yeah, it was good enough for Dick."

"I need two dollars for a guard to send a letter to Dick's father," Josie said.

Blackburn took off his shoe and gave him one. Tucker gave him the other.

"Thanks. Now, there's something you all need to know. Last night, 'fore all this happened, Dick was telling me about the water here." Josie saw that Sweet wasn't paying attention to him. "Thomas? Thomas, you want to pay attention over here?"

Sweet still didn't answer, but at that moment Gleason and Tobias arrived with the meal and the two pieces of wood, interrupting the meeting.

Suddenly Sweet stood up. "I'm going to get it back," he said. He started moving toward the Raiders.

Gleason, seeing what he was doing, reached out and grabbed him. "What're you doing, Sweet? Don't be a fool. There's ten of them for every one of us. Besides . . ."

Sweet pulled loose, then continued walking purposefully toward the Raiders.

"Day, you'd better stop him," Gleason called.

Josie stood up quickly. "Thomas!" he called. "Thomas, you get back here, right now! That's an order, Sweet!"

Sweet continued toward the Raiders like a man possessed. No entreaties, and no orders, would stop him.

"What's he doing?" Tucker asked.

"I don't know, but whatever he's doing, we can't let him do it alone," Josie said, starting after him.

"I agree," McSpadden added. He tried to get up, but he was still too weak. The men stood there for a moment, as if waiting for orders from their sergeant. Then, though no definite words were spoken, the men of I Company of the

19th Massachusetts realized that the torch of command had passed. McSpadden was no longer giving orders. Josie was. First Tucker, then Blackburn, then all the others, including Gleason, began to follow Josie, unwilling to let him go alone.

McSpadden, not yet ready to relinquish command, got to his knees, then, in a wobbly effort, managed to stand up. He, too, started after them, not as a leader now but as a follower.

"Hey," one of the Raiders said when he saw Josie and the group coming over. "Hey, you men, lookit what's comin'."

The music slowed, then stopped.

"What is it? What'd you stop playin' for?" Collins asked, interrupting his dance.

The banjo player nodded toward the men coming toward them.

"I do believe them boys is comin' over here to pick a fight with us," Curtis said.

"You'd think they'd-a had enough of us last night," Munn suggested.

Collins turned toward them, then put his hands on his hips and smiled. Sweet and Blackburn arrived first. Sweet pointed to the Raider who had been playing the banjo.

"That belongs to him," Sweet said, nodding toward Blackburn. "And we want it back."

Collins smiled evilly. "Oh, you do, do you?" He looked at the little group of men who had shown the audacity to challenge the Raiders. "All right, I'll tell you what we'll do. Who's your best man?"

"He is," Josie said, nodding toward Sweet.

"And who're you? You their leader?"

"I'm . . . one of them," Josie replied, not yet ready to admit that he had assumed the role of leader. "And what're you?"

"What am I?" Collins turned to look at his men. "Boys, he wants to know what I am." He turned back to Josie. "What do I look like?"

"With that jacket? Mister, to me you look just like a big old green-tailed fly sitting on top of a pile of shit."

Several men laughed nervously. Collins' eyes narrowed menacingly, then opened wide, and he smiled.

"Well, boy, now, that's prob'ly right. But when you get right down to it, this here whole place is nothing but a big dung heap." He took in the entire prison camp with a wave of his arm. "And, if you ever notice, those big ol' green-tailed flies generally get the biggest turd for themselves." Collins laughed out loud. He pointed to Sweet. "You still say he's your best man, huh?"

Josie nodded.

"Hell, he's a baby!"

"Runt of the litter," Munn put in.

"All right, boys, draw the ring," Collins said. "Hey, Georgie!"

At Collins' beckoning, Georgie stepped out of the crowd. When Josie saw him, he suddenly began to have second thoughts. Georgie was the biggest, roughest-looking man Josie had ever seen. As big as Sweet was, Georgie had height, weight, and years on him. He also had something else, a streak of cruelty in him. He would have to, in order to belong to this group.

"Fight! Fight, ever'body! There's a fight!" someone shouted, and people began to gather—though, because it involved the Raiders, far fewer came than Josie would have thought.

"Well, I'll be," Gleason said, as the crowd started gathering.

"What is it?" Josie asked.

Gleason nodded toward a tall, rangy, bearded man who came up with the others. "That's Limber Jim."

"Who?"

"Limber Jim. Stays to himself, mostly. But he's a good man. A damn good man. I'm glad to see he's here."

Curtis, seeing the other prisoners approach, stepped

toward them, then held up his hand to stop them from coming any closer.

"That's far enough! You folks just stop right there."

At Curtis' warning, the other prisoners stopped. Only Limber Jim continued forward, glaring at Curtis, challenging him to stop him.

"I'm with them," Limber Jim growled, nodding his head toward Josie, Gleason, and the group.

Curtis looked at him for a moment, deciding whether he wanted to accept the challenge. Then, licking his lips, he allowed himself a smile.

"Sure, Limber Jim. Come on ahead, seein' as how they's only one of you."

Collins looked toward the crowd. "Any the rest of you gents wants to come in for a good look, come ahead." When a few of the men started forward, Collins smiled broadly. "Only cost you five dollars a man," he added, laughing.

The few who had started forward stopped, grumbling at the conditions Collins had put on watching the fight. Only Patrick Shay paid no attention to Collins, or to the stopped crowd. He picked his way through them, then slid up beside the Massachusetts and Pennsylvania group.

"What about the boy?" someone called. "You let him through."

"Ahh, he's just a boy," Collins said, waving his hand in dismissal.

Sweet had not taken his eyes off Georgie since the big champion of the Raiders arrived. Josie studied Sweet's face, to see if he could detect any sign of fear. Sweet was showing none.

Blackburn was frightened, however, for he had seen Georgie fight before. "Look out for him, Thomas," he whispered. "He's a bad 'un. He's killed men in fights in here."

"Whatever you do, don't turn your back on him," Limber Jim warned.

"He don't fight fair," Patrick added.

Sweet nodded in response to the warnings. But as he did so, he was pulling his shirt over his head. When the shirt completely covered his face, Collins nodded at Georgie, who stepped in without warning and drove a powerful blow into Sweet's stomach, knocking him down.

"Hey! What the hell!" Josie shouted.

"That's cheating!" Patrick yelled.

"If you're going to fight a man, fight 'im fair!" Limber Jim cried.

The Raiders cheered the knockdown, then laughed as Georgie strutted around inside the ring that had been drawn on the ground, holding his arms over his head in victory.

"Damn, Georgie, maybe we should get you three of 'em to fight next time. That's 'bout the only way we could make it a fair fight."

Mad Matthew began cheering and cackling, dancing around Sweet, who was still on the ground. In the nearest turkey roost, one of the Confederate guards poked the other to call his attention to the fight.

"Get up, Thomas!" Blackburn said. "Get up before he has another shot at you!"

Sweet got onto his hands and knees, and he stayed there for just a minute, getting his breath back. Josie kept a close eye on all of the Raiders, to make certain that none of them stepped inside the ring to take advantage of Sweet. So far, they seemed content to be spectators, confident that Georgie could easily finish off this overgrown, baby-faced inter-loper.

"You can do it, Thomas," Josie said reassuringly. "I've seen you whip tougher men than this."

Slowly, Sweet managed to get to his feet. He had just done so when Georgie charged toward him a second time, swinging a roundhouse right that sent Sweet down again. This time Georgie followed through by kicking him, knocking Sweet backward.

Again the Raiders cheered, and urged their champion on.

"Give it up, Thomas!" Blackburn pleaded. "Give it up! It's not worth gettin' yourself killed over."

Sweet got onto his hands and knees again. One of his eyes was swelling shut, and his lip was badly puffed. He struggled to his feet again, and this time Georgie was overconfident. He moved in for what he thought would be the easy kill, swinging a powerful punch that Sweet ducked. Sweet countered with a swift left jab that caught Georgie square in the face. Despite the power of the blow, however, Georgie managed to laugh it off. But it did push him back far enough to allow Sweet to regain his balance for the first time since the fight began.

"That's it, Thomas, that's it!" Tucker shouted. "You're givin' it to him now!"

"Quit playin' around with him, Georgie," Collins said. "Knock the son of a bitch's head off and get it over with!"

Georgie charged again, scoring again, dropping Sweet to his knees, then putting him on his back with another roundhouse right.

When Sweet went down this time, Georgie thought he had finished him off. As before, he turned around and clasped his hands over his head in a victory pose.

But Sweet, with one eye nearly shut, his lip twice its normal size, and a big bruise on the side of his face, managed to get to his feet one more time. He shook his head, then stood unsteadily for a moment, raising his hands in front of his face in the pose of a prizefighter.

"Boy, when you goin' to learn?" Georgie asked. "When I knock you down, stay down."

"It takes more'n you got to knock him down, mister!" Billy shouted. "He's goin' to whip your ass. I seen him fight before!"

"Yeah!" some of the others who were supporting Sweet yelled.

"Is that right, boy? You goin' to whip ol' Georgie's ass?" Georgie mocked. He feinted twice, then danced in and out, but Sweet didn't respond. In fact, Sweet did nothing but hold his fists in front of his face and watch the antics of his opponent.

"Boy, I'm tired of messin' around with you," Georgie said. "You're beginnin' to get on my nerves." He moved in with another clublike swing. Again Sweet managed to avoid it, and again he counterpunched with a quick, straight jab. The next time Georgie swung at him, Sweet managed a left jab that caused Georgie to drop his guard slightly, then a hard right cross that snapped Georgie's head back.

"Yeah!" Josie yelled in excitement. "That's the way it's done, Thomas!"

The smile left Georgie's face. With a bellow like a bull, he charged, but Sweet stepped nimbly to one side, then hit Georgie in the nose with a hard left. Georgie's already flat nose went even flatter. It had been broken, the latest in what appeared to be a long line of breaks. Georgie's nose started bleeding profusely, and the blood ran down into his beard. Georgie continued to grin wickedly, seemingly unperturbed by his injury.

Sweet tried to hit the nose again, but now Georgie was protecting it. Georgie continued to throw great swinging blows toward Sweet, who was now managing to avoid any real impact, catching them on his forearms and shoulders. Josie feared that if just one more connected, Sweet would be finished.

By now the noise was deafening as the partisans of both sides shouted their encouragement and support. Fights inside the prison grounds were not uncommon. But a fight of this magnitude, pitting two powerful men against each other, drew a large following.

A moment later, Sweet managed to get another sharp, bruising jab through to Georgie's nose, and for the first time Georgie let out a bellow of pain. But it was clear that the triumph would be momentary, for the thunderous punches that had repeatedly landed on Sweet's shoulders and forearms were beginning to tell, and he began to move more

103

slowly. Then Georgie managed to land a straight, short right, and again Sweet fell to his hands and knees.

"Finish the son of a bitch off now!" Collins shouted.

"Kill him!" Curtis added.

"Take off his head!" Munn screamed.

With a yell of victory, Georgie rushed over and tried to kick him, but at the last second, Sweet rolled to one side. He hopped up before Georgie could recover for a second kick, and while the big man was still off balance, sent a brutal punch straight into Georgie's groin.

When Georgie instinctively dropped both hands, Sweet hit him with two powerful left jabs.

"Now you've got him, Thomas!" Blackburn yelled excitedly.

"Finish him!" Limber Jim shouted.

Georgie was no longer fighting back. He was glassy-eyed and trying to stay on his feet. Sweet drew his right back for the final blow. Then, suddenly, Munn stepped behind him and swung a heavy club at the back of his head. Sweet went down instantly.

"You son of a bitch!" Josie yelled, starting toward Munn. Tucker, Limber Jim, and all the other Massachusetts and Pennsylvania men followed him.

"Collins!" Munn yelled in fright.

"Hold 'em, boys, hold 'em!" Collins yelled, and a score of Raiders stepped in to grab Josie and his friends while the rest of the Raiders, all of them armed, turned menacingly toward the prisoners who had gathered to watch and were protesting the way the fight ended.

Once again Sweet got to his hands and knees.

"What the hell does it take to keep you down, boy?" Collins asked, stepping over to him and kicking him savagely in the side.

Sweet let out a whoosh of breath and fell, face down.

Josie, Blackburn, Limber Jim, and even McSpadden struggled with the ones who were holding them, trying desperately to get loose.

"You cowardly bastard!" Limber Jim shouted

"Let me have a crack at 'im," Munn said. He kicked Sweet hard in the side, and would have kicked him in the head if Sweet hadn't managed to put his arms up at the last moment.

"That's enough!" Josie yelled, breaking free and running to the middle of the ring. He pushed Munn away, then raised his fists. "Why don't you try fighting someone who's standing up, Munn?" he challenged.

At first Munn's face registered surprise that Josie had managed to get free, then fear that he might actually have to fight him. He took several steps back, until he was standing in line with a group of armed Raiders, who, brandishing their clubs, started toward Josie. The expression of fear on Munn's face was replaced by a broad, evil grin.

"All right, if you want a little of it. We'll give it to you."

Suddenly Collins held up his hand, laughing.

"What the hell, boys?" he shouted. "We've had our fun for today, eh? You want to leave something for tomorrow, don't you?"

All action stopped, and in the quiet that followed, Collins walked over to Sweet, and with the toe of his boot, almost gently flipped him onto his back.

"He's all yours," he said to Josie. Then, to the others, "C'mon, boys, let's go."

The Raiders moved back to give the Massachusetts and Pennsylvania men a little room. Josie, Blackburn, and Limber Jim picked up Sweet, and started carrying him away.

"Remember what you learned, next time you boys got a bone to pick with us," Collins called to them. "And don't send a boy to do a man's job."

The Raiders laughed uproariously.

When Josie and the others reached the shebang, he looked over at Limber Jim.

"Listen, uh, Jim. I want to thank—" Josie started, but Limber Jim interrupted him.

"You're the ones went down there," he said. Then, content that they had brought Sweet safely home, Limber Jim nodded and turned to go.

Josie watched him walk away, fixing his name and image in his mind. Limber Jim was a good man who obviously could be counted on. Josie had a feeling the time might come when he would need to know whom he could count on, and whom he couldn't.

"Did we get it?" Sweet asked.

"Thomas, you all right?" Blackburn asked.

"Yeah," Sweet replied. He put his hand gingerly to the back of his head, feeling the wound inflicted by Munn's club. "Don't quite know how Georgie managed to hit me back there, though."

"Georgie didn't," Josie said. "Munn did. With a club. You're lucky you aren't dead."

Sweet brought his fingers around and examined the blood. What little blood there had been was already beginning to coagulate. "The banjo," Sweet said again. "We didn't get it back, did we?"

"No," Blackburn said.

Sweet shook his head. "I'm sorry, Martin."

"We'll get it next time."

"No!" Gleason said, shaking his head angrily. "There will be no next time, do you hear me? There'll be no more fighting, no more worrying about the Raiders, no wasting time, no wasting strength, no anything. Do you want to live?"

Sweet nodded.

"Then tunnel!" Gleason demanded, shoving a canteen half at him.

"Give him time, John, have a heart," one of the other Pennsylvania men said.

"You, too!" Gleason ordered angrily. "Tunnel!"

Sweet spit out one of his teeth, then wiped the back of his

hand across his cut and swollen lip. After that he took the canteen half and crawled into the shebang. One of the others went in with him.

Josie was sitting with McSpadden near the entrance to the tunnel, just inside the shebang. He was holding a pad and pencil, but the events with the Raiders still so dominated his mind that he couldn't write. Blackburn and Tobias came out of the tunnel. As soon as they were out, Billy and Sweet went in.

Josie closed his eyes for a moment. It would be so easy to just sit here and do nothing, like so many of the others. It wouldn't take much food and water to sustain him if he didn't expend any energy.

He thought back to when he was on the train. Somehow, during that trip, he had managed to separate body and soul. It didn't last very long, but he had been able to do it.

If he tried, he could do it again, and he was sure he could make it last longer . . . a lot longer. He might even be able to make it last until he got out of here. Then what difference would it make how his body might suffer? As long as there was barely enough food and barely enough water to keep his body alive, he would survive, for his soul would be free.

Sweet came out of the hole, carrying several bags full of dirt. His appearance surprised Josie, who thought he had just gone in. He realized then that he had been thinking about the separation of his soul and body for longer than it seemed. Maybe the separation had occurred without his realizing it.

Billy also emerged with bags of dirt.

"No more for you, Billy," Gleason said. "You've been down there three times today."

"It's not so bad down there. No Rebs." Then Billy smiled. "And the quicker we get it dug!" Passing off the bags of dirt, he turned and crawled back into the tunnel.

"What're you going to do about him, Sergeant?" Blackburn asked.

Gleason shrugged. "Nothin'," he said. "Hell, if the boy wants to work that much, let 'im work."

Josie turned his attention back to the task at hand, staring at the blank page in frustration.

"What do I write to Dick's father? Do I say, 'Wasn't the Rebs killed him, sir. Our own boys in here did it'?"

"Sorry, Josie, I don't have an answer for that," said Gleason.

Blackburn shrugged.

Josie put the paper down. "Tell me, how many Raiders are there?"

"Not sure," Gleason replied. "Two, three, four, maybe as many as five hundred."

"There are that many evil men in here?"

Blackburn shook his head. "Most of 'em are more frightened than evil, I'd say. More keep going over to 'em every day, when they get hungry, or scared."

"So what you're sayin' is, if we got any dispute with the Raiders, we need to take it out with the head men."

"Why so interested?" Gleason asked.

"'Cause the way I see it, they're the enemy now. Before we got here, it was the Rebels. Now, in here, it's the Raiders, just as much. What they did to Dick . . . that can't happen to any more of our men, ever. Else we're not fit to wear the uniform. That's the way I see it."

Blackburn nodded in approval, but Gleason grew angry.

"Tell Dick's father any damn thing you want, but first, you listen to me, Corporal. You've got to get ahold of yourself. A lot of good men have died in here . . . more than you know. And a lot more are going to.

"But getting my men out of here, through this hole in the ground, is the most important thing on my mind, so we're not going back over there to kill Raiders or do anything else. We're tunneling, do you understand? You have something else in mind, like getting together with some others to keep a watch on what they're doing, that's fine. But that's all. Do you understand me?"

Josie nodded, then looked down at the ground in shame. He had assumed command of the Massachusetts bunch until McSpadden was totally on his feet again. And as the man in charge, he should have been thinking about what was the greater good for the group, just as Gleason was doing for his men. Instead, he was dwelling on the temporary satisfaction of getting revenge.

"I'm sorry, Sergeant. You won't have any more trouble with me."

Gleason smiled, then put his hand on Josie's shoulder. "Hell, do you think I don't know what you're going through? I'd like nothing better than to break a few heads over there myself. But we can't let that get in the way. Especially men like you and me. We have more than ourselves to take care of. We're responsible for what happens to everyone under us."

"Yes, Sergeant." Josie realized that at that moment, Gleason had given tacit approval of his taking over command of the Massachusetts group from the wounded Sergeant McSpadden.

Chapter 7

Night:

At night, the camp was much quieter than during the day. So quiet, in fact, that the hushed conversation of the thousands of prisoners became little more than the whisper of a soft evening wind.

Sweet and Blackburn were sitting outside the Pennsylvania shebang. Sweet, bruised from his fight, and dirty from his time in the tunnel, looked over at his new friend.

"Martin, how do you do it?"

Blackburn looked at him questioningly.

"I mean, how do you stay under the ground, digging, without losing your mind? A few minutes and I . . ."

"It's what I do."

"You mean it doesn't scare you? Being down there?"

Blackburn shrugged and shook his head.

"Was it hard, the first time you went down?"

Blackburn pulled up a blade of grass, then sucked on the tender root stem. "My father took me," he said. "I wanted to go. All his friends worked in the mine. . . . Sergeant Gleason's father, Tobias' father, too. I couldn't wait."

"How'd you learn to play the banjo?"

"My father taught me that, too."

"You really think I can learn?"

Blackburn smiled and nodded. "I'm sure you can. I could tell the other night. Could tell right away. You'll be good. Real good."

Sweet smiled happily.

Still later that night, in another part of the camp, Josie, Blackburn, and Tobias were squatting in a circle, conferring with a dozen or so other prisoners. Limber Jim was there, too, and a one-legged firebrand named Samson. So was Willens, a cautious and contemplative sergeant. Sitting on the edge of the group, listening to what everyone was saying but adding nothing of his own, was a silent man named Grundy.

Josie had used Limber Jim and Martin Blackburn, and even Patrick Shay, to help him round up the men he needed to talk to, men he could trust. In quick, urgent tones, he told them of his plan to set up a way to keep the Raiders always under watch.

"You can count on us, Day," Willens said. "We'll stand watch with you."

"Long overdue, I say," Samson added.

"Well, I say, why just a watch?" Limber Jim put in. He looked intently at the others. "I mean, why not just wade into 'em, knock their heads off? You ask me, that's what we ought to be talking about!"

"Shhh! Keep your voice down," Willens cautioned. Everyone was quiet for a moment, and Willens looked around before he began talking again. Then, in a low voice he said, "You can't just wade into 'em, there's too many."

"We'll get every man here," Samson suggested. "Should-a

done it two months ago." He snorted in disgust. "Just that everyone thought we was goin' to get exchanged." He paused, then added, sarcastically, "Did it when we should-a, my brother'd still be alive."

"Josie," Tobias said, "what do you think? Maybe we *should* take 'em on."

"What're we a-feard of?" Limber Jim asked. "We're not little girls, y'know."

Josie listened to their entreaties, and he agreed with every one of them. But he also knew the importance of what Gleason had said to him about having responsibilities beyond one's own wishes, so he said nothing.

"Anyhow, you can't keep a secret in a place like this," Willens said. "You start to put a thousand men together to take 'em on . . . ."

"A thousand?" Josie asked in surprise.

Willens nodded. "That's what you'd need. Only they'll get you first. And there's a reason I don't want to do anything just now. Some of us are working on a tunnel out of here."

"Well, so are we, but . . . ," Tobias started, then looked at Josie. "What do you think?"

Blackburn gave Tobias a swift kick and a sharp look, warning him against saying anything else. There was a long moment of silence, and everyone looked at Josie, expecting him to speak.

"For now," Josie said, "we'll all keep watch, not go after 'em. But any of the Raiders come for any of us, the others'll help out. We'll all stand up for each other." He studied their expressions to see how they were taking his suggestion. "Don't anybody say yes if you don't mean it. Every word of it. It's like a commitment you're making."

The men exchanged glances, then nodded.

"Yes," Limber Jack said.

"Yes," Samson said.

"Yes," Willens said. One by one, as if taking a vow, the

113

men made the first step in taking back control of their own lives.

"I agreed to this," Limber Jim told the others, "'cause I believe something really needs to be done about the Raiders. Something more than just standing watch. But if right now standing watch is all we can do, then so be it. And if the Raiders come after one of our'n, so much the better."

Samson cleared his throat. "I said yes, also. And you can count on me when the goin' gets rough. But I agree with Jim. We ought to be doin' something more than just standin' watch."

Josie stood up. "Then it's a deal. Let's shake on it." He extended his hand, and Limber Jim was first to take it.

Later, walking back to their own shebangs, Josie spoke to Tobias. "You shouldn't have said that, Toby. About us working on a tunnel, I mean."

"I know," Tobias said contritely. "I knew, soon as I said it."

"There's tunnel traitors here who'll turn you in for half an apple," Blackburn said angrily.

"I just thought . . . ," Tobias started, then let out a long sigh. "I mean, I know it don't justify nothin', but I was gettin' the feelin' they were makin' all these excuses about why we shouldn't—"

"We'll have to tell Gleason," Josie interrupted. "We have no choice. We may have been compromised."

"Yeah," Tobias said. "I know. It doesn't make me feel any better 'cause I know, but I know."

Gleason was angrily pacing back and forth outside the Pennsylvania shebang. He ran his hand through his hair in an effort to calm himself.

"What the hell were you *thinking* about? Will you tell me that, Tobias?"

Tobias sighed. "I don't know, Sergeant."

"Well, all right, we're all going to have to work double

shifts," Gleason said, outlining what he saw as the solution to the problem. "The tunnel has to be rushed now. Whether we're hungry or tired, it doesn't matter. We don't have a month anymore."

"I'm sorry, John. I know I . . ."

Gleason waved Tobias' apology away. "It's done. We can't unring a bell. You three," he said to Josie, Blackburn, and the contrite Tobias, "you know who was at that meeting, so get outside and watch everyone who was there listening. If any of 'em is a tunnel traitor and goes near a Reb . . . ." Gleason paused for a moment. "Well, you know what to do."

Josie and Blackburn went outside. Tobias followed, but just before he left the shebang, he looked once more toward Gleason, hoping for absolution. Gleason turned away, still angry, to the only other man in the shebang.

"Tyce," he said. "Get some plates. We're going down."

That evening, Josie got out his paper and pencil, and began writing:

> When I was a child, the parameters of my existence were established by my mother. "Don't leave the front yard," my mother would say, and I would stay there, for her words were as restrictive as any fence.
>
> When I became an adult, my horizons were unlimited. There was the town, the county, the state, the nation, and the world. It required only a pair of shoes, or a horse, or the cost of a train or steamship ticket to move from one to the other.
>
> Then came the war, and my world was the army. My little corner of it was I Company of the 19th Massachusetts.
>
> When I became a prisoner of the Rebs, my world shrank again. It is now small enough to be confined within a thirty-two-acre field. And yet I have voluntarily made my world even smaller, for those who are outside

*the Massachusetts or Pennsylvania shebangs are foreign-
ers to me. They are as citizens of other states or other
countries. With most, we coexist peacefully. But there are
those who are evil and disruptive. These are the ones who
call themselves "The Raiders."*

Noon, the following day:

Josie was standing watch just outside the Pennsylvania
shebang. He had developed a method of scanning which
ensured that no part of his area of responsibility would go
unobserved. First he looked toward the turkey roosts, to see
if the guards were unusually alert. Then, when he was
satisfied that the guards were showing no more than a casual
interest, he let his gaze come back across the no-man's-land
between the stockade wall and the Deadline. After that was
covered, he slowly perused the camp itself. This extended
the boundaries of the world he had written about in his letter
the day before, and with this perspective, the magnitude
of the suffering of all the prisoners was clearly discernible.

Most noticeable was the thousands upon thousands of
lethargic men wasting away, dying slowly. He could see the
sick call, a long line that barely moved, and he could see the
ball-and-chain gang, which did move, but only rarely and
then in unison.

Down at the Swamp several naked men were standing
knee-deep in the water, bathing. More energetic were the
men working in one of the many Swampside laundries.
They did a brisk business because the cleaner the clothes,
the fewer the chiggers. Josie admired their industriousness.

But while Josie could admire the enterprise of the camp's
many laundrymen, barbers, and tailors, he abhorred the evil
industry practiced by the Raiders. He looked toward the
Raiders' area and saw Collins, in his bright green coat,
holding court with half a dozen sycophants who were
hanging on his every word. Then he let his eyes continue to

sweep across the compound, taking in shebangs of every size, shape, and hue.

Inexplicably, he chuckled.

"What're you laughing at?" Blackburn asked. He and Tobias were standing watch with Josie, each of them responsible for his own area.

"I was thinking how much this place looks like the refuse heap they got just outside town, back home. Because of the smell and the flies, I used to hate going by there. But right now, I think being there would be a hundred times better. The things people throw away there would be useful to us here."

Blackburn and Tobias laughed.

"Josie," Blackburn said, "all those letters home that you write? How do you send 'em?"

"I don't. No money."

"What's the point of writing 'em, then?" Tobias asked. "I mean, who'd want to hear about this stinkhole, anyway?"

They were silent for a moment while Josie watched the guards in one of the turkey roosts confer with a new guard who had climbed the ladder to talk to them. He paid close attention to see if it indicated anything he should be aware of. It didn't seem to.

"You write about Wirz? And the Raiders?" Tobias asked.

Josie shrugged. "Sometimes."

"What else, Josie?" Blackburn asked. "I managed to get a letter out to my wife and children when I first got here, telling 'em I was all right. I was thinking about them. What do you write about?"

"My friends. Just some things I think about."

"Like what?" Blackburn's curiosity had been raised now.

"Oh," Josie started, then paused. He wasn't anxious to share too much of his personal self with others yet. He was thinking how to answer Blackburn's question without really answering it, and also without hurting his new friend's feelings. "I write about how it's hard to understand how a place can be as bad as this, but how there's good here, too."

117

"Good?" Tobias was surprised by Josie's statement. "Here? The only good in here is getting out of here. And the sooner the better."

"Here comes Patrick," Blackburn said. A huge smile was spread across Patrick's face.

"Wonder what he's so happy about," Josie mused.

"You fellas hear what happened?" Patrick asked.

"No," Blackburn answered for all of them.

"Well, sir, one of the Minnesota boys fainted dead away. They thought he was gone for sure, so they took him to the Deadhouse and laid him out. Toe tag and all. An hour later . . . whoops! He sits up!"

"He sat up?" Blackburn said.

"He sat up. And this Reb pup they got in there jumps about six feet straight up in the air. About comes out of his own scaredy skin." Patrick was laughing so hard that it was difficult for him to finish the story.

Patrick mimicked the young Confederate guard. "H-h-h-hey there, Y-y-y-y-ank. If you ain't d-d-d-ead, you get back inside!"

Josie and Blackburn laughed appreciatively at the story. Tobias failed to see the humor.

"I'll see you fellas," Patrick said, still laughing. "This story is too good to keep to myself. I got to spread it around some."

Josie, Blackburn, and Tobias hadn't stopped studying the compound as Patrick was talking to them, and they continued to do so as they resumed their conversation.

"Josie, like what?" Blackburn asked.

"Beg your pardon?"

"You said there was good in here. What's good in here?"

"Oh, friends who'll help you, no matter what. People who'll be your friend, like you and Thomas are friends, no matter what."

"Yeah, I, uh . . ." Blackburn was embarrassed at being singled out as one of the good things.

For the next several minutes no conversation passed

among the three men as they applied themselves to the task at hand. Josie's eyes roamed over the depressing scenery again and again. The naked bodies being washed at the edge of the Swamp might change, but from Josie's perspective they were the same. It was a slowly turning kaleidoscope of rickety shebangs, emaciated men, and a sluggish stream, all watched over by cold, impersonal guards.

Then something changed, and Josie was immediately alert. He saw Grundy moving slowly along a meandering route, trying not to be conspicuous but the more conspicuous because of it, toward the turkey roost that held Lieutenant Barrett.

"Son of a bitch," Josie said quietly.

"What is it?"

"There." Blackburn and Tobias looked in the direction Josie indicated.

"That's Grundy," Blackburn said.

"He heard us talking last night," Josie said. "That means he knows about the tunnel."

"I'd better warn them," Tobias muttered grimly.

When Tobias stuck his head inside the shebang, Gleason was kneeling at the mouth of the tunnel, receiving platefuls of dirt from Tyce.

"John, you'd better come here."

Gleason didn't ask why, and Tobias didn't need to explain. Quickly, Gleason got up and followed him outside.

"What?" he asked when they got outside.

Josie pointed toward Grundy, who was still moving toward Lieutenant Barrett's turkey roost.

"You go that way," Josie said.

Gleason nodded. To Tobias and Blackburn he said, "Quickly. Quickly now."

The four men started out, Josie going in one direction while the others flanked him, spreading out so that if Grundy suddenly became suspicious, he would have nowhere to run.

Josie moved rapidly down the little hill, maintaining as

119

straight a line as he could, which meant disregarding the ethics of respecting other people's territory.

"Hey, watch where you're goin'!" someone called angrily.

Josie didn't take the time to answer. He had Grundy in sight, and he wasn't going to lose him.

Gleason was leading the others down the hill, also pushing people aside in order to stay in sight of Grundy.

"Be ready," Gleason said to all the prisoners as he passed through them. "Look lively, lads, look lively. Be ready."

Seeing the concentration on the faces of Josie, Gleason, and the others, the prisoners began getting up and drifting behind them, wondering what was going on.

Grundy had just about completed his meandering through the prison compound. Now he was at the Deadline, very close to the turkey roost occupied by Lieutenant Barrett. Frightened to call out loud, Grundy whispered, "Lieutenant . . . Lieutenant!"

Barrett, who was looking out over the compound, didn't see Grundy, nor did he hear him.

Josie was now moving fast, with Gleason and the others advancing just as quickly. Patrick joined them, as did a handful of the other prisoners, some of whom had figured out that Grundy was about to snitch on someone.

Thinking he was safe, and unable to raise Barrett by whispering, Grundy shouted aloud to him. "Lieutenant! Hey, Lieutenant!"

Barrett heard him this time, and he moved to the edge of the guard tower.

"Got somethin' for you," Grundy said.

"What you got for me, Yank?"

"I'll meet you at the gate. Right now. All right?"

Barrett studied Grundy for a moment. "Tell me what you got, first."

"I can't," Grundy yelled up at him. He looked around furtively. "I got informa—" He stopped, and gasped when he saw Josie right behind him. The blood left his face, and he nervously licked his lips.

"What do you want?" Lieutenant Barrett asked Josie.

Thinking fast, Josie reached into his jacket pocket for his letter. "I got a letter to be mailed, sir. Can you help me with it? I'm told it takes two greenbacks." He held up the letter and the two dollars for Barrett to see.

"Is the letter unsealed? 'Cause I'm goin' to read it."

"Yes, sir, it is."

"All right. Meet me at the gate," Barrett said. He looked at Grundy. "You, too."

At that moment, Blackburn, Tobias, and Gleason caught up with Grundy. Quickly, Gleason wrapped his coat around Grundy's head, then grabbed him by the head as Tobias and Blackburn grabbed him by the feet. They began carrying him away from the Deadline, into the massed crowd of prisoners. Having figured out what was going on, the crowd of prisoners opened to make room for Gleason and the others, then closed around them, swallowing them up like the Red Sea closing over the Egyptians.

"Hey! What the hell!" Barrett shouted, pulling his pistol from its holster. "What's going on there? Where you taking that man?"

The prisoners who closed ranks around Gleason, and the others, managed to look perfectly innocent, as if they had no idea of what was going on. Patrick, however, wasn't content to leave it that way. Fired with the zeal of youth, he started dancing around, thumbing his nose at the Rebel lieutenant.

"What'cha lookin' for, Lieutenant?" he mocked. "Lose something, did you?"

"I'll tell you what he's lookin' for! He's lookin' for a thirty-day furlough, the Rebel son of a bitch!" one of the prisoners shouted.

Having accomplished his mission of preventing Grundy from telling about the tunnel, Josie melted back into the crowd.

Barrett, who had not come down from his tower, leaned

out with his pistol at the ready and stared down into the crowd, but he could see nothing.

In the middle of the sheltering mass, flat on the ground, Gleason held the struggling Grundy still.

Chapter 8

Several days later:

The moon was a sliver of silver. Josie watched a cloud drift across, take on a soft glow for a moment, then move on. He wrapped his arms around his knees and gazed at the now familiar camp as the thousands of men settled in for the night. He looked up at the guard towers looming darkly against the sky, and at the great slab of wall that marked the borders of their world.

Finally, Josie turned his eyes back to his own group, where McSpadden was sitting on one side of him and Billy on the other. McSpadden had come through the immediate danger, but his wound had taken a lot out of him . . . not only physically, but mentally and emotionally as well.

In addition to McSpadden and Billy, there was Tucker, 2nd Wisconsin, Tyce, 60th Ohio, Sweet, Blackburn, Wisnovsky, Tobias, and, nearest the entrance, Benton. Only

Gleason, their leader, was absent. All were covered with dirt, evidence of the fact that they had been digging.

"What do you think, Josie?" Billy asked. "Will it work?"

"That's something Sergeant Gleason will have to decide."

"I don't care what he says, I'm going anyway," Billy said. "I mean, I haven't been doing all that work for nothing."

"You can't go if the tunnel ain't no good," Wisnovsky said.

"It's been good enough for us to work in, hasn't it?" Billy asked, looking for support. "Well, hasn't it?"

"Billy," Sweet said, "these men—Martin, Wisnovsky, Sergeant Gleason—they know what they're about. If they say it's all right, it's all right. But if they say no . . ."

"Quiet," Benton said. "Here he comes!"

Quickly the men went into the shebang as a gleam of golden light moved out of the tunnel. A moment later Gleason appeared, carrying a lantern made from half a canteen and a bit of candle. He crawled out of the hole, handed the lantern to Blackburn, then sat up and spit dirt.

"Well?" Billy asked.

Though the others said nothing, their expressions showed that they were just as anxious as Billy.

Gleason looked around, then smiled. "It's a good tunnel. It'll hold."

There was a united sigh of relief. Then the Pennsylvania men, who had started the tunnel and who had done most of the work on it, began smiling and congratulating each other. Tobias seemed most pleased.

"Considering the little time and tools we had, we did—" he started, but Gleason cut him off.

"It's good enough for what we need." Gleason looked around. "All right, first men out have the best chance. More time before they sound the alarm."

"And more time to get away from their damned hounds," Wisnovsky said.

The others nodded, then turned to Gleason, who had

become the leader not only of the Pennsylvania group but of all of them.

"We'll draw lots to fix the order we go in," Gleason continued.

"Sergeant Gleason," Josie said, "we've talked it over . . . that is, the Massachusetts men, and we think you should go first. It's your tunnel."

"You helped us dig it." Gleason looked at Billy, the dirtiest of them all, and smiled. "And you, Billy. You're a tunneling fool, did you know that? You ever get to Pennsylvania, I'll have to work for you."

Billy shook his head. "No, I'm never going underground again. I'm going to New Bedford, where I can breathe good, clean, salt air."

"Fair's fair, Sergeant. You first," Josie insisted.

"All right," Gleason said. "Agreed. We need one strong man to be last, to brace up the beam. That way, we'll be sure everyone gets through before the support gives way. And if we have a cave-in, he's got to drag us out fast."

"I'm prob'ly the strongest one here," Sweet said. "I'll do it."

"No," Gleason said, shaking his head. "Appreciate the offer, Sweet, but it has to be a mining man . . . has to be someone who can see a cave-in coming."

"I'll stay with 'im," Blackburn volunteered. He reached over and put his hand on Sweet's shoulder. "We'll make a good team, Thomas. Your brawn and my experience."

"Thanks, Martin," Sweet said.

"All right, that takes care of that," Gleason said.

"What do we do with him?" Wisnovsky asked, jerking his head toward the back corner of the shebang, where Grundy lay tied and gagged.

"Leave him tied up here for another week," 60th Ohio said. "It'll be good for him."

"I say we kill the son of a bitch," Wisnovsky proposed.

"Yeah," Tyce agreed. "Cut his scummy throat for him."

Wisnovsky reached into his pocket, pulled out a jack-knife, and, with his thumb, flipped open the blade. Tyce moved to the corner and grabbed Grundy by the hair, yanking his head back to expose his throat to Wisnovsky. Grundy struggled, the gag muffling his protests of terror.

"No," McSpadden spoke for the first time. "Leave him be, he's not going anywhere. I'll keep watch on him."

"How you plan to do that?" Gleason asked.

"Easy," McSpadden replied. "I'm staying here."

"James, no!" It was the first time Josie had ever called his sergeant by his first name.

"Better this way, Josie, lad. I'm not fit to go. Really, I'm not."

"Sergeant, you can't stay!" Billy protested.

"We need you," Sweet added.

"Don't stay here for this bastard," Tyce said, still holding Grundy's head up.

"All we have to do is get to the river," Josie said. "Once we get there, we've got it made." He glanced toward Gleason. "And what is that? A mile or two? No more."

Gleason shook his head. "Can't really tell from the map," he admitted.

Grundy's eyes were wide in terror as he watched and listened to these men discussing his fate.

"Leave him tied," Josie said. "Someone'll find him in the morning." He turned to McSpadden. "You're coming with us."

McSpadden shrugged, then nodded. "I just don't want to hold you boys back, is all."

"You won't be holding us back." Josie smiled broadly. "Hell, if he has to, ol' Sweet could pick you up and carry you with no more trouble than if he was carryin' a haversack."

"That's true, Sergeant," Sweet agreed. "You wouldn't be no trouble to carry."

"That's settled," Josie said. "Now, how soon do we go?"

"Looked to me like we only have a few more feet to dig," Gleason replied. "I think we can break through in an hour."

Billy's smile spread from ear to ear. Excitedly, he grabbed Josie's shoulder. "You hear that, Josie? We'll be through in an hour!"

Josie smiled at him. "Yeah, Billy, I heard."

"We should go first chance we get, John," Wisnovsky said. "Those hyena Raiders over there, they may come after us any time."

Tyce, who had let Grundy's head drop to the ground, kicked him hard in the side. "Or sell us to the Rebs for a crust of moldy bread, like this sorry bastard was going to," he said.

Tyce noticed that Grundy was wearing good boots. "What the hell are you doing with boots that good?" he asked. He reached down and grabbed Grundy's bound legs, then roughly rolled him over. He wrestled the boots off Grundy's feet, then sat down and pulled off his own boots. They were torn and nearly worthless, the sole flapping loosely on one of them. Tyce held up the good boots, looked at them for a second, then put them on, jamming his old boots in his belt. He sat down and leaned back, pleased with his acquisition.

Tobias looked at his own bare feet, then at the boots Tyce stuck into his belt.

"What you goin' to do with them old boots, Tyce?" he asked.

Tyce looked coldly at Tobias but said nothing.

"Are you just going to . . . ," Tobias started, then let the question drop. He looked at everyone else in the shebang. It was obvious that none of them approved of Tyce's behavior, but no one made any effort to interfere. Instead, they looked away, avoiding Tobias' gaze. Sighing, Tobias settled back. "Well, I've gone this long without them," he said to no one in particular.

Wisnovsky looked again at Grundy. "You boys know we're going to have to kill him. We can't leave him to turn traitor on someone else's tunnel."

Grundy rolled over and began looking at everyone with eyes opened wide in fear.

Gleason ran his hand through his hair. After a long moment of contemplation, he let out a resigned sigh. "Much as I hate to agree with him on this, Josie, I'm afraid he's right."

Wisnovsky took out his knife again. "Should-a killed him soon's we caught him." He started toward Grundy, who was shaking so badly that he was almost in convulsions. He was pleading with his eyes, making whimpering sounds behind his gag, and shaking his head.

Wisnovsky stopped.

"Do it, damn you! Do it!" Tyce cried. "I want to get out of here! Out of here! Out of here!"

"No, Wisnovsky, don't do it," Josie said, holding up his hand to stop him. For a long moment there was a stalemate between the two factions within the group. Opinions were almost equally divided as to whether or not they should kill Grundy.

The final decision was Gleason's, and his expression showed that he wished he could pass this cup. Finally he held his hand out to Wisnovsky. "Give me the knife. Don't worry, Josie," he added, "I'm not going to kill him."

Gleason stepped over to Grundy, who was screaming in muffled terror. He knelt beside him, made slashing movements with the knife, then stood up. There was blood on the knife blade and on his hand. And there were two bloody Ts slashed in Grundy's forehead.

"There," Gleason said, looking at his handiwork. "All the boys see that, they'll know he's a tunnel traitor. Don't expect he'll get the opportunity to turn anyone else in." He closed the bloody knife, then he turned to Benton, who was closest to the opening of the shebang. "Take a look around outside, Benton," he ordered. "And check how's the moon."

Benton stepped outside.

Everyone was quiet for a moment while they were

waiting for Benton to come back in. Josie looked over at the now still form of Grundy.

"Boys, we get any thinner we can escape out of a worm hole, 'stead of a tunnel," Blackburn said, making a macabre joke to fill the silence.

Benton stepped inside. "Don't see anyone prowling around. And what little moon there is, is sometimes covered by clouds."

"Good," Gleason said. He pulled out the hand-drawn map and passed it around so that everyone could get a look at it. "Nobody can take this map," he cautioned. "If you're caught, it'd lead 'em right to the rest of us. So study it till you know the way."

One by one the men looked at the map, fixing the details in their memory, then passing it to the next person. While Billy was waiting his turn, he spoke quietly to Josie.

"Josie, you need help with sergeant?"

"No, I'll take care of him. I want you to be the first Massachusetts man out. Soon as you're clear, you run for the river."

Billy nodded. "I will. And I'm going to get there, too."

"Yes, you are."

While the men silently studied the map, Gleason stared hard at Tyce. Sensing it, Tyce looked up, then looked away.

Gleason was unrelenting. He continued to stare at Tyce. Finally he spoke. "Give him your old boots." He nodded toward Tobias. "Give them to him."

Tyce looked away—defensive, stubborn, and angry. Then he saw that everyone was staring at him. He was alone in his defiance. Finally he looked at Tobias.

"You got anything to swap?"

Tobias shook his head. "No, I've got nothing but the pants and shirt I'm wearing."

"Well, do you expect me to just . . . ?" Out of the corner of his eye, Tobias saw Gleason snap open the knife. "What the hell?"

Gleason glared at Tyce, then sliced three brass buttons off his coat. He held them out.

"Now, do it, damn you," he said in cold anger.

Tyce shrugged, then looked at the buttons. Finally a small smile spread across his face. The three buttons were worth far more than his worn-out boots. He took the buttons, dropped them into his pocket, then removed his old boots from his belt and held them out toward Tobias.

"Thanks," Tobias said.

"Don't thank me, I was . . ."

Tobias looked up at him coldly. "Wasn't thanking you, pissant. I was thanking the sergeant."

After studying the map, Josie passed it to the next man.

"Let's make 'em divide their forces, John," he suggested. "Once we get outside, you boys go right, we'll go left."

Gleason nodded. "Good idea. Now, there's one more thing. We won't all get away. But anyone who does, is honor bound to get to Grant or Sherman. Tell 'em what it's like in here, and how many of our men are dying. Tell 'em they've got to exchange for us."

All agreed with a nod.

"All right, we'll go in two hours. With God's help, we'll meet at the river."

"Don't count on God," Tyce said dryly.

"Tyce, you ever been in a church?" Wisnovsky asked.

Tyce didn't answer.

Gleason reached over to shake hands, first with Josie and then with McSpadden. After that, the men left.

As Josie and the others started across the short distance that separated the Pennsylvania shebang from their own, they met Patrick Shay, the young drummer boy. Looking around to make certain he couldn't be overheard, Patrick stepped close and whispered, "Good luck tonight."

"What?" Billy was startled by Patrick's words. "You know?"

"There's not much in here Patrick doesn't know," Josie

said. "Patrick, may be room for one more. I could ask Sergeant Gleason."

Patrick shook his head. "Nah, thanks anyway, Josie. Some of the boys in here, they kind of depend on me, you know? I think I'd better stay."

"All right, if you feel that way. But you're welcome to come with us."

"Hope you make it."

Josie watched Patrick move quickly through the camp, stopping here and there to speak to people, always welcome.

"Hope he makes it through to the end," Josie said. "He's a good man."

"Man?" Billy snorted. "You call him a man? He's nothin' but a boy."

"A boy who's better than most of the men I've ever met."

"Yeah," Billy agreed. "Yeah, I guess he is at that."

Two hours later:

A rabbit momentarily stopped foraging when it heard something. It raised its ears, then lifted its head, its nose twitching nervously.

From the rabbit's perspective, this night was no different from any other night. There was a long expanse of open ground that ran between the woods and the stockaded walls and towers of the prison. The guards in the towers were dark shadows whose movements back and forth were not threatening.

And yet something, a sound or a movement, had disturbed the rabbit. It was about to relax when once again it sensed danger, and this time it let its instincts take over. With a mighty thrust of its powerful hind legs, the rabbit bounded away, heading for the woods.

A moment later the source of the rabbit's fright appeared. Grass moved, and dirt shifted, then a hole opened in the earth and Gleason's head poked out. Very carefully, Gleason examined the area, checking in all directions. Then he hoisted himself out of the hole. He glanced toward the towers, and satisfied that none of the guards were looking in this direction, he pulled up Wisnovsky. As soon as Wisnovsky was out, the two of them started off to the right, running in a crouch.

The guards continued to watch the inside of the prison compound.

Tobias came out, pulling Benton up behind him. They checked the towers, then took off to the right, just behind Gleason and Wisnovsky.

Billy and Tucker came up next, then Tyce, then 2nd Wisconsin and 60th Ohio. They ran to the left.

The guards continued to watch the inside of the prison, still unaware that an escape was in progress.

Josie and McSpadden came up. Josie emerged first, then turned and helped McSpadden out. The guards were still looking away. He signaled McSpadden, and the two of them started off to the left, toward the trees some 150 yards away.

Halfway there, McSpadden's foot caught a tree root, and he fell on his face, then slid across the ground on his healing wound. He hit so hard and painfully that he was unable to prevent a short, sharp cry.

Hearing him, Josie stopped and looked around. He ran back, intending to help him up, when he heard one of the guards call out.

Private Allen had been plagued with a recurring dream. In it he could see his brother, Jubal, and the Yank prisoner he had shot. Jubal and the Yank prisoner were laughing at him.

"Michael, you was always so dumb you couldn't pour piss out of a boot," his brother was saying to him. "Here you've gone and kilt Ethan for no good reason. Ethan ain't the one shot me, you dumb shit. Ethan's my friend! Why, he even brung me this corn to eat!"

If the prisoner he shot wasn't the Yank soldier who killed Jubal, then his brother's real killer was still inside.

"I'll find out which'n you are," Allen said under his breath. "An' when I do, you won't need to cross no Deadline for me to shoot you. I'm goin' to shoot you soon's I find you."

"Allen! Allen!"

The guard in the next tower was calling him.

"What you want?"

"I think I heard something."

"Sergeant, stay down!" Josie hissed. He went flat on his stomach, with only his head raised, and looked toward the towers.

"What you think you heard, Bobby Roy?"

"Don't know. Wisht the moon was out fuller, so's we could see better."

"You all right?" Josie whispered.

"Yeah. Damn fool stunt, falling like that."

The two guards were trying to determine whether they had actually heard anything.

"Think we ought to call Sergeant Martindale?" Allen asked.

"Don't know yet," Bobby Roy replied. "Keep lookin' out there, see if you see somethin'."

"Ah, it's probably nothin'," Allen said. "You can look out there if you want to, but I'm keepin' my eyes on the ones that's inside. That's where he is."

"That's where who is?"

"The Yankee son of a bitch that shot my brother."

"Allen, you're as full of shit as a Christmas goose."

Josie continued to keep his eyes on the guard towers. Both guards turned back to the inside of the prison.

"All right, they're lookin' back inside now," Josie whispered. "Think you can get up?"

"Yeah, I think so," McSpadden said, wincing as he got to his feet.

Back at the hole, Blackburn came out, but instead of crouching, he stood upright as he turned to help Sweet exit.

"Get down!" Josie whispered, but he was too far away for Blackburn to hear him, and he dared not speak any louder for fear the guards would hear him. "Get down!" he whispered again. "Don't stand up like that! If the guards turn around again, they'll see you!"

Sweet was big, almost bigger than the hole, and he was having a hard time getting out. Blackburn was smaller than average, and helping Sweet out was more of a task than he was prepared for. The two men strained until, finally, Sweet came out, with an audible grunt of exertion.

"Hey!" Allen shouted, turning around quickly. "Hey, Bobby Roy, turn around! They *is* somethin' out there! I see 'em!"

From Allen's tower a brilliant light flashed as he fired his rifle. The boom followed shortly thereafter, and Josie heard the angry whine of the bullet as it flew past his ear.

"Yankees escaping!" Bobby Roy shouted. "Outside the walls! East wall, east wall!"

Now Bobby Roy fired, and again there was a flash of light and a loud bang.

"Come on! Let's get out of here!" Josie called, tugging on McSpadden as they started across the field on a dead run.

Private Allen saw two men running in the distance, and two much closer. One of the two closer men was much larger than the other. Having reloaded, Allen aimed at the larger and more tempting target.

Sweet and Blackburn were running when Allen fired his second shot.

Suddenly there was a blow to the middle of Sweet's back.

It was hard and heavy, but it didn't hurt. Instead, it spread an immediate circle of numbness through him. Sweet felt his legs turn to rubber, and he fell.

"Martin!" he shouted. "I'm shot!"

Blackburn had been a few feet in front of Sweet. When he turned and saw Sweet fall, he came to a complete stop.

Josie had turned just as Sweet was going down, and he saw Blackburn stop.

"No, Martin! Don't stop! Run, Martin! Run!" Josie shouted.

"Come on, Martin!" McSpadden added.

With a mighty effort, Sweet managed to get to his hands and knees. Then, seeing Blackburn coming back for him, he waved a hand, trying to get his friend to stop.

"No, don't come back! You go on, Martin!" he shouted. "Leave me! Get out of here! Run!"

Two more rifles cracked, and the flame patterns of their muzzle blasts washed the trees in light, as if lightning streaks were shooting down from the night sky.

A bullet hit the dirt a few feet from Josie and McSpadden.

"Come on, Sergeant, they have our range!" Josie called.

"What about Blackburn?"

"Leave him! There's nothing we can do for him or for Sweet!"

The two men looked at each other for a moment, and McSpadden nodded, acknowledging that Josie was right and, despite the difference in rank and age, was in command.

Blackburn had returned to Sweet and, ignoring the guards who were now firing from the towers, sat down on the ground to cradle his friend's head in his lap.

"I'm here, Thomas," he said, weeping over his dying friend. "I'm here."

Josie and McSpadden continued to run toward the trees, but McSpadden, slowed by his fall, wasn't moving well. Josie kept looking over his shoulder at him. Every instinct

135

in his body told Josie to run, to leave McSpadden to shift for himself. But time and again he stopped and helped.

The bullets were getting closer, singing past their heads, digging up the dirt around them, popping through the limbs and leaves of the trees just beyond.

By now the rest of the guard had been alerted, and the gates to the prison swung open. Josie saw several guards moving toward them. He also heard the barking and baying of the hounds, and could see them pulling at their leashes, barely controlled by their handlers.

Then he saw Lieutenant Barrett coming after them, pulling up his galluses as he ran.

The barking and braying of the dogs intensified, and they began running around, sniffing the ground, getting the scent of the escaping prisoners.

"Come on, James, we're in the woods!" Josie shouted, then, looking back, saw that McSpadden was still in the open. The other thing Josie saw filled him with fear: Lieutenant Barrett and half a dozen other soldiers were now mounted, bent low over their horses' necks as they urged their steeds to a gallop. They flew past the guards on foot, and quickly caught up to the dogs.

The dogs and their handlers reached the exit of the tunnel, then stopped.

"Let 'em go!" Barrett shouted. "Let the dogs go!"

The handlers knelt for a moment, then separated the leashes from the dogs' collars. They stood up, then raised their arms with a flourish.

"Sic 'em, dogs!" they shouted. "Go get them Yankees!" The dogs barked and howled as they milled around, getting the prisoners' scents, then went in two directions, one group heading south toward Gleason and the Pennsylvania men and the other group heading north, toward Josie and the Massachusetts men.

McSpadden made it to the edge of the woods, panting and wheezing, and holding his shoulder. He leaned against a tree to get his breath. Every survival instinct in Josie's body screamed at him to go on, to get through the woods and into the swamp beyond. But he was determined not to leave McSpadden on his own, so he stopped and waited with him.

Behind them the dogs continued to bay, and the guards continued to shout.

"Dogs," McSpadden managed to say as he regained his breath. "How I hate those goddamned dogs!"

At the tunnel exit, Blackburn was still sitting on the ground, cradling Sweet, when the dogs hit. They leaped on them, knocking Blackburn away by the force of their impact. Growling, with fangs bared, the dogs sank their sharp teeth into their helpless victims, tearing out chunks of flesh.

Sweet, though badly wounded, managed to get to his knees. He reached for one of the dogs that was attacking Blackburn, grabbed it by the throat, and pulled it off. With the last reserve of his tremendous strength he crushed the dog's windpipe, killing the animal just as a guard thrust his bayonet into Sweet's back and penetrated his heart. Sweet looked down at the bloody spike protruding from his chest, reached for it, then fell forward.

One of the handlers reached down to grab his dogs, pulling them back from the bloody and terrified Blackburn.

"This one's dead," the guard who had stabbed Sweet told Lieutenant Barrett.

Barrett nodded.

"Lieutenant, the dogs is still wantin' to run," one of the handlers said.

"That's because there are more of the escaped Yankees out there. Let 'em loose. Let 'em run." Barrett took a quick look at Blackburn. "And take that one back!"

"Yes, sir."

Two guards moved over Blackburn, then roughly jerked him to his feet. They started marching him back toward the stockade. Barrett watched them for no more than a second, then whirled his horse around and started after the dogs.

•   •   •

By now Josie and McSpadden were deep into the swamp. They ran through a carpet of bladderwort, then splashed through a shallow pond filled with protruding cypress knees. McSpadden's breath was coming in great, ragged gasps, and it was becoming harder and harder for him to keep going. Finally, in desperation, McSpadden held out his hand, pleading with Josie to stop. Josie did, though his heart was pounding in fear, and every fiber in his body was urging him on.

"Listen!" McSpadden gasped.

Josie cocked his head to hear beyond McSpadden's wheezing as he tried to regain his breath. In the distance the baying of the hounds reached another peak, like the one when they attacked Sweet and Blackburn. Then, above the yelping dogs, they could hear the sound of men crying in terror and pain.

"They caught some of the others, poor devils," McSpadden said.

"Sergeant, we've got to go. We can't stop here."

"I know, I know," McSpadden said, gasping. He made a motion with his hand, signaling that he was ready.

Once again, Josie and McSpadden started running, staggering forward through the patches of open water and clots of floating plants, past thickets of brush and shrubs, beneath the moss-hung branches of huge cypress trees. Moving was becoming more and more difficult.

Behind them, the dogs had started their baying again, taking up a new chase. This time the dogs were coming after them.

"The dogs are after us now," Josie said, though he knew that McSpadden understood that as well.

Finally McSpadden came to a stop.

"No!" Josie said. "You can't stop now!"

"How far, lad?" McSpadden gasped through ragged, wheezing breaths. "How far's the river?"

"Wait," Josie said. He saw a little hill ahead of them. "I'll see what I can see."

Josie ran up to the top of the hill. Not more than a quarter of a mile away he could see the water, winking blackly under the dim light of the new moon. "I can see it!" he cried.

He ran back to McSpadden, who was leaning against a tree, barely able to stay on his feet.

"Sergeant, come on! The river's just ahead! I can see it!"

McSpadden shook his head. "Can't make it," he said between gasps. "Go on . . . without me. . . . Go, Josie."

But Josie refused to listen to him. He bent down, picked McSpadden up, put him on his back, then carried him up the hill. They barely made it to the top. Then, cresting the hill, they plunged down the other side, toward the river, which lay across an open field.

Back in the swamp, Lieutenant Barrett and his mounted guards were finding the going as difficult as had Josie and McSpadden. Only the hounds seemed undeterred. They bounded over bogs and splashed through shallow pools of water, baying and howling as they moved toward their quarry.

Josie started across the field with McSpadden on his back. The field was about a hundred yards wide, open and flat except for a tree right in the middle. Weakened by weeks of malnutrition, and exhausted by his effort tonight, Josie was finding it more and more difficult to keep going. Behind them, the dogs had broken out of the swamp and were having easier going in the open field.

"Those dogs, Josie! Please don't let them get me! I don't want them tearing into me!"

The dogs were getting closer. The intensity of their baying showed that they knew they were almost upon the two men.

"For God's sake, Josie!" McSpadden said again, his voice on the edge of terror.

"All right, hang on!" Josie had no choice now. Instead of heading for the river, he headed for the tree. Reaching it, he

139

let McSpadden down, then climbed to the first tier of branches. He turned and reached toward McSpadden.

"Grab hold!" he called.

McSpaden grabbed hold, then, using all his strength, Josie pulled him up. The first dog reached the tree just at that moment. It leaped toward McSpadden, snapping its jaws shut just inches below his leg.

Josie helped McSpadden climb a few more limbs higher, then moved behind him, positioning himself between his sergeant and the dogs. He put his arms around McSpadden, hugging him close to prevent him from falling from their perch.

"I've got you, Sergeant. I've got you."

Despite Josie's reassurance, McSpadden was terrified, and he kicked out to keep the jumping dogs away.

By now Barrett and his horse soldiers had reached the top of the hill. Seeing that the dogs had someone treed, he started forward at a gallop. When he reached them, he raised his pistol and took careful aim. Josie closed his eyes and braced himself for the bullet . . . but it didn't come. When he opened his eyes a moment later, he saw that Barrett had lowered his pistol.

The dogs were still baying and jumping and snapping at their treed prey while soldiers were circling around. In despair, Josie looked toward their goal—the river was right there, so close and yet so unattainable, just a few yards away, glistening black and silver in the sparse moonlight.

"Take 'em back," Barrett ordered.

Chapter 9

The middle of the next day, just outside the stockade:

Josie, Sergeant McSpadden, Billy, Tyce, Tucker, Blackburn, Wisnovsky, Tobias, Benton, 2nd Wisconsin, and 60th Ohio were in the stocks. As the sun beat down upon them, the would-be escapees grew thirstier, and felt the agonizing pain of muscle and bone being held in one position for too long.

All day, Josie had been trying to use the trick he had developed on the train. Then, he had been able to separate his mind from his body. Unfortunately, he had not been able to do that since being hauled back and slapped into this torture device.

A few new prisoners arrived and, seeing so many men being so brutally treated, became even more frightened.

The guards changed, passing the stocks without so much as a second glance.

A wagon rolled by, carrying the prisoners' ration of cornmeal. Like the guards, the wagon driver paid no attention to the men in the stocks.

The sun grew hotter, and flies and gnats buzzed around them. A few, who had been badly mauled by the dogs, whimpered in pain.

Josie continued to try and separate his mind from his body.

From the star fort came a discordant sound. It was supposed to be music from a fife-and-drum military band, but it was little more than noise.

Colonel Chandler and Lieutenant Dahlgren hurried by, heading for the fort. Chandler glanced toward the stocks. Distaste for what he was seeing was clear on his face, but he made no move to ease their situation. Josie wanted to call out to him, to ask him how, if he was indeed an inspecting officer, he could let this go on. Wasn't this inhumane? Didn't this means of punishment, and the deplorable conditions of the prison itself, violate all standards of human behavior?

Josie wanted to call that out to him, but he didn't have the strength. It was taking everything he had just to hang on.

Inside the star fort, the fife-and-drum corps, composed of both Confederate soldiers and Yankee prisoners, none of them older than sixteen, continued to play what passed for music. Marching to this cacophony, in a formation and at a pace just as incompetent, was a formation of soldiers.

Captain Wirz, his face twisted in a scowl of rage, turned to Barrett. "These 'musicians,' they must be better. Much better! And this . . . what you call marching! Until dark you will drill them, and after dark, if necessary. By tomorrow they must be ready!"

"Absolutely, Captain. They will be better."

The young bandsmen, who had heard Wirz's tirades before, continued to play and march in the only way they knew how.

At that moment Chandler and Dahlgren came into the star fort. Chandler looked at Wirz, and then at the band and the drilling soldiers. His face registered total contempt.

"So, Colonel," Wirz said, moving quickly to greet him. "I hope you do not have to leave before we have welcomed back General Winder."

"Leaving tomorrow morning," Chandler said.

"Ah, that is too bad. The musicians will improve very much bef—"

Chandler interrupted him. "If you and your officers spent one hour a day improving the conditions of the stockade instead of . . . of planning these ridiculous little ceremonies—" He let the implied sentence hang, then, with a shrug of disgust, turned and walked away with Dahlgren.

Wirz paled at the criticism, and for a moment he stared after them. Suddenly he started after them, rushing to catch up with Chandler.

"Colonel, excuse me, you must know. I am in charge of the guard force here. So their perfor—"

"You are also responsible for the operation of the prison."

"Well, yes, in part. But, of course, Colonel. . . ."

"May I ask you a personal question, Captain Wirz? Something I need to know for my report?"

"Of course, Colonel. You may ask me anything."

"I have heard that before you came here from Switzerland ten years ago, you had medical training."

"*Ja*, it is true, Colonel. I am fully qualified to—"

"To what?" Chandler snapped. He pointed toward the stockade. "To allow this . . . this *disgrace* to civilization to exist?"

"Colonel, please. You must not say such things in front of my men."

"They'll hear soon enough, Captain. I'm filing my report this—"

"Please!" Wirz held up his good hand. "There are things

I must say to you. But not in front of the men. I must talk to you, please."

Chandler looked at Wirz, then stared out the window, looking at the escaped prisoners in the stocks. After a long moment, he turned back and saw the anxious, pleading expression on Wirz's face. Reluctantly, he nodded.

"Thank you, Colonel, thank you," Wirz said. "And now, if you will, please come with me to my quarters."

Leading the way, Wirz left the star fort, with Chandler and Dahlgren close behind him. They walked quickly past the prisoners who were being punished, without so much as a glance in their direction, then went into Wirz's quarters.

"Lieutenant, open a window," Chandler said. "It's stuffy in here."

"Yes, sir."

It did not escape Wirz's attention that these were his quarters and that, technically, Chandler had no right to open a window, or do anything else, without Wirz's permission. But because he wanted Chandler to listen to what he had to say, he said nothing.

"You must know, Colonel, that General Winder is in charge here. Totally. Of food, of quarters, of medicines, supplies . . . of all, he is in charge."

"I will report to the government what I believe the general's responsibility is. If you want to discuss your own responsibility for the deaths of more than one hundred men in your care each day. . . ."

"Of course, I only meant. . . ."

"Captain, in one week you could have finished dams across the streams . . . made floodgates to flush out the waste. You could have built another camp to relieve crowding."

"Ah, but you see, Colonel, we have no tools. No saws, no axes. For these things I have asked, not one time but ten times."

"You do have some tools, Captain. I've taken inventory.

144

And you could parole prisoners to bring in wood from the forest and food from nearby plantations."

"I did, Colonel. Earlier. They ran."

". . . under guard!" Chandler continued. "And let the prisoners build shelters!"

Wirz shook his head. "We have not enough lumber for barracks, and no canvas for tents."

Exasperated by Wirz's excuses, Chandler pointed to the woods. "Then get more wood, Captain!"

"I wanted them to have wood. But General Winder, he ordered all the trees cut down so there'd be no shade."

"Captain Wirz, I said I won't speak to you about the general. Now, have you anything else to say on your own behalf?"

Wirz stood there for a long moment, looking totally defeated. Seeing that the commandant had nothing more to say, Chandler signaled Dahlgren, and the two officers started to leave.

"I . . . most respectfully," Wirz called after him. Chandler stopped, then turned back toward the commandant.

"Yes, Captain?"

Wirz gathered himself, straining to speak as clearly as he could, thinking hard to find the right words, with the least accent, so Chandler could understand him more easily.

"Please, you must tell them, there is no one, absolutely no one, in this war who has to deal with the circumstances I have to deal with. You have seen. You know that. But tell them I do not complain. I am a soldier, Colonel. I know my duty, and I do it faithfully." Wirz held up his wounded arm. "Look at this arm of mine. It was shattered in the Battle of Seven Pines."

"Yes, you are a soldier, Captain." Chandler pointed toward the outside. "So, when you personally ordered stocks to be built, and the ball and chain. . . ."

"Only for escaped prisoners, so they won't run."

"You knew you were violating the Articles of War. As you

knew you were violating them when you withheld food from prisoners as punishment."

There was a long silence.

"Was there anything else you wanted to say, Captain?"

Wirz looked at the floor. Turning, he walked away a few steps, then stopped and turned back toward Chandler. He took a deep breath.

"Yes?" Chandler asked.

"It is true, Colonel. Of course it is. It is all true."

Believing that he was finally getting something out of Wirz, Chandler came back into the room.

"I know it will not surprise you that I agree with what you say. I try. I try very hard." Wirz pointed out the window. "Those young boys in the fife-and-drum corps out there. I paroled them so they would not have to stay in that wretched stockade. I did that. I ordered the hospital moved outside the walls, where the air is better. General Winder did not approve. He became very angry with me, but I did it anyway. And I ordered the stockade made bigger.

"But you know the problem, Colonel. They just send us, all the time, more prisoners, on General Winder's orders. Thirty-three thousand now, when we were built for only eight thousand.

"So, of course, I agree with you. With the proper help we could do much more. The problem is, I need people. Can you help us, Colonel? Perhaps, if I were major instead of only captain, then I would have more staff assigned to me. We could start to solve these problems later.

"They listen to you in Richmond, Colonel. I think if you put that recommendation in your report, it would be most definitely helpful."

Wirz's suggestion that the solution to the problem would be to promote him left Chandler speechless. He looked at Dahlgren as if to see if Dahlgren heard what he heard. Then, without a further word, he turned and left Wirz's quarters.

Outside the stockade walls, late that night:

Josie looked around, surprised to see that it was dark. When did it get dark? He couldn't remember the sun going down. Perhaps he had been able to separate body and soul after all, for he could remember seeing the Confederate inspection team go into Wirz's quarters. He was aware of nothing else until this very moment.

To the best of his ability, restricted as he was, Josie looked around at the men here with him: McSpadden, Tucker, Blackburn, Wisnovsky, Tyce, and 2nd Wisconsin. When he turned his head in the other direction, he could see that Tobias, Benton, and 60th Ohio also were there. By now, several of them were being kept from falling flat only by the stocks themselves.

Moving his gaze in front of him, Josie saw a flatbed cart parked near the stocks. This was the kind of cart they used to take people to the Deadhouse, and he wondered if they had it sitting out here for that purpose—for them.

"Take your damn cart! Take it back, do you hear me? I won't be on it! No, by God, I won't be on it!"

Josie thought he was shouting the words loud enough to be heard all the way to the turkey roosts, but not one of the sentries on duty looked toward him. Neither did any of the other prisoners look around. Josie began to wonder if he had said anything at all.

The two inspecting officers came out of the stockade, heading toward the star fort, where temporary quarters had been established for them. They stopped near the stocks and looked at the men there.

Colonel Chandler sighed. "There will be those who know we tell the truth and will want to act on it. But men have other things on their minds these days, and I fear that, in the end, nothing will be done."

"Perhaps not, sir," Dahlgren agreed.

"Yes, well, good night, Lieutenant."

"And good night to you, sir," Dahlgren replied.

Leaving Chandler, Dahlgren walked past the stocks. He stopped, then walked over to have a closer look. Examining two of the men, he called out. "Colonel?"

"Yes?"

"Colonel, couple of these men are dead. Legs gave out and they strangled themselves."

"You think Captain Wirz knows?" Colonel Chandler asked.

"I don't know if he does or not, sir," the lieutenant answered.

"Then by all means go tell him, Lieutenant. By God, I want to see him weasel out of this one."

"Yes, sir."

"Not that it will make any difference," Chandler added.

Who was dead? Josie wondered. Was McSpadden dead? He was in bad enough shape before they started. Surely he couldn't have survived.

But Josie couldn't turn his head far enough to see who was alive and who was dead.

Across the way, Dahlgren arrived at Wirz's quarters. He returned the salute of the two sentries, then spoke to one of them. The sentry turned and knocked on the door to Wirz's building, then disappeared inside. Dahlgren was forced to wait outside.

Josie waited to see what was going to happen next. Finally Wirz appeared in his nightclothes. He and Dahlgren had a brief discussion, then Wirz said something to the sentries. They saluted, and Wirz went back inside.

Dahlgren led the sentries back to the stocks.

"Take them down," Dahlgren ordered.

"Yes, sir," one of the sentries replied. One by one, Dahlgren and the sentries went to the stocks to open them and free the men.

As soon as Josie was free, he looked around to see who

had survived. It was difficult to tell now, because none of them could stand on his own. All of them fell to the ground the moment they were released.

One of the sentries bent over to check the prisoners, going from man to man, reaching down to feel for a pulse. He came to Josie, who felt the hand on his neck. He tried hard to turn over, to tell the sentry he was still alive, but he couldn't make himself move or speak.

"I'm not dead! Don't put me in the Deadhouse! I'm not dead!" he screamed as loud as he could. But the words were in his mind only, for not one sound came from his lips. Then he began to wonder if perhaps he really was dead.

"These here is still alive, I think," the sentry called to Dahlgren.

Josie breathed a quick prayer of thanks. He was one of those the sentry was talking about. If the guard thought he was alive, then he must be.

"But them two're gone," the sentry continued. "Lieutenant, sir, would you mind helping me get these here live ones back inside the walls? Eugene," he called to the other sentry, "you get them an' take 'em to the Deadhouse."

"We're going to use the cart?" Dahlgren asked.

"Yes, sir. Can't do it no other way. Don't expect any of these fellas can walk."

Josie felt himself being picked up and put onto the cart. At first he was filled with panic, equating the cart with the Deadhouse. Then he realized that the ones being loaded onto the cart were alive.

But who was dead?

Josie's brain, muddled by pain and exhaustion, finally told him how to determine who was still alive and who wasn't. Those who were loaded into the cart were alive. Those who were dead would be left behind. He would simply wait and see who was still on the ground.

When the cart was fully loaded a moment later, the two men remaining on the ground were Tucker and 60th Ohio.

Oh, Tucker, Josie thought. *I just wish there was more I could have done for you.* He tried to cry for his friend, but he could not. He was so dry that no tears would come.

Chapter 10

Inside the stockade, a few days later:

As Limber Jim walked past the front gate, he heard Captain Wirz giving his welcoming speech to a group of new prisoners. The men, in shock from being captured, were thrown into even more shock by the scene that greeted them, and were looking around in fear and despair.

"Those who are not shot are caught by the dogs without fail and put in the stocks, or ball and chain. And if you escape the dogs, what then? To go hundreds of miles to your own army?" Wirz shook his head and held up his good hand. "Not possible."

Limber Jim continued his walk through the prison camp, bound for the Massachusetts shebang, where for the last few days he had been feeding the men who were recovering from their ordeal after their escape attempt.

"Jim, how're them Massachusetts and Pennsylvania boys doing?" someone asked.

"Tolerably better."

"Are they going to make it?" another asked.

"I think so, yes."

"Here," still another said, giving Limber Jim a small sack of cornmeal. "Know none of 'em can get around on their own yet. That bein' so, thought they might be having trouble gettin' their share of the rations."

"Me 'n' the boys 'preciate your kindness." Limber Jim took the proffered sack.

He moved up the little hill to the Massachusetts shebang. There he saw Josie and McSpadden, still on their backs, barely able to move.

"Got some mush here," Limber Jim said, settling down between them. "Been listenin' to folks talk all over the camp. Ever'body's real proud of you. They're all sayin' you got real close. Closer than anyone ever did."

"Saw the river," McSpadden said. His voice was little more than a croak.

Limber Jim dipped out a spoonful of mush, then held it out to Josie. "Could Sergeant Gleason really have gotten away? Really away?" he asked.

"Maybe," McSpadden said. "Maybe."

The next spoonful went to McSpadden.

"Good chance," Josie said.

"Lordy, lordy, wouldn't that be somethin'?" Limber Jim said. He held out another spoonful of mush to Josie. "Well, now, we get some of this good food in you, I'll have you boys back on your feet in no time."

"You call that good food?" McSpadden croaked.

"Why, sure, it's roast pork, just drippin' with apple sauce." Limber Jim laughed at his own joke. "Open wide, here comes another bite."

There followed a period of silence as Limber Jim continued to feed his two charges. Patrick arrived, also carrying a container of mush.

"How they doin'?" he asked.

"Some better," Limber Jim said. He got up and moved to the opening of the shebang, where he stood looking down at the newly arrived prisoners. Wirz was still talking, but he couldn't be heard.

"You lookin' at the new men?" Patrick asked.

"Yeah."

"Don't you feel sorry for them when they first get here and see what they have gotten themselves into?" Patrick asked.

Limber Jim chuckled, then turned around and looked back at Patrick, who was getting into position to feed Billy. "What do you mean, do I feel sorry for them? Why should I? They're just gettin' here. Look how long we been here already."

"That's my point," Patrick said. "We know what it's like in this place. That makes it much easier for us to bear than it is for them."

"Nothing makes this place easy to bear," Limber Jim insisted.

Patrick held a spoonful of mush toward Billy. Billy was lying with his back to the others, staring into nothingness through dull, vacant eyes. Of all the group, he was by far the most despondent.

"Come on, Billy. I took all the cob out, so the mush isn't really that bad today," Patrick said, trying to get Billy to turn over and eat.

"Don't want it," Billy mumbled. "Go away."

McSpadden raised up on his elbows and looked over toward Billy. "Eat, Billy. You can't live without eating."

"Don't want to live. Not here. Soon as I can stand, I'm goin' to walk across the Deadline. Goin' to die anyway. Might as well make it quick and easy."

"Doesn't have to be that way," McSpadden said.

"Yes, Sergeant, it does."

"Goin' to leave the rest of us in here alone, are you, Billy?" Josie asked.

"Yes. I'm going to leave the rest of you in here."

"No, you're not, because I'm not going to let you," Josie said, resolutely. "We're going to get through this together, Billy. Or we won't. But whichever it is, it will be together."

"Can't," Billy said, with a dry sob deep in the back of his throat. "I just can't."

"Yes you can, Billy. Don't make it easy for 'em, do you hear me? Don't you dare make it easy for these Rebel bastards. Now, eat." Josie said the last two words with all the force of command that he could muster.

For a long moment Josie, McSpadden, and Limber Jim waited anxiously to see what Billy would do. At first Billy didn't move. Then, finally, he forced himself to sit up, and when Patrick extended a spoonful of mush to him, he nodded his acceptance.

With Billy now eating, Limber Jim left the shebang and walked back toward the gate, where Wirz was still talking to the new prisoners. Unused to his German accent, they were straining to understand what he was saying.

"Tunnels are useless," Wirz was telling the new men. "Even if you are outside, I give any two men a twelve-hour start and then track you with dogs . . . and you suffer the consequences."

Now Wirz smiled and began speaking in a more conciliatory tone. The smile, tone, and words were practiced. By now, Limber Jim believed he could do them himself.

"But why bother trying to escape anyway?" Wirz asked. "I know, absolutely, that there are talks going on this very moment for prisoner exchange. Any day now you will all be paroled, and in quick order, too. So, we understand each other."

When he finished the welcoming speech, Wirz, Barrett, and the detail of guards withdrew. As the big gate closed behind them, Munn and several of the Raiders began drifting toward the new men.

"Hey, fresh fish!" Munn called, jovially. "Welcome to

Andersonville. Fine-looking place, don't you think? For a hog pen, maybe." He laughed. "Where'd you boys get catched at? Virginia? That's good. Means Grant's goin' forward, Bobby Lee's goin' backward. Come on, bet you're hungry. I'll get you something to eat. Let me show you around. You'll wanna be up near the wall, away from the Swamp. Lots better up there."

Limber Jim watched the new prisoners. They were willing to follow Munn without the slightest hesitation. In fact, they seemed grateful that someone had taken charge of their lives, for they were still so dispirited from having been captured that they could not.

Limber Jim wanted to warn them, to tell them that many of them might well be heading to their doom, but he said nothing. Anyway, what could he do to help? He was only one man, and he had learned that the new prisoners wouldn't listen to the warnings. They were still too much in shock to comprehend the warning, and the Raiders knew this. The Raiders took advantage of the situation by establishing their presence immediately, moving in where the Confederate guards left off.

Limber Jim saw Samson swinging past on his crutches. He had a great deal of respect for Samson, who, even though he had only one leg, was one of the most active men in the entire prison.

"Them fellas that tried to escape," Samson said, "I hear you're takin' care of 'em."

"Yeah, but I'm not the only one. There's others helpin', too."

"How they gettin' along?"

"Tolerably well."

Limber Jim's answers were short because he was gazing intently at the new prisoners and their welcoming committee.

"Somethin's got to be done about that," he said, nodding toward the new prisoners. "It ain't right for us to just sit back here an' let that kind of thing happen."

"I agree. But what do we do about it?"

"I don't know. Haven't figured it out yet. But somethin's got to be done."

With Sergeant Gleason:

Gleason managed to beat off the dogs and reach the river. Once in the water, he grabbed a log floating downstream. The current was swift, and the water was deep enough to allow him to move with it. He was a good three miles downstream before he left the river and started across country.

Gleason kept going after sunup, deciding that it would be best to keep away from roads and, whenever possible, stay in woods. If there were no woods, he would work his way through high brush, or cornfields, or anything that would provide cover. By doing this, he was able to walk all day without coming into contact with another person.

By nightfall Gleason had covered some thirty miles. His original plan was to continue through that night, then sleep all the next day. But by midnight he was too exhausted to go any further. He had to get some sleep. The problem was where to go. If he lay down under a tree, he would be visible to anyone who might happen by. He needed a place where he could get some rest, a place where he wouldn't be discovered.

As if in answer to his silent prayer, a large haystack loomed just in front of him. He moved quickly toward it, then climbed halfway up. As he burrowed into the straw, its softness and aroma gave him a deep-rooted sense of returning to the womb. He was asleep within moments.

Gleason was awakened the next morning by the sound of voices. When he poked his head up to look around, he saw several soldiers . . . Confederate soldiers! After he had gone to sleep, a company of infantry must have bivouacked beside the haystack.

"Hey, Charley," one of the soldiers called, "get me some of that there straw to help get this fire goin', will you? I'll make us some cornbread for breakfast."

"Cornbread? Well, now, there's a switch."

"What's the matter with you? Cornbread not good enough for you? You think you got to have biscuits an' gravy ever' day?"

"Ever' day? Hell, I'd like to have 'em just one day. Cornbread, cornbread, cornbread. Damn me if I ain't gettin' pretty tired of cornbread."

As Charley came toward the haystack, Gleason very quietly pulled some hay over himself.

A couple of the others came over and began relieving themselves on the haystack, very close to Charley.

"Hey, you fellas watch where at you're a-pissin'. I'm a-tryin' to get some dry straw here."

"Hell, Charley, you ought to get some o' that straw Billy's pissin' on. He done drunk so much pinetop last night, he's prob'ly pissin' coal oil," someone said, and several men laughed.

The straw that had been aromatic and inviting last night was now drawing more than a few insects, and Gleason was growing uncomfortable. He wanted to get out of there, but he had to remain perfectly still. After Charley took his straw, others came as well, some to get their own straw and some to relieve themselves. In fact, the haystack became the main urination point for the entire company.

"Bet them cows is really goin' to like this straw," someone said. Everyone laughed.

"Hey, Cap'n, where we goin' now?"

"We're goin' to Atlanta."

"What for?"

"'Cause more'n likely the Yankees is goin' to try 'n' take it."

"Well, hell, let the damn Yankees have Atlanta, for all I care. Never liked the snooty bunch o' bastards that live there anyway."

There was more laughter.

"Hey, Cap'n, how long we goin' to be hangin' around in this here hay field?"

"Till we get orders to move."

"That could be all day."

"What you complainin' about, Steve? Lyin' aroun' on our asses all day sure beats ridin' shanks mare, don't it?"

"I guess so. Just don't like waitin' aroun', that's all. If a fella could just find some way to take out all the waitin' around, why, we'd-a had this war over in a week."

The Confederate soldiers remained for most of the day, which meant that Gleason had to stay in the haystack. Finally, in midafternoon, he heard someone shouting.

"All right, men, on your feet! Let's go!"

"It's about damn time. I'm gettin' tired of waitin'."

"Damn, Muley, you'd bitch if'en you was hung with a new rope."

Gleason waited a full hour after everyone else had left before he very cautiously emerged from the haystack. Sore and itching, he brushed himself off, then started out. According to the position of the sun, he calculated it to be about four in the afternoon.

By now Gleason was well into his second day without food. He was getting weaker and weaker, and didn't know how much longer he would be able to go on. He had to find something to eat, and he had to find it soon.

When the sun was very low on the horizon, Gleason saw a farmhouse and started toward it. It was slow going because he was avoiding not only roads but also open fields. As a result, he sometimes had to walk four hundred yards or more to cover what would have been one hundred if he could travel in a direct line. Finally he reached a stand of trees very near the house and he stood well back, shielded by the trees as he watched a woman and a little girl feed chickens.

The woman was wearing a bonnet, from which protruded several tendrils of brown hair. She was in her late twenties or early thirties and very pretty.

"Mama, Daddy won't ever be comin' back home, will he?"

"Honey, he's with us all the time now."

"Where? Why can't I see him?"

"Because God has made him an angel, and you can't see angels. But that doesn't mean he isn't there."

"Can he see me?"

The woman put her arms around the little girl. "Yes, darlin'. He can see you now."

"I'd rather have him be a daddy than an angel."

"I know, darlin'. So would I."

The woman's husband was a Rebel, perhaps one of those who had tried to kill him . . . or maybe even one of those he had killed. Seeing the grieving of a Rebel soldier's wife and child gave Gleason a different perspective on the war.

"Come on, sweetheart," the mother said. "It's time for supper."

"All right, Mama."

Gleason stayed motionless until the woman and the girl were inside. When the door to the house was closed and he was certain they would not come out again, he started toward the chicken coop, staying just inside the line of trees as long as he could. By now he was so light-headed from hunger that he felt almost drunk.

Finally, Gleason reached the point in the woods nearest the chicken coop. But between it and the coop was an open space of seventy-five yards or more. It would have to be crossed, and crossed quickly.

Gleason breathed a quick prayer, then took a deep breath and started running as hard as he could across the open space. His boot crushed a cow pile, but he barely smelled it, so fixed was he upon reaching the chicken coop.

He made it!

Gleason pushed the door open and stepped inside, gasping for breath, inhaling the smell of chicken manure, feathers, and ground-up corn. The inside of the coop was illuminated by a few red bars of the setting sun, which stabbed at crazy angles through the cracks between the boards. Half a dozen chickens were at the back of the coop. Gleason managed to take a few steps toward them before he passed out.

For a moment Gleason thought he was back in his parents' home. He was lying in bed between clean sheets, his head on a pillow. He lay there for a long moment, then sat up so quickly that his head began to spin. He put his hand to his forehead until the dizziness passed.

There was a candle on the table beside the bed, and by its soft, wavering light, Gleason began to examine the room. It was about twelve feet square. The walls were wide planks of unpainted pine. There was a window on one wall, and a shelf on another.

Where was he? And how did he get here?

As John made a long, slow examination of the room, a little girl suddenly appeared in the doorway. Seeing that Gleason was sitting up, she gasped, then turned and ran. "Mama! Mama, he's awake!"

A moment later a woman came into the room. It was the woman he had watched feeding chickens. Gleason knew, now, how he got here. He could vaguely remember passing out in the hen house, then later, with her support, walking toward the house. He couldn't remember anything beyond that, though he must have walked in here by himself, for he was reasonably certain she couldn't have carried him.

"You'd better lie back down," the woman said, easily. She put her hand on his forehead and gently pushed him back onto the bed. Her hand felt cool to his skin.

"Who are you?" Gleason asked.

The woman brushed errant tendrils of hair back from her

face. "My name is Claudia Hughes," she said. "My husband and I . . ." she paused for a moment, took a breath, then continued. "That is . . . I . . . own this farm. Now it's my turn to ask who you are."

"I am Sergeant John Gleason."

"Are you a deserter from the army, Sergeant John Gleason?"

"No, ma'am, I'm not a deserter."

"You have the look of someone who's running away from something. And Lord knows, from the looks of you, you have a right to be running. I had no idea conditions were so bad that the men in the army were starving to death."

"I haven't had too much to eat, of late."

"Is that why you were in the chicken coop? Were you planning to steal some eggs from me? Or a chicken, perhaps?"

"I'm ashamed to admit I was," John said. "I'm sorry, Mrs. Hughes. I was desperate."

"I understand, and I forgive you. I would like to think if my Carl had ever become that desperate, someone would have helped him." A wistful look crossed her face for a moment, then, forcing that thought away, she smiled at him. "I've made some potato soup. Would you like some?"

"Yes, ma'am, please," John said.

"I'll be right back."

When Claudia left, Gleason saw the little girl standing in the other room, peeking around the edge of the door frame. He waved at her, and she quickly jerked back.

A moment later Claudia returned with a tray on which were a bowl of soup and a biscuit. She set the tray on the bed, and Gleason reached for the spoon. When he tried to pick it up, however, his hand was shaking so badly that he couldn't hold the spoon. He dropped it, then picked it up and tried again. This time he managed to get the spoon into the soup, but he spilled it all while conveying it to his mouth.

"Would you let me feed you?" Claudia asked.

"Yes, ma'am."

She took the spoon, dipped it into the soup, then held it to his mouth. He took it.

"Thank you, ma'am. That's the most delicious thing I've ever eaten in my life."

"It's just plain old potato soup, Sergeant." She held the spoon to his lips again.

Gleason ate all the soup and the biscuit.

"My, my, Sergeant, you certainly make a woman feel like her cooking is appreciated," Claudia said in her soft drawl. "Now, you rest, while I go into the other room and take care of the dishes. If you need anything, just holler, you hear?"

"Yes, ma'am."

"And you don't have to say 'ma'am' to me every other breath."

"No, ma'am," John said, then they both laughed.

Gleason lay back on the bed, his stomach satisfyingly full for the first time in almost two years. All of a sudden the warm, full feeling turned to very painful cramps. He got out of bed and moved quickly to the door of the bedroom. The woman was standing at a table in the kitchen, pouring water into a dishpan.

"Ma'am?" Gleason said, holding his hand over his stomach. His face was contorted in pain, and she knew at once what was wrong.

"The privy is out back, Sergeant. Through that door."

Gleason moved quickly, barely making it to the outhouse in time. He stayed there for a long while. When the cramps and the diarrhea had finally run their course, he got up and returned weakly to the house.

"Here," Claudia said, handing him a steaming cup. "I want you to drink this."

"No, I'd better not."

"It's sassafras. It'll be good for what ails you. And you've got to get something in you. I'm afraid the soup was just too rich."

"It was delicious."

"Drink this. I've sweetened it with honey."

Gleason nodded his thanks, then began sipping the tea. "It's good."

"Sergeant, how bad is it? Is everyone in the whole army starving to death?"

"I . . . can't speak for everyone in the army. I can only speak for myself."

"Look at you. You're skin and bones. And your stomach is so unused to food that you can't even hold it down. Have things come to that? What in the world is going on? What unit are you with?"

"The 184th Pennsylvania."

"The 184th Pennsylvania?" Claudia gasped. "Is that in the Yankee army?"

"Yes, ma'am."

"Good Lord. I'm givin' aid and comfort to the enemy!"

"Yes, ma'am, I suppose you are. Don't want to trouble you none, so I'll be movin' on."

"Were you at Gettysburg, Sergeant?"

"Yes, ma'am."

"My husband died at Gettysburg."

"A lot of good men . . . on both sides . . . died at Gettysburg."

"I . . . I reckon that's so. Still, I'd hate to think that you might have. . . . I mean. . . ."

"I know what you mean, ma'am. Who was your husband with?"

"General Dole's brigade."

Gleason shook his head. "If it'll put your mind any at ease, ma'am, we were never across from General Dole."

"I'm glad."

"Yes, ma'am. I am, too."

"You know, Sergeant. I had no idea the Yankees were this close."

"I don't know that we are. I have no idea where my regiment is."

"But I don't understand. What are you doing here?"

"I am—or I was, until I escaped—a prisoner of war,

163

ma'am. I'm in this condition because, for nearly a year now, I've been in Andersonville Prison."

"Prisoner of war? You mean that is why you are in such condition? Sergeant, are you telling me that the South is starving its prisoners?"

"Yes, ma'am. That's exactly what I'm saying. Back in the prison my friends are dying at the rate of a hundred or more every day."

"But that can't be true. Surely your condition is an exception."

"Yes, ma'am, I'm an exception. I'm much better off than most. That's why I was able to escape. Only about half of those who are still alive can walk at all. And only half of *those* could walk as much as a mile. And now, if you'll excuse me, I must be going."

"Going? Going where?"

"I told you, ma'am, I'm an escaped prisoner. I can't stay here. I have to make my way back to my own people."

"But you're in no condition to travel. Whether you like it or not, Sergeant, you're one of those people who couldn't walk a mile."

"I reckon you may be right, ma'am, but I have no choice. Now that you know my secret, I must go. I have no intention of letting you turn me in to the authorities. And since I have neither the strength nor the means to defend myself, my only chance is to go now."

"Don't be ridiculous. I have no intention of turning you in to the authorities. You're going to stay right here until you regain your strength."

"Why?"

"I beg your pardon?"

"Why would you want to keep me here? Like you said, I'm an enemy. Your husband was killed at Gettysburg, and while I don't think I did it, I certainly could have, and would have, killed him had the opportunity presented itself."

"You may be my enemy, but you're also a human being," Claudia said, easily. "And it's time for the hate to stop.

There is no excuse for . . ." Claudia stopped in mid-sentence, then bit her lips for a moment. "The truth is, Sergeant, I'm ashamed of the way you've been treated. I don't know what kind of cruel, evil monster they have running that prison, but Southerners—true Southerners—aren't like that. If you will allow me, I want to make it up to you in some way."

Chapter 11

Andersonville Prison:

In the distance, Josie could see that the leaves of the trees were turning yellow. That was good, Josie decided, because it meant relief from the long, hot Georgia summer. Sitting outside and using his knees as a desk, he began to write:

Although I have no idea what will eventually become of these letters, I continue to write them in the hopes that they will eventually be delivered. That means everything I write could be read by the guards, so I must be very careful not to say anything of use to the enemy. But I know that those of our enemy who are honorable will understand this, and will not hold it against me.

I am saddened to report that Thomas Sweet and Tucker were both killed while trying to escape. [That wasn't exactly true. Tucker died after being brought back and put in the stocks. But he knew he couldn't write it that way, not if he had any serious hopes of the letter getting to its destination.]

There are now only three with me who were with me when I was captured, they being Sergeant McSpadden, Billy, and Tyce.

Sergeant McSpadden was wounded in the battle in which we were captured, and has been very slow in recovering. Billy was not wounded in the body, but I fear he has suffered mightily in spirit. While I have been able to doctor Sergeant McSpadden's wounds, Billy's wound has been more difficult to treat.

Private Tyce is a strange one. He is one of my men (I have mostly taken over command during Sergeant McSpadden's long recovery), and so I feel that I must look after him. But he is sullen and quick to anger. He makes friends with no one and he trusts no one. I think his basic instincts are probably good. He has always been loyal to our little group, he has always done his work without complaint, and he is a ferocious fighter. I can't help but feel that there must be some tragic secret in his background to have made him so withdrawn and so unwilling to share himself with anyone.

Josie paused in his writing. It was very quiet inside the prison, and had been for some time. Even the Raiders seemed content with preying upon only the newly arrived, satisfied that no one else could possibly have anything they would want. And there had been no more escape attempts, so the stocks were empty.

Josie looked at his fellow inmates, aware that he was now totally integrated into the prison population. He was no longer set apart as one who had recently arrived, nor was he one who was notable for his escape attempt. The other prisoners, sunburned, with cracked lips and flaming shoulders and necks, sat singly or in groups, bored, staring at the ground, scratching, cleaning their toenails, or shaking lice out of their hair and beards. A few were walking around aimlessly. None seemed to have any particular purpose.

When his gaze reached the Swamp, Josie saw 2nd Wisconsin on all fours, his head down in the stream, drinking the fouled water like an animal. He finished drinking, then stood painfully and looked around. No one else seemed to notice, or to care.

Josie had seen 2nd Wisconsin drink from the Swamp before, and he had warned him about it. The first time, Wisconsin denied doing it. The second time he admitted doing it, but reminded Josie that it was none of his business. "You got no say-so over me, Corporal. I ain't in the 19th Massachusetts," he said angrily. "For that matter, ain't never been to Massachusetts."

He was right, Josie thought. It wasn't any of his business.

Josie sharpened the pencil stub with his teeth, smoothed the paper on his knee, then went back to his writing.

It is now some weeks since we tried to get away from here, and since our time in the stocks without food or water. I am now able to write and even to move around for a short time.

Wisnovsky limped by. Since Gleason had not been brought back from the escape attempt, Wisnovsky had assumed the role of leader of the Pennsylvania group. McSpadden, who was sitting nearby, raised a stiff arm to get Wisnovsky's attention.

"Wisnovsky," he called out.

Wisnovsky stopped. "Sergeant McSpadden, how are you doing?"

"Sit a minute, will you?" McSpadden invited, patting the ground beside him.

"Sure." Wisnovsky sat down near Josie and McSpadden. He picked up a tiny handful of dirt and let it cascade from one hand to the other.

"You went out the tunnel with Gleason," McSpadden said.

"Yes."

"So, what *did* happen to him?"

Wisnovsky looked around before he answered. "The dogs," he said. "The dogs got him. I got up a tree, but John wouldn't stop. Kept runnin' for the river, swingin' a stick at those dogs." Wisnovsky shook his head. "You can't outrun dogs."

"Damn," McSpadden said with a sigh. "I heard 'em get someone. Glad I didn't see it."

Wisnovsky nodded. "I didn't see it neither. Didn't want to." He jerked his head toward the Pennsylvania shebang. "I'm not tellin' them what I think, Sergeant. No point in it. John was like a father to 'em, so I just tell 'em I don't know. Anyhow, I suppose it's possible he could've gotten away. I didn't really see."

Although McSpadden and Wisnovsky were speaking very quietly, Josie overheard everything they said. He breathed a little prayer that John Gleason did make it to freedom, then he returned to his writing.

It is autumn now, the fourth autumn since I Company of the 19th Massachusetts was formed. So much has happened since then, yet I can still remember how exciting it all was in the beginning. I can remember the parades, the cheering crowds, the young boys who ran alongside us as we marched, and the pretty girls who stood on the side of the street, throwing flowers.

Tucker caught one of the flowers, then declared to the rest of us that he was in love with the girl who threw it. He told Bob, Peter, Tinsdale, Quinn, Dick, Sweet, and me that when he returned from the war, he was going to marry her.

At the time, we were eating our supper, using as a table a fallen tree which lay in a grassy glen. The birds were singing, and a nearby brook was splashing over polished

*stones. Tucker was declaiming his love for the young
woman who had thrown the flower, and we were teasing
him about it, though I believe that many of us, myself
included, secretly wished it had been we who caught the
blossom.*

*The war was far away then, and no one had any idea
of what an evil thing it was going to be. We thought only
of blowing bugles and waving flags . . . of blue uniforms with brass buttons that flashed in the sun, of
parades and pretty young women.*

*We didn't know, then, how easily a minié ball could
take off a man's kneecap, or blow away the back of his
head. We had not yet seen an explosive shell rip open a
man's belly and spill his intestines onto the dirt. None of
us had tasted fear or smelled death.*

*And now all those fine young men are gone. Tinsdale
was killed at Antietam, Quinn at Gettysburg, Bob and
Peter at Cold Harbor. And Dick, Sweet, and Tucker here,
at Andersonville Prison.*

*The children of those fine young men, their children's
children . . . and their children as well, will never be
born. An entire world of farmers and fishermen, artists
and tailors, physicians and mechanics, musicians and
clergy, politicians and teachers has been lost. I know now
what I did not know then. I know that war is the destroyer
of worlds, not only of the brave young soldiers who die in
battle, but of entire generations who will never be.*

Billy was sitting some distance away, his knees drawn up
in front of him and his arms wrapped around his legs. Josie
smiled at him and Billy tried to smile back, but he could
hold the smile for only a second or two before despair
reappeared in his face.

About a hundred feet away, Mad Matthew was trying to
eat his food. Tyce was sitting next to him, talking. Josie
couldn't hear what Tyce was saying, but from Mad Mat-

thew's reaction he realized that Tyce was trying to wheedle food from him.

Mad Matthew turned away from Tyce and hunched his shoulders in an attempt to protect his food. Undeterred, Tyce reached around for it.

Someone nearby called something out to Tyce. It must have been an admonishment, for he heard Tyce's angry reply.

"Mind your own damn business," Tyce snapped. Once again he tried to get Mad Matthew's food, and once again Mad Matthew twisted around to put his body between Tyce and his plate.

Josie put his pencil and paper down, securing the paper with a rock, then got up and limped toward Tyce. McSpadden too, managed to get up, though he was still in no condition to move down the hill toward Tyce.

Tyce was so busy trying to steal Mad Matthew's food that he neither saw nor heard Josie approach him. Josie put his hand on Tyce's shoulder.

"Leave him alone, Tyce."

"I wasn't doing anything."

"Then go somewhere else to not do anything. Get away from him."

Tyce glared at Josie. Silently, he got up and walked away.

"It's all right, Matthew," Josie said. "Tyce won't bother you anymore."

Mad Matthew, not fully comprehending what had just happened, made no attempt to thank Josie. Instead, he curled his arm protectively around his plate and continued eating.

Josie limped back to the shebang and sat down beside McSpadden. He pulled up a blade of grass, then began sucking on the root. He continued to do that for a long moment, then he sighed.

"It's not all caused by the Rebs, you know," he finally said.

"Pardon?" McSpadden replied.

"It's not the Rebs make 'em do these things. It's not the Rebs, not the Raiders. It's having nothing to do."

"What are you talking about, Josie?"

Josie took in the camp and the prisoners with a wave of his hand. "It's having nothing to do all day long. That's what eats at us in here."

"You may be right," McSpadden said. "You know what they say. Idle hands are the Devil's workshop."

Tyce found a place some distance away from the others. He sat down, then drew his knees up in front of him, wrapped his arms around his legs, put his head down, and closed his eyes. That was when he heard the voice, as clearly as if someone had spoken the words in his ear.

"Have you no shame, Coley?"

"What?" Tyce asked, raising his head.

There was no one there. Looking around, he saw Mad Matthew finishing his meal, Billy sitting by himself, and Josie and Sergeant McSpadden engaged in conversation. No one seemed to be paying any attention to him. Yet someone clearly spoke to him.

"Did you say something to me, Corporal Day?" Tyce asked.

"No, I said nothing."

"Thought I heard something." Tyce put his head down on his knees again.

"Have you no shame at all?"

"Damn it, Corporal Day, if you have something to say to me, spit it out!" Tyce demanded. This time he said the words loudly enough that everyone looked at him. "Don't be sneaking around about it!"

"I didn't say anything to you, Tyce."

"The hell you didn't. Or at least, somebody did. God-damn it, I heard it with my own ears!"

"Nobody said anything to you," Josie repeated. "You must be hearing things."

"Someone called me Coley."

"Coley?" Josie said. He chuckled. "Well, it sure wasn't me. I don't think I even knew what your first name was. I know I've never heard anyone use it."

"Only one person ever did," Tyce said. "But it couldn't be him because . . ."

Suddenly Tyce felt a chill pass over him. He knew now who said his name, not only because he was the only one ever to call him that, but also because he could recognize the voice.

"It was Father Bonnington."

"Father Bonnington? You mean a priest?" Josie asked. "'S funny, Tyce, the way you're always spouting off about there being no God, I wouldn't think you would even know a priest."

"I knew one once," Tyce said to Josie. Then, as if speaking to himself, he added, "The finest man I ever knew." He put his head down on his knees again.

"Coley, you don't need to answer me aloud."

"Father Bonnington, it is you!"

"Yes, Coley."

"But, I don't understand. Where are you?"

"I'm in here . . . in your mind . . . in your heart."

"In my soul?"

"You might say that, though in truth, my son, there is very little of your soul left. That's why I'm here. I've come to save what remains of it."

"Are you really talking to me? Or is this my imagination?"

"Perhaps I'm talking to you through your imagination. But what difference does it make? The important thing is, I'm talking to you."

"What do you want?"

"I want to save what's left of your soul."

"It's too late to save my soul."

"It's never too late with God."

"There is no. . . ."

"No, Coley, don't say it. You have no idea how much pain it causes me when you say that. What has happened to you, to make you so bitter?"

"Surely you, of all people, should know. It's because you were killed. You were a good man, seeking only to serve your Lord, but He let you die. How could your God do that?"

"Don't try to limit Him by saying He's my God. He is God of us all. And if I died, what of it? Death is nothing, Coley. It's as insignificant as a sneeze."

"No, death is not insignificant. Life is all we have, and death is the end of that."

"Look around you, my son. Haven't you seen enough death now to know that it's all a part of our voyage toward eternity?"

"I fear death, Father."

"Many people do. The trick is not to fear death but to love life."

"I'll try."

"Do you believe again, Coley?"

"I suppose I do."

"That's not enough. You must believe totally and unequivocally."

"Yes, yes, I believe. Otherwise, how could I be talking to you?"

"And will you now ask the Lord to forgive you for your sin of disbelief?"

"Yes, Father, I will ask for forgiveness."

"Then do so at once. Get on your knees, Coley."

Getting on his knees, Tyce crossed himself, then said aloud: *"Indulgentiam plenariam et remissionem omnium peccatorum tibi concedo. In nomine Patris, et Filii, et Spiritus Sancti. Amen."*

When Tyce finished, he was, for the first time in many years, at peace with himself.

On the Hughes farm:

During Gleason's days on Claudia Hughes's farm, he had recovered from diarrhea and was now able to keep his food down.

And what food he was given!

Claudia had fried chicken for him, made biscuits to serve with honey and butter, fixed black-eyed peas with salt pork, baked pies, and made soups. Since coming here, Gleason had eaten more than in the previous three months. He could feel his strength increasing with each passing day.

He was standing just outside the back door, thinking of the others back in Andersonville. He was sure Wisnovsky hadn't made it, because he saw them take him out of the tree. He didn't know if any of the others had made it, and he wondered if some of them were out there, trying to work their way north. And if any of them were out there, had they been as lucky as he had been? He studied the hills to the north and east. He would have to get over those in order to reach his own people.

"I hope you like chicken and dumplin's," Claudia said, coming out to join him.

John held up his hand. "Mrs. Hughes, you've done so much for me now that I'm beginning to be ashamed of myself for staying as long as I have."

"Nonsense, you haven't been in any condition to leave."

"Perhaps not, but I am now." He nodded toward the hills. "I'm leaving tonight."

"Tonight?"

"Yes, ma'am. I have a long way to go, and I've prevailed upon your hospitality for too long."

"You've more than paid your way, Sergeant. You fixed the door to the privy, you repaired the roof of the barn, and you mended the fence."

Gleason pointed toward a pile of firewood. "I'm going to

chop some wood for you before I leave. Come winter time, you'll be puttin' more of a demand on it than you are now. It'll start going down pretty fast."

"You don't need to do that. Mr. Johnson said he'd send Willie over to take care of it."

"Willie?"

"His handyman."

"Slave?"

Claudia laughed. "Sergeant, not too many people in the county own slaves. Mr. Johnson doesn't, and we never did. Willie's a freeman."

"I'm surprised by that."

"Why? Do you think everyone in the South owns slaves?"

"I don't know," John replied. "I'm not sure that I ever really thought about it before. I suppose I thought so. Otherwise, why would you people be willing to fight in a war to keep slaves?"

"Is that what you believe? That Southerners are fighting this war just so they can keep their slaves?"

"Yes, I guess it is what I believed."

Claudia shook her head. "It's not just that we couldn't afford to own slaves. We didn't have any because Carl didn't believe in slavery."

"He didn't?"

"No. Neither do I."

"Then why did he . . . ?"

"I don't know why he went to war. I suppose it had something to do with honor."

"Did you approve of his going?"

Claudia raised her hand to her hair, and when she did, it caused her breasts to stand out in bold relief against the dress she was wearing.

"I don't know. I didn't want him to leave, but I, too, thought it was the honorable thing to do. Although, if I had known then what I know now . . . if I had known he would never be coming back, I would have tried with everything in my power to stop him."

"Mrs. Hughes, if we had all known then what we know now . . . I don't think this war would ever have been fought." Gleason pointed to the pile of wood. "I'm going to cut some wood for you."

"I'll call you when it's supper," Claudia said.

Gleason cut wood for nearly two hours, chopping it into short lengths, then using the wedge and the back of the axe to split it into manageable chunks. By the time the sun was an orange ball, low in the west, he had built a sizable pile.

"Sergeant," Claudia called from the back door, "supper's on the table."

Gleason stopped just outside the back door and washed his face and hands in the basin Claudia had set out for him. She stepped outside and handed him a towel.

"Thanks."

"Your uniform is clean and repaired. But it seems to me you'd be better off if you continued to wear Carl's clothes."

"I can't. If I get caught in my uniform, I'm an escaped prisoner, and they'll send me back to prison. In these clothes"—he indicated the shirt and pants he was wearing—"I could be hanged as a spy."

"Oh, my," Claudia said, shivering. "Let's not even talk about that."

Gleason followed Claudia inside, then sat at the table. He smiled as she served him a generous helping of chicken and dumplings.

Half an hour later he pushed his plate back, having eaten three helpings.

"I'm stuffed. If I stayed here long enough, I could actually get fat."

"You could stay."

Gleason looked up in surprise.

"Just until the war is over, I mean."

"I couldn't do that, Mrs. Hughes."

"Claudia."

"I couldn't do that, Claudia. I have to get back."

"To what? The war?"

"To my own side."

"Your side doesn't need you, John. They're winning the war without you. And if you try to get back, you might get caught. You might have the confidence that your army uniform will keep you from being hanged, but I don't. Anyone who would starve their prisoners wouldn't have second thoughts about hanging one of them."

"I *have* to get back. I owe it to those I left behind me in prison. I have to get to General Grant or General Sherman, and tell them that our men must be exchanged."

"But what if you don't make it back? What good will you be to the prisoners then? At least here you're safe."

"I might be safe, but I'd be without honor."

"Honor? You mean the kind of honor that killed Carl at Gettysburg?"

"Claudia, please understand."

"Oh, I understand. Believe me, I understand."

"I'm sorry."

"No," Claudia said with a resigned sigh. "It is I who should apologize. I had no right to expect that of you. I had no right even to ask it of you. Please forgive me. And forget I ever brought it up."

John put his hand over Claudia's. "There's nothing to forgive. And I don't want to forget it. It pleases me that you would even want me to stay."

"When are you going to leave?"

"A couple of hours after it gets dark."

"I'll pack some food for you."

"No, don't do that. I don't want to deprive you."

"We've got food, John. Maybe the Confederate money is no good, but living on a farm, we do have food."

"That's very kind of you."

After supper John entertained the little girl, whose name was Ellen, by showing her tricks with a piece of twine.

"This is called Jacob's Ladder," he said. "And this one is Rock the Cradle."

"Show me, show me!" Ellen squealed in delight.

"Sweetheart, I think it's about time you got to bed now, don't you think?" Claudia said.

"All right, Mama." She smiled broadly. "Mama, can Sergeant John say my prayers with me?"

"Well, I don't know," Claudia said. "I would say you have to ask Sergeant John."

"I'd be glad to say your prayers with you, Ellen."

Smiling, Ellen held out her hand to John, then led him back to her tiny bedroom. She knelt beside her bed, folded her hands, and began to pray.

"Now I lay me down to sleep. I pray the Lord my soul to keep. If I should die before I wake, I pray the Lord my soul to take. God bless Mama. God bless Daddy, who's in heaven. God bless all the Daddies who're Southern soldiers. And God bless Sergeant John, even if he is a Yankee. Amen."

Ellen climbed into her bed, then reached for a little rag doll on the bed beside her. She held the doll up. "This is Marcie," she said. "Marcie said her prayers, too, and she asked God to bless you, too."

"Thank you, Ellen. And thank Marcie for me."

On impulse, Gleason bent down and kissed the girl on the forehead. He started to leave, but Ellen held up her doll. "Marcie wants a kiss too," she said.

Smiling, Gleason kissed the doll, then left the bedroom. It was dark now, and the house was lit only by a few candles and the glow from the kitchen stove. He stood in the shadows, watching. He thought about the turn his life had taken over the last few days. He had gone from being a starving prisoner to a pampered house guest.

He hadn't been entirely truthful with Claudia when he said that his regiment hadn't faced General Dole. His regiment was across from General Rodes's division, and Dole was on Rodes's right. It was entirely possible, during the heat of battle, that some of the lines were crossed, and one of the Confederate soldiers who lay dead on the slopes and in the meadows in front of him could very well have been Carl Hughes. All things considered, he would just as soon not know the truth. Until now, Rebels had been either the wild-eyed, screaming men who charged them in battle or the cold-eyed, murderous guards who manned the towers and parapet at Andersonville Prison. It was easier dealing with that kind of Rebel than it was with this kind.

Claudia turned around and saw Gleason watching her. She smiled self-consciously and wiped a tendril of hair back from her forehead. It was a movement she had made so often in the short time he had known her that it had become the thing he most associated with her.

"I'm heating some water," she said. "I thought you might want a bath before you put on your uniform."

"A bath? My God! Do you know how long it's been since I had a real bath?"

"A long time, I would think." Claudia nodded toward the back door. "I have a big tub out on the back porch. Haven't used it in a while . . . it's too big for me to handle alone. Ellen and I have been using a washtub. If you bring it into the kitchen, I'll start filling it."

"All right. I'll get it right now."

A moment later, Gleason dragged the tub inside. It was a large copper tub, as large as any he had ever seen.

"This is quite a tub."

"Carl bought it in Atlanta. Had it brought by train to Marietta, then hauled it here in a wagon. He planned to build a special room just for the tub. He was going to call it a bathing room. I told him that was the dumbest thing I ever heard. Put it over there."

Gleason set the tub down, and a moment later Claudia brought over one of the big pots of boiling water and poured it in. Two more pots of boiling water put about six inches of water in the bottom of the tub. After that, Gleason brought in buckets of well water until the tub was more than a third full.

Claudia handed him a bar of soap and a towel, then turned her back.

"Get undressed and get in. I won't look."

Gleason quickly got out of his clothes, then stepped into the water. He wet the bar of soap and slid it over his body; within a few moments, he was covered with lather. He bathed happily, so content with the sensation that he almost forgot Claudia was even there.

The realization that Claudia was there, too, was brought sharply into focus a moment later when, totally nude, she slipped into the water. She smiled shyly at him.

"It seems a shame to waste the bathwater," she said, reaching for the soap.

"Yes, it does, doesn't it?"

On her knees in the tub, Claudia came to him, plastering her wet, nude body against his as she kissed him full on the mouth.

"Is there any way I can talk you into staying just a few hours longer?" she asked breathlessly when she pulled her lips away from his.

Chapter 12

Andersonville Prison:

"Fresh fish!" a loud voice called from the Raiders' area.

Another new batch of Union prisoners was arriving. Men who had seen their share of hard fighting and were still in fighting trim, well fed and healthy, were brought through the gates of the prison to be introduced to Andersonville in the same way as thousands before them, including Josie.

And Wirz, as he did with all new prisoners, came out to welcome them with his familiar speech. Josie wasn't close enough to hear more than bits and pieces of the speech, but he did pick up several well-worn lines: "Those who are not shot are caught by the dogs without fail and put in stocks or ball and chain. And, still, if you escape the dogs . . . to go hundreds of miles to your own army? Not possible."

Also, during the speech there began a now familiar ritual, the gathering of Munn, Collins, and fifty or more of the

Raiders. Listening to Wirz from close by, they looked at the new men with a malevolent light in their eyes, ready to pounce on them at the first opportunity. And as Wirz continued to speak, Munn and the Raiders began inching closer to the "fresh fish."

"I know for absolute fact that at this very moment talks are going on for exchange of prisoners," Wirz was saying.

Tobias cupped his hands around his mouth and shouted as loudly as he could, "You're a damn liar, Wirz!"

"I don't know, Toby," Benton said. "If John Gleason does make it back to Uncle Billy or ol' Ulysses . . ." Benton looked around at the others. "Then we'll get exchanged. You can bet on it. Sergeant Gleason won't leave his men in here to starve."

Limber Jim glared at the Raiders with ill-concealed anger. "I've had about enough of this," he said.

"Beg pardon?"

"The bastards!" Limber Jim growled.

"Who's that, Jim?" someone asked.

Limber Jim pointed toward the Raiders. "Look at those vultures, just waitin' to rob and murder the new boys. Look at 'em, the dirty little cowards."

Josie, McSpadden, Blackburn, and the others who had been sitting, or lying around, stretched their necks to look.

Limber Jim had called them vultures, but Josie believed wolves would be a better analogy, for the Raiders gathered in packs, watching the new prisoners and waiting for Wirz to finish his speech.

"So, we understand each other," Wirz concluded his speech. Escorted by his protective detail of guards, he left.

As soon as the gates were closed behind him, Munn moved forward to greet the new men. "Hey, fresh fish!" he called, forcing a wide smile. "Welcome to Andersonville." He turned to take in the compound with an expansive wave, continuing a speech that was as familiar to the long-time prisoners as that of Captain Wirz.

"Fine-looking place, don't you think? For a hog pen,

maybe." He laughed out loud. "So, you some of Grant's men? From up in Virginia? That where you get catched at?"

Munn started steering the new men, all of whom followed without question, toward an area where the Raiders were lying in wait for them.

"Let me show you around . . . get you a decent place to stay. The thing is, see, you want to be up away from the Swamp."

The Raiders, waiting with hidden clubs and knives, watched Collins. They were ready to pounce as soon as he gave the signal.

Josie and the entire camp watched as Munn started to lead the new lambs to slaughter. Josie knew that every man in camp hated what was going on as much as he did, but there was nothing anyone could do about it. Except for the Raiders, the prisoners were weak, disorganized, lifeless, and helpless.

Limber Jim had not taken his eyes from the Raiders from the moment they started stalking the prisoners, and he was getting angrier and angrier. The situation was clearly becoming more than he could bear. "We can't let this go on," he growled.

"You think any of the rest of us like it?" Tobias asked. "But what can we do about it?"

"Something," Limber Jim replied. "Anything!" Looking around in desperation, he spied a rock as big as his fist. He picked it up and got to his feet. "By God, I'm not going to let it go on any longer."

"What can you do, Jim? There's a thousand of 'em," Tobias said. "And they've got knives and clubs and . . ."

Limber Jim stood on the highest part of the hill and held the rock over his head. "Who's with me?" he shouted.

Josie, McSpadden, and Blackburn looked at each other, not knowing what to do. Limber Jim was silhouetted, an avenging angel, against the bright blue sky. Again he thrust the rock over his head. "Whooooooo?" he shouted.

Suddenly Josie realized what Limber Jim intended to do,

and he was frightened for his friend. "No, Jim," he said under his breath. "No, don't do this."

By now Munn had just about finished delivering the "fresh fish" welcoming speech.

"Whooooo? Who's with me?" Limber Jim called again, his scream now like that of a banshee. "Whoooooo?"

The Raiders and the new prisoners had not yet come together. Instead, both groups stopped and stared at the howling apparition on the hill.

None of his fellow prisoners responded to Limber Jim's call for help. Undaunted by his lack of support, he started down the hill alone, holding the rock high over his head.

"Whooo?" Jim screamed as he ran, so that the word was now a war cry as well as a challenge.

McSpadden struggled to stand, muttering as much to himself as to the group, "We're with you, Jim. We're with you."

He fell back. Josie got to his feet, then reached down to pull McSpadden up. Seeing McSpadden and Josie on their feet, Blackburn and Tyce also began to rise.

Limber Jim didn't know if the entire camp was behind him . . . or if no one was. By now he didn't care. There was blood lust in his eyes, and he was heading right for Munn and the other Raiders.

"Whoooo?" he screamed at the top of his lungs.

The Raiders looked up the hill, shocked that one man would be so foolish as to challenge them. The newly arrived prisoners, who didn't understand what was going on, were thrown into confusion.

Somewhere inside the compound, a prisoner stood up and shouted, his voice carrying loud and clear across the yard. "I'm with you, Jim!"

Twenty yards away, another man got to his feet and yelled, "I'm with you!"

Josie and McSpadden started forward with difficulty.

"Whoooo?" Limber Jim shouted.

"Here! Me! I'm with you!"

"I'm with you!"

"Me!"

"Me, too!"

"We're with you, Jim!"

"Come on, boys! Come on!" one of the new recruits called. "Join us! Come on! Hurrah for Jim! Hurrah for the flag!"

Rising from their lethargy, one here, three there, a dozen more, then a score, then three score, then by the hundreds, the prisoners stood and started moving, en masse, toward the Raiders.

From the perspective of the guards in the towers, the movement of people looked like a landside as entire sections began to converge on one point.

"Sergeant of the guard!" Private Allen shouted nervously. "Sergeant Martindale! Somethin's goin' on!"

Munn and Collins, seeing the mass of men coming toward them, sensed immediately that this was out of the ordinary . . . that this might indeed be something to fear.

"Collins! Collins! What the hell is that? What's goin' on!" Munn asked fearfully.

"Form up!" Collins shouted nervously to the Raiders. "Form up!"

Limber Jim was no longer alone. He had been joined by a few men, lame, crippled, and weak, then by stronger men, all struggling to catch up, those who were limping being passed by those in better shape.

Samson, the one-legged man, came swinging hard downhill on his crutches, passing many others as the impromptu army grew by quantum factors. Even young Patrick Shay, the drummer boy, had joined with the group.

Limber Jim's yells were being drowned out by the full-throated roar of an army that numbered over a thousand men. All were racing down the hill on a collision course with the Raiders. Tobias, Benton, 2nd Wisconsin, and Tyce were in the ranks.

Desperately the Raiders tried to form themselves into a tight defensive circle.

"Georgie!" Collins commanded, "you take the point!"

Georgie didn't have to be told. His eyes were wide and bright, and he stood ready to do battle, to turn back anyone who would have the audacity to challenge the supremacy of the Raiders.

"Don't worry, boys!" Collins shouted. "Stand together! They'll show tail. They always have!"

But the angry group of old prisoners didn't show tail. Instead, they swept in like a tidal wave, bowling over many of the men who were in the front ranks. Limber Jim took a special delight in smashing into Georgie. He brought his rock down hard onto Georgie's head, knocking him off his feet. With Georgie down, the Raiders' first line of defense crumbled, unable to stand against the overwhelming number of prisoners attacking them.

Nearly everyone on both sides was armed. Anything and everything was employed as a weapon: clubs, knives, slingshots, a shovel, pointed stakes, and rocks. Those without weapons used their hands and teeth, ripping out chunks of flesh. Blood ran from their mouths and into their beards.

Munn realized very quickly that the battle was going against them, and he started worming his way backward, putting as many Raiders between himself and the attackers as he could.

The newly arrived prisoners stood by in shock, unsure with which side they should ally themselves. Every now and then, one or two of them looked ready to mix into the fray. They were held in check, however, by their sergeants, who, for the first time since being captured, had begun to exercise some command and control over the men under them.

"Stay out of it, men!" a first sergeant with the new group shouted. "Noncommissioned officers, keep your men out of it!"

The other noncommissioned officers started carrying out his orders.

"Stay out of it till we learn which side we're on!"

With the new prisoners standing by as spectators, the Raiders and the spontaneously formed Avengers continued to flail away at each other. Samson, balancing himself precariously on one leg, was one of the most savage warriors on the field. Hopping about like a maddened stork, he swung his crutch here and there, catching, and almost decapitating, Munn.

Then, much more quickly than anyone would have thought possible, the battle turned into a mopping-up action. Scores of Raiders, reading the signs of defeat, began slipping away, dissociating themselves from the group that for many months had been their protector.

With each passing second, the ranks of Avengers increased while those of the Raiders decreased.

"Shit, boys! It's ever' man for himself!" Collins shouted, and although he had fought savagely, he now made an effort to get away. Limber Jim caught him and knocked him down, then fell upon him and began to choke him. The two men struggled on the ground for a long moment, Collins strengthened by his fear and Limber Jim by his rage. Finally Limber Jim prevailed, grabbing the long stick of wood Collins had been using as a club and jamming it crosswise into Collins' mouth. Then, with the help of two other Avengers, he secured the stick by tying it to Collins' arms, so that it became a halter bit, restraining both his teeth and his hands.

The fight, now overwhelmingly one-sided, continued around them. The Raiders, so long a dreaded part of the prison population, were struggling to keep from being wiped out.

Curtis was the last leader of the Raiders remaining on his feet. Grabbing a spade, he began swinging it viciously back and forth, opening up a path as the prisoners fell back from him.

Watching Curtis break out of the pack, Josie moved into position to intercept him. He stood his ground as Curtis, spade held high, rushed him, swinging hard.

Josie caught the spade, held it, then forced it back until Curtis was down, with Josie on top of him, holding the spade handle across the Raider's throat. McSpadden, who had been beside Josie for the entire battle, took off his shirt and ripped it into strips so it could be used to tie Curtis up.

As the fight went on, the Confederate guard poured out of the barracks and rushed up the ladders to the towers, their muskets loaded, ready to put down the riot.

"Hold your fire!" Lieutenant Barrett ordered. "Let them fight it out! Hold your fire unless they charge the walls!"

Shocked and fascinated by what was going on, the guards filled the towers and climbed to the top of the walls to find vantage points from which to watch the battle. Private Allen was especially excited. As far as he was concerned, it was Yankees killing Yankees. And if anyone tried to take advantage of the fight to escape, he was ready for that, too.

"You've already tasted blood a couple of times," he said to his rifle, stroking its barrel almost as if it were a living thing. "Let them Yankees come, and I'll kill the son of a bitch that kilt my brother."

And then, almost as suddenly as it had started, the battle was over. The last of the Raiders put down their weapons and raised their hands as they fell to their knees and started begging for mercy.

Josie and McSpadden pushed the bound Curtis ahead of them, forcing him into the pack with the other Raiders who were now prisoners of the Avengers. Mad Matthew, not fully comprehending what had just happened, began jumping up and down in excitement.

The last act of the battle was a mighty triumphant roar, rising from every quarter, shaking the prison, as those who fought, and those who were too weak to fight, cheered the results. And there were many, even among the Confederate guards, who applauded the fact that at least one evil of the prison had been summarily and totally eliminated.

Chapter 13

Approximately one hour after the battle:

A quiet had settled over the prison. There were still twice as many guards on duty as there normally were, but none of them seemed nervous, for now there was nothing about the prisoners' behavior that could be construed as frightening.

"Never seen nothin' like it," Bobby Roy said to Private Allen. "I mean, they come together like it was a battle or somethin'. I thought they was goin' to come against us next."

"Wisht they would-a tried." Allen licked his thumb, then rubbed his sight. "Done kilt me two o' them sons of bitches. I'd-a kilt me a bunch more if'n they started after us."

"That's where me an' you is different. I don't want to kill no one, if I can help it."

"I do," Private Allen replied. "I want to kill the ones that kilt my brother."

"How you know who that was?"

"It was all of 'em."

Bobby Roy looked out over the prison grounds. "What think they're doin' out there now?"

"Nothin'. They're just millin' around, is all."

"Looks to me like they're holdin' some of 'em prisoners over there."

Bobby Roy pointed to a hundred or more Raiders, more frightened, some surly, sitting jammed together on the ground with their hands tied. They were being watched by a group of fifty of the victors armed with the clubs, pocket knives, and rocks they had captured.

Private Allen laughed.

"What you laughin' at?"

"Them Yankees is double prisoners. They're prisoners of prisoners."

Near the group of captive Raiders, Josie stood with few hundred of the Avengers, looking down at a veritable treasure trove. All the booty was stored in a huge excavation the Raiders had been using as their vault. There were uniforms, haversacks, utensils, weapons, watches, books, food, even Martin Blackburn's banjo. Josie looked around the perimeter of the pit, studying the faces of the other prisoners. Some were open-mouthed in surprise, others were tight-lipped in anger. Many were so overwhelmed at being close to so much, when they had done with so little for so long, that they could barely hold back the tears.

The banjo lay on a pile of shirts. "That's Martin's banjo," Tobias said.

"And that's my greatcoat," another prisoner added. He pointed to one of the coats piled in the pit. "I recognize it from the tear in my sleeve."

"Wait till everyone's here before anyone takes anything," Patrick continued.

"Listen, fellas, that's mostly stuff we got from them that's already died," Munn tried to explain. "We was thinkin', what with winter comin' on afore too long, we'd divide it up amongst ever'one. We was gettin' ready to do that very thing when you boys jumped us today."

"Munn, shut your mouth, you lying bastard!" Benton said angrily. He took a step toward Munn. "You talk again before anyone tells you to, and I'm going to bash your head in."

Josie walked over to the Raider prisoners. The six acknowledged leaders—Munn, Collins, Curtis, and three others—occupied a position of dubious honor in the front row. All of them, badly bruised and scarred, were trussed. Each also had his own guard. In every case, the guard was a former victim.

Walking continuously around the entire band was the man whose call to action had tumbled the Raiders from power. Limber Jim, still caught up in the rage that had driven him to spark the revolt, was holding a length of rope that he kept snapping in front of the captured Raiders, as if testing its strength.

"Hang 'em!" Limber Jim shouted, his nostrils flared and his eyes wide and wild. "Hang 'em all!"

Munn began shaking his head, crying and babbling. Collins continued to stare at the Avengers with eyes full of hate. When one of the prisoners with a long-standing grievance came over to kick him, he didn't even flinch.

"String 'em up!" Samson shouted. "String 'em up, the murderin' devils!"

"I've got the rope!" Limber Jim shouted, holding the piece of rope aloft. "I'll do it! I'll hang 'em with my own two hands."

McSpadden, who was standing close by with Josie, Blackburn, and the others from the Massachusetts and Pennsylvania shebangs, reached over to put a gentle hand on Limber Jim's arm.

"Jim, Jim, we're not murderers."

"Murder?" Limber Jim shouted back. "Are you sayin' it's murder to hang *them?*"

"'Twouldn't be murder to hang the bastards. 'Twould be justice!" someone else shouted.

"Yes, justice! Send their souls to hell!"

"What *they* did was murder," Samson added.

"We're not hangmen," McSpadden insisted.

"The hell you say!" Limber Jim screamed. He turned to the others. "Anyone wants to help, come ahead! Nobody has the sand for it, I'll do it myself." He kicked Collins. "Starting with you!"

"What about them?" Josie asked.

"Who?"

"The other Raiders. Not the ringleaders, the followers. Do we hang them, too? And if we do, where do we stop? Do we begin making a list of everyone who's wronged us and hang them as well?"

"If we have to," Limber Jim replied defiantly.

"You do that, Jim, and you're committin' murder," McSpadden said.

By now the cries for hanging had died down, even among the most vocal. Some were beginning to have second thoughts, and Limber Jim could sense that his base of support was eroding.

"It's not murder," Limber Jim insisted.

"It's justice," Samson stated.

Martin Blackburn had been quiet during it all. Now he held his hand up, keeping it raised until the others saw him and finally grew quiet. They turned to him.

"You're a fair man, Pennsylvania," McSpadden said, calling out Blackburn's state so that the others would know that he wasn't one of his Massachusetts men, and thus was speaking independently.

"Yeah, what do you have to say, Martin?" Samson asked.

"The first thing we must do . . . before anything else," Blackburn said, "is give these men a trial. A fair trial."

"A fair trial?" someone shouted, as if it were the most outlandish thing he had ever heard. "Why should we do that? I ask you, when were they ever fair to us? The murderin' sons of bitches!"

"Yeah, if you have a trial, you have to have witnesses and all that."

"Witnesses? What do we need with witnesses? Hell, ever'one in this here prison has seen 'em murderin' and stealin' with their own eyes! Don't need no eyewitnesses!"

"Oh, but we do," Blackburn insisted. "If we try this case, we're going to try it properly. And whoever is the prosecutor is going to have to make his case!"

"I say we show the bastards the same fairness they showed my brother!" Limber Jim shouted.

"They killed over a hundred men in here!" Samson cried.

"Yeah! Does that make the case for you?"

By now the debate had moved out into the crowd. Groups of prisoners on both sides shouted back and forth, each one trying to be heard, no one listening to the other.

"Hang the bastards!"

"They deserve killin'."

"You need someone to jerk the rope, I'll do it!"

"It's justice we want, not revenge!" someone shouted.

"Revenge *is* justice!"

Josie looked at Munn, Carter, and Collins. By now Munn had dissolved into such fear that he had wet his pants, and he was crying from the shame and misery of it all. Curtis was nearly as frightened as Munn, and showed it. Collins was still openly defiant. He stared malevolently at Limber Jim, who drew his leg back to administer a vicious kick.

Josie put his hand on Jim's shoulder. "No, Jim, that's enough. Don't do that anymore. It makes us no better than them."

"Hell, Josie. I thought you knew," Limber Jim replied. "We *aren't* any better than they are, and we never were."

"I say we just go down the line behind them, bashing their heads in," someone suggested. "There's no sense wasting good rope on such sorry bastards."

"No! We must put them on trial," Blackburn said again,

more resolutely than before. "A fair trial, with witnesses and a jury."

"Trial, hell! They don't deserve a trial!"

"Hell, no! Why you want to waste time with them?"

Blackburn was quiet while the others debated the issue by shouting back and forth. Josie waited until there was a relative lull in the argument, then spoke to Blackburn in a loud, clear voice so that it would register on the others.

"Tell us why, Martin. Tell us why you think they ought to have a trial."

Blackburn, seeing for the first time that there were people willing to listen to him, cleared his throat. "I ask you. If we do this, are we so much better? I mean, if we do to them as they did to us?"

Gradually, more and more people listened. Some began to agree, and many started to change their minds. But Limber Jim and Samson remained steadfast in their opposition to the idea of a trial.

"You're actin' like we was back in Philadelphia, New York, or Boston, or some such place," Limber Jim said. "Sure, back there, we could take them to court. But in case you fellows haven't noticed, we ain't back there. We're here . . . in prison . . . and we don't have any such laws."

"Then let's make us some laws," Blackburn suggested. "We have enough people here for a good-size city. If we put our minds to it, we could have our own court, following our own laws."

"Yeah, Blackburn does have a point there," someone said. "Hell, I've read of whole states forming with fewer people than we have in this prison."

"I'm for givin' it a chance," someone else chimed in.

"All right, but this is going to take time," Josie said. "And what are we going to do with our prisoners in the meantime? If we try and keep 'em here"—he paused and looked pointedly at Limber Jim and Samson—"someone will kill them."

"You got that right. You leave those bastards in here, and you won't have to be worryin' none about no court. 'Cause I'll kill 'em my own self."

"I hadn't considered that possibility, Josie, but you are right," McSpadden said. "They won't be safe in here."

Josie looked at the Avengers gathered around the pit containing the Raiders' booty. Some of them wanted instant and extreme punishment—right here, right now—and were already positioning themselves to be in on the kill or to be able to see it happen.

"I'd like a show of hands. How many people will be willing to support a trial?" Josie asked.

The count revealed that a vast majority wanted the trial so that the whole thing would have at least the semblance of legality.

"What will we do with the prisoners while we're waitin', Josie?" McSpadden asked. "I mean, we've already decided we can't keep 'em in here."

"I don't know. I guess I haven't figured that part out yet."

"Well, if we can't keep 'em in here, why don't we ask Wirz to keep them under guard outside the walls? He can deliver them back to us for trial when we're ready," Blackburn suggested.

At first, the idea seemed so far-fetched that the prisoners laughed. Then a few began to understand the concept, and they explained it to friends, who explained it to their friends, until finally it seemed to be the ideal solution.

"Well, I don't know. Do you think Wirz'll do it?" Benton asked.

"Josie, what do you think?" said McSpadden. Everyone stared at Josie, waiting for his decision.

Aware of the stakes, Josie nodded. "Let's do it. We'll let Captain Wirz see how we conduct ourselves when we have men at our mercy."

"Yeah," agreed a man who had been one of the most vocal for killing them outright.

"I'll go along with it," another said. A few more came

over, until finally everyone, including Limber Jim and Samson, agreed that a trial might be the best way to proceed.

"All right, Martin, you've won us over," Josie said. "What do we do now?"

"We go see Captain Wirz. I'd like you to lead the delegation, Josie. Sergeant McSpadden, you come as well." Blackburn looked out over the group of prisoners. "And maybe two or three others. No more."

"I'd like to go," Tyce said.

"You, Tyce?" Josie asked. "I would've thought you'd be one of those calling for blood now."

"I've changed."

Josie and Tyce locked gazes for a long moment while Josie tried to decide if Tyce was serious, or whether he wanted to be included with the negotiating team so he could somehow cause it to fail.

"I really have changed, Josie." It was the first time Tyce had called Josie by his first name, and there was a ring of sincerity in his voice that Josie had never heard before.

"All right . . . Coley. If you'd like to come with us, you'll be more than welcome."

"I'll go, too," another added. "When?"

Josie sighed. " Well, far as I'm concerned, there's no time like the present. Let's go now."

The men walked over to the Deadline at the gate, then stopped.

"What you Yankees want?" one of the guards called down.

"We want to see Lieutenant Barrett," Josie replied.

Barrett appeared immediately.

"What do you want, Corporal?"

"Sir, we request permission to speak with Captain Wirz."

"All of you?"

"Yes, sir," Josie said. He looked at the men with him. "I think it's going to take all of us to get our point across."

Barrett studied them for a long moment, then nodded to the guard at the gate.

"Let 'em through."

The guard opened the gate. Josie and the rest passed through.

Barrett led them through the sally port to Captain Wirz's office. "Wait here," he ordered.

Wirz's office was furnished with a settee and chairs, pictures on the wall, kerosene lamps on the tables, and a bookshelf crammed full of books. All this reminded Josie that there was a real world outside, something beyond the Swamp and the shebangs, and the three-quarters of a cup of cornmeal and ground husk a day.

A few moments later, Wirz came into the room, adjusting his sword belt. "Is this about what went on inside the prison today?" he asked.

"Yes, sir," Josie replied.

Wirz shook his head. "Don't approve of that," he said angrily. "Don't approve of it at all. We almost had a riot."

"Yes, sir. But it's all under control now. At least it will be, with your help."

Wirz looked up in surprise. "My help? What are you talking about? How do you need my help?"

"Captain Wirz, we want to hold court. We want to put some men on trial."

"And for what are these men to be tried?"

"For murder and treason," Josie answered. "Some, for lesser crimes."

"Who are these . . . murderers and traitors?"

"They call themselves the Raiders, sir," Blackburn explained. "For too long, they've been running roughshod over everyone."

"And if they are found guilty, we want you to execute them," McSpadden said.

Wirz ran his hand through his hair. "How would be conducted this trial?"

"According to the rule of law, Captain. Both sides would

have lawyers to speak for them," Blackburn explained. "The Raiders would be allowed to speak for themselves, and question the witnesses."

"You would have a jury?"

"Yes, sir," Blackburn said.

"Impossible," Barrett interjected. "After what happened out there today, how would you get a jury who could be impartial?"

"I've thought about that, sir," Blackburn said. "And I think I know a way."

"How?" Wirz asked.

"We'd use new prisoners, Captain," Blackburn answered. "We'll select the jury from among men who come in after today. That way, none of them will have had any direct dealings with the Raiders. They won't be prejudiced against the defendants."

"I don't know," Wirz said, shaking his head. "I have never in my life heard of anything like this." He looked over at Barrett. "These men, these Raiders, they're as bad as they say?"

Barrett nodded. "They're animals, Captain. They're cut-throats and murderers. Even as Yankees go, these are the worst of the worst."

"And if this trial I allow, it will make your task easier?" Wirz asked Barrett. "Keeping order in the stockade?"

Again Barrett nodded. "Might do that, sir. Like I said, they're the worst of the troublemakers."

Wirz began pacing around the room, trying to decide whether to allow this trial to take place. He looked at the prisoners, casually at first, then did a double take when he saw Josie. He stepped closer, for a better look.

"You, I've seen before, haven't I?"

Josie returned Wirz's steady gaze. "Yes, sir, you have. I was one of the men you caught escaping. As punishment, you put my friends and me in the stocks for a week."

Wirz nodded and smiled, as if it were a reunion of old

friends. "Ah, yes, I remember now. You won't be making that mistake again, ah?"

"I will not make the mistake again." Josie could make the statement with a clear conscience, for the mistake he intended not to make again was getting caught.

"*Gut, gut.* If more from you would learn, less trouble we would have."

After that, Wirz strolled around the room for a long time without speaking. Blackburn started to say something to further their argument, but Josie, seeing that Wirz was contemplating the matter, held up his hand to prevent Blackburn from speaking. After perhaps two minutes, Wirz turned toward them.

"All right. The trial I will allow, if properly you will do it. I will get you the law books." He paused for a moment, then raised his good hand. "The proceedings, you must keep in writing. *Und* to me, the findings and the sentences you will send. If everything is in order, the sentence will be ordered for execution."

"There's one more thing, sir," Josie said.

Wirz looked at him.

"We would like for you to keep the ringleaders . . . that is, the ones we are going to try, in a separate place from the other prisoners."

"Why is that?"

McSpadden cleared his throat, then spoke for the first time. "Quite frankly, sir, we're afraid that some of our boys will take justice into their own hands."

Wirz nodded, then looked at Barrett. " Keep the ringleaders under lock and key until they ask for them."

"Yes, sir."

Wirz looked at Josie and the rest of the delegation. "Go. The trial you may have."

"Thank you, Captain," the prisoners answered as one. They saluted; Wirz returned their salute, then nodded at the guards, who gave the command for the prisoners to return to the stockade.

With Sergeant John Gleason:

A thunderstorm boomed and flashed over the north Georgia hills. The rain came down in sheets, causing rivulets to cascade down the hills and form deep pools in the valleys.

Gleason brushed his hair back from his forehead in an attempt to keep the rain out of his eyes. He shivered in the cold, and looked around for a place that would give him shelter . . . a cave or an overhang. He wished he had a poncho or a piece of canvas, but wishing didn't make it so. He had no choice but to continue to make his way through the rain.

He wasn't sure where he was, though he was reasonably certain he was headed north by northeast. He had maintained his course by the position of the sun, when he could see it, and by the moss that grew on the north side of trees. The problem was that hills made any true course impossible to follow; therefore he had to make frequent course adjustments, sometimes going due east, sometimes going due west, but always, or at least as much as possible, going north.

Inside his jacket, wrapped in oilcloth, were the last two biscuits Claudia had made for him. It was almost a week since he left the Hughes farm, and he had sustained himself so far with the biscuit and bacon sandwiches she had fixed on that last night, allowing himself just one a day.

Even in the cold rain, Gleason was warmed by his memories of what had happened between them the last night he was there. They had moved from bathing each other in the big copper bathtub onto the iron bed, where they made love. Afterward, they lay side by side without touching and without speaking, lost in their own thoughts as they stared into the darkness. Claudia spoke first.

"John, what did you do in Pennsylvania before the war?"

"I was a coal miner."

"Did you like being a coal miner?"

"I don't know. I don't have anything to compare it to. I've never done anything but mine coal and soldier. My father was a coal miner, and now I am."

"Have you ever thought about being a farmer?"

"No."

"You could be, you know. I have 120 acres. We could make a good living here."

"We?"

"If you would marry me."

Gleason was startled by her suggestion, and there was a long silence before he spoke again. "Claudia . . ."

"No," she said quickly. "Don't answer me now. You don't have to answer now." She raised up on her elbow and looked down at him. He could see her in the dim light of the moon, her body a shadowed work of art limned in silver, with one of the erect nipples highlighted and glowing. "I know you have to go back to your army now, and I understand that. But afterward, when this war is over, I want you to come back here to me, and to Ellen."

"Claudia, I know you were hurt bad when Carl was killed. And now you want to look for someone to come home to you again. I could be that person. You don't know how easy it would be for me to be that person. But I don't want to take advantage of you. This has all happened so fast. What if I came back here after the war, and you didn't feel this way anymore?"

"I *will* feel this way," Claudia insisted. "I've fallen in love with you, John Gleason."

"But you've known me for only three days."

"Three days is enough time to know my heart," Claudia insisted. She leaned down to kiss him, brushing the nipple of her small, well-formed breast against his bare chest as she did so. "I told you. I love you, John Gleason."

"I love you, Claudia Hughes," Gleason had said then. He repeated those same words now, though his voice sounded small and tinny in the roar of the rain.

Just ahead, Gleason saw a hollow place in the side of a hill, not quite a cave but a deep enough indentation to afford him some protection from the rain. Breathing a quick prayer of gratitude, he started toward it.

Chapter 14

Inside the stockade:

Josie, McSpadden, Blackburn, and Limber Jim were waiting just inside the gate when the new batch of prisoners arrived. Battle-weary and still dazed from their capture and transport, they looked around at the prison grounds with predictable reactions. McSpadden pointed out a grizzled veteran with the three stripes of a sergeant.

"There," he said. "What about him?"

The other three looked, then nodded.

"He'll do," Josie said.

McSpadden stepped toward the newly arrived sergeant. "Sergeant, I'm Sergeant James McSpadden of the 19th Massachusetts. We"—he took in those with him with a wave of his hand—"represent all of the prisoners here at Andersonville. We're going to ask you to do something for us."

"And would you be for tellin' me what that might be?" the new sergeant asked suspiciously.

"We need you to be the foreman of a jury," Blackburn said.

"And we need you to select a jury from these new men," Josie added.

"A jury, is it?" the new sergeant said. "And what is the purpose of this jury?"

"Same as any jury. We're goin' to have a trial," McSpadden explained. "But at this point, I don't want to tell you too much about it, 'cause I don't want to prejudice you for or against the defendants."

"Aye, and who might the defendants be?"

"They're prisoners, like ourselves," McSpadden said.

"Would you be for tellin' me, lad, whether this might be somethin' for the Rebels, to give some legitimacy to some foul deed they might have in mind? For if 'tis, you can count Mickey Cavanaugh out. I'll not lend one hand to their evil design."

"No," Josie said quickly. "It's nothing like that, Sergeant Cavanaugh, I promise you. We have permission from the prison commandant to conduct the trial, but granting that permission is his only participation in it."

"This is strictly our deal," McSpadden added.

"Then I don't understand why you want me. 'Tis plain for anyone to see that I just arrived in this place."

"That's exactly why we want you," Blackburn said. "Only someone who has just arrived can render an honest verdict to the trial."

"And we do want an honest verdict," McSpadden insisted.

"Before we hang the sons of bitches," Limber Jim added.

"And so, 'tis a hangin' you're wantin', is it?" Sergeant Cavanaugh said, holding up his hand. "You'll be needin' to find someone else for that, too. I don't intend to be part of a trumped-up trial, just so's you can hang someone. In my book that'd be murder, and Colleen Cavanaugh didn't raise her son to commit murder."

"It's not like that, Sergeant Cavanaugh, I promise you," McSpadden said. "We want you and the jury to hear all the evidence, then we want you to arrive at a verdict. Whether you find them guilty or innocent, we will accept your verdict."

Cavanaugh looked over the newly arrived prisoners. "And you say I can pick the jury?"

"We *want* you to pick the jury," Josie said. "Sergeant Cavanaugh, we're dead serious about this. We want this trial to be as fair and impartial as any trial would be in the outside world."

Cavanaugh scratched his beard for a moment, then he turned and looked out over the prison compound, as if seeing it for the first time. "Jesus, Mary, and Joseph," he said. "What kind of purgatory is this place?"

"I won't kid you, Mickey," McSpadden said. "You've come to a place that's as bad as any place you can possibly imagine. That's why we want to have this trial. It'll give us an opportunity to reestablish some sense of reality."

"This trial is that important to you, is it?"

"Sergeant Cavanaugh, if you had been here for a month, you wouldn't have to ask that question," Josie replied. "On the other hand, if you had been here for a month, you couldn't be the foreman of the jury, because you would already know what you're going to learn at the trial, and you wouldn't be able to reach a fair decision."

"The defendants, they'll be having a lawyer, will they? 'Tis a real lawyer I'm speakin' of, not someone connivin' to deliver them to the hangman."

"They will have a real lawyer," McSpadden said. "I promise you."

"All right, lads, if it's an honest trial you're wantin', then Mickey Cavanaugh is your man. I'll be your foreman. Let me pick the jury, and you'll have your trial."

McSpadden reached out to shake Sergeant Cavanaugh's

hand. "Thank you, Sergeant. You'll be doin' everyone here a great service."

The 102nd New York shebang was in the extreme southeast corner of the prison yard, so far from the Michigan and Pennsylvania shebangs that Josie had never been in this part of the yard before. It was also so far away that McSpadden didn't come over, fearing that the walk might be too difficult for him. Josie, not wanting to go alone, had invited Billy to accompany him.

In front of the shebang they had been directed to, three men were sitting on the ground. One was wearing a shirt but no shoes. The other two were wearing shoes but no shirts. They scarcely looked up when Josie and Billy arrived.

"Lookin' for the 102nd New York," Josie said.

No one answered.

"The 102nd New York?" Josie said again.

One of the men picked up a stick and started scratching at the ground. A second continued to stare off into space. After a long moment, the third man finally looked up at Josie.

"What do you want with 'im?" he asked.

"I was told I could find Jared Hopkins in the 102nd," Josie answered.

"What you want with 'im?"

Josie was beginning to get a little irritated with the lack of responsiveness from these people. "I'd say that's between Hopkins and me," he said, rather shortly.

"He's in there," the man with the stick said, nodding toward the shebang.

"Thanks."

Josie crawled into the shebang. There, stretched out on the ground, was a tall, cadaverous-looking man with sunken jaws and a wild patch of dark hair. He was lying so still that for a moment Josie thought he might be dead. Then a fly landed on his nose, and the man twitched his nose.

"Mr. Hopkins?" Josie asked.

The man opened one eye.

210

"What do you want?"

"Are you Mr. Hopkins?"

"Mr. Hopkins, is it?" He sat up. "Well, I don't know. It's been a long time since anyone called me that. Now I'm just Private Hopkins." He looked around the shebang, then let out what might have been a laugh. "Actually, I guess I'm not even that anymore. Now I'm Prisoner Hopkins."

Hopkins ran his hand through his unruly hair and looked at Josie and Billy.

"What do you boys want with me?"

"I hear you're a lawyer," Josie said.

"A lawyer? Oh, yes. At least, I was before I became an infantryman-cum-prisoner."

"Are you a good one?" Billy asked.

"Good one what, son? Infantryman? Or prisoner?"

"Good lawyer," Billy said.

"Oh, hell, son, I was the best. I got people off when they already had the gallows built and measured for them."

"Then you sound like the very man we need," Josie said.

"Need for what?"

"To defend the men we're putting on trial."

"You are talking about the disturbance from the other day? The Raiders? I wasn't a part of that. Stood right here and looked out across the grounds to watch, but I didn't participate."

"That's good," Josie said. "It would be rather difficult for you to defend them if you'd been one of the ones who fought them."

"I'd rather prosecute then defend."

"I'm sure you would, Mr. Hopkins," Josie said. "But I've checked around, and everyone tells me you're the best defense attorney in Andersonville. And, regardless of what these men have done, they have a right to a defense . . . the best defense possible. That would be you."

"That's true. But I also have a right to decide who I will defend and who I will not defend."

"We'll pay you for it," Billy said. "We've collected sixty dollars. Ten dollars for each defendant."

"It's not a question of money." Hopkins stared at Billy for a moment. "Is that money in federal greenback dollars?"

"Yes, sir."

Hopkins stroked his chin. "I don't know. Defending lowlife scum like those men isn't going to make me very popular in here."

"That's true," Josie agreed. "Doing the right thing isn't always popular. But it's always right."

Hopkins smiled. "Damn, boy. You should be the one defending them."

Josie shook his head. "Has to be a real lawyer."

Hopkins pointed toward the rear of the shebang. "Do you see those two boys over there?"

"Yes, sir."

"They're brothers from Illinois. There were three of them when they arrived. They were jumped by Mosby and his Raiders the moment they came through the gate. One of them was killed. Now, you tell me, how'm I going to face them if I defend the man who killed their brother?"

"Mosby?" Josie asked in confusion.

"That's what the men used to call Collins. Mosby, as in Mosby's Raiders. They called him that after the Rebel Mosby. Then they decided calling him after a Rebel was too good for him." He paused. "You didn't answer my question, son. How'm I going to face those men if I defend Collins?"

"How will you face yourself if you don't defend him?" Josie asked. "In fact, Mr. Hopkins, how would you ever be able to practice law again, knowing that you withheld your services from someone who needed you and had no other means of defense?"

"Damn, boy, are you *sure* you aren't a lawyer?"

"I'm not a lawyer. But where there is law, I respect it."

"Where there's law . . . ," Hopkins mused. "Hmmm, an interesting point."

"Beg pardon?"

"You have the sixty dollars with you?"

"Yes."

Hopkins held out his hand. "All right, give it to me."

"You'll do it?"

"Yes."

"You have my respect, Mr. Hopkins," Josie said, taking out the money and handing it to him. "I don't envy you . . . but you do have my respect."

Hopkins began counting his money. "We'll see how much respect remains after I start the defense."

"Horace Trimble, 9th Indiana Volunteers," the sergeant said, sticking out his hand when Josie and Blackburn approached him. "And I think I know why you're here. Unless I miss my guess, you want me to act as a lawyer in the trial for the Raiders."

"We've been told that you are a lawyer."

"I am, indeed. Duly admitted to the bar in the state of Indiana, and prosecuting attorney in and for Wabash County."

"I'm glad you have experience as a prosecutor, because we want you to be the prosecutor in this case."

"Wait a minute. You want me to prosecute?"

"Yes."

"I thought you wanted me to act as defense attorney. I'll be glad to do that. But prosecute?" Trimble shook his head. "Won't prosecute. You're going to have to get somebody else for that job."

Josie blinked in surprise. "I beg your pardon."

"You heard me, son. I said get someone else."

"But I don't understand," Josie said. "You are perfect for it. You are a lawyer with experience as a prosecutor. And, as far as we were able to determine, you, personally, have never had any encounter with any of the Raiders."

"That's all true."

"So why do you not want to be the prosecutor?"

"It's a simple matter of saving my skin."

"Are you frightened of them? Because if you are, there's no need to be. We have them well secured. They'll never again be a menace."

"It's my professional and political skin I'm frightened for," Trimble said. When he saw that they didn't understand, he continued, "Boys, what you have constructed here is a situation in which nobody is going to come out clean."

"Why do you say that?"

"Consider this. If we conduct a trial and hang these men without proper judicial authority, I'll be guilty of murder and conspiracy to murder. On the other hand, if we conduct a trial and hang these men using the judicial authority of the Confederate government, I will, in effect, be committing treason by cooperating with an entity that is in a state of war with the United States. Doubly so, as the victims are United States servicemen, who are being held prisoners by a belligerent force."

"But Sergeant Trimble, if we don't conduct this trial, we'll be admitting that we no longer have the right to govern ourselves, nor to behave as responsible citizens," Josie said.

"It's a dilemma, isn't it, Corporal?"

"If it's a choice between two equally balanced alternatives, then the majority has chosen the trial," Josie said. "And if we conduct the trial, then we have the responsibility to do so with the best legal representation for the prosecution, and for the defense, that we can make available. Jared Hopkins has agreed to act as defense, and we must have someone of his stature to act as prosecutor. You, Sergeant Trimble, are the only one in Andersonville who meets that criterion."

Trimble was silent for a long moment, then laughed out loud. "All right, Corporal Day, I'll prosecute your demons for you. And if I'm ever brought before the bar to defend my actions, by God, lad, I want you to speak as a witness on my behalf."

Josie smiled, then stuck out his hand. "It would be an

honor and a privilege to bear witness for you, Sergeant Trimble."

In the hills of northern Georgia:

When it was light enough to see the next morning, Gleason found some dry pine needles and sticks in the back of the shelter. After spinning a stick between his hands, he was able to get a fire going, and now he was sitting beside that fire, completely nude, his clothes spread on some nearby rocks to dry.

Persimmons and black walnuts provided his breakfast, allowing him to save the two remaining biscuits, which he was also drying.

"Hey!" somebody called. "Hey, anyone down there?" The shout came from the top of the hill above his shelter. "I see your smoke."

Gleason looked around, trying to find a place to hide or a way to escape, but there was none.

"You don't mind, I'm goin' to climb on down there and dry myself by your fire," the voice called. "Got some coffee I'm willin' to share."

"All right, come on down," Gleason replied. Looking around, he found a rock that was about the size of his fist, wrapped his hand around it, then held it behind him.

There was a scraping, then the sound of sliding rocks, and finally a small waterfall of stone and sand cascaded across the mouth of the shelter. A moment later a pair of gray-clad legs dangled down.

This was his chance. The man was extremely vulnerable, and it would be very easy for Gleason to grab him, pull him into the shelter, and bash his head in with the rock.

And there were several compelling reasons for doing just that. If the soldier had anything that would aid Gleason in getting back to his own army, such as a weapon, food, map, or compass, it was his duty to take it. And because the prisoners in Andersonville were depending upon Gleason's getting back to report on their condition, it was his duty to prevent this soldier from reporting him to the Confederate authorities.

Gleason moved to the mouth of the shelter and waited, holding the rock cocked over his head, ready to strike. Suddenly little Ellen's prayer came back to him: *"God bless Mama. God bless Daddy, who's in heaven. God bless all the Daddies who're Southern soldiers. And God bless Sergeant John, even if he is a Yankee. Amen."*

Gleason put down the rock just as the soldier dropped onto the lip of the shelter. Blond and bearded, he appeared to be in his mid-thirties. He was a private in the Confederate cavalry. When he saw Gleason, he smiled.

"Man, does that fire look good. Feels good, too." He leaned his rifle against the wall of the shelter beside Gleason, then walked over to hold his hands above the flame. "Don't know how you managed to get it goin' what with the rain 'n' all. I had me some lucifers, but I couldn't keep 'em dry last night. And this mornin' I couldn't find me nothin' dry to burn. Was hopin' I'd find a little holler like this'n." He turned toward Gleason and stuck his hand out. "Don't normally shake hands with naked men," he said. "The name is Culpepper. Amos Culpepper."

"John Gleason."

"Where you from, John?"

"From near Marietta." Claudia had mentioned Marietta as being fairly close.

"Hey, no kidding! Got a first cousin lives there, name of Tommy Calhoun. Know 'im?"

"Fairly tall, light brown hair, blue eyes?" Gleason bluffed.

"Not all that tall. Guess he looks taller'n he is, 'cause he's so damn skinny."

"Who isn't?"

"That's the truth, the way they feedin' us in this army. Who you runnin' messages for?"

"Beg pardon?"

"You out here all by your lonesome. Figure you must be runnin' messages for someone, just like me."

"Yes, I am."

"Who?"

"Don't know as I should tell you that. How do I know you ain't a Yankee?"

"Shit, that's a good one, John." Amos held out his haversack. "Some coffee in there. Got 'nything to make it in?"

"Lost all my stuff in the storm."

"That's all right. You can use my pot."

Gleason took a handful of the beans and placed them in the pot.

"Who you with, John?"

"Dole's division."

Amos let out a low whistle. "You boys sure had it rough at Gettysburg. Was you there?"

"Yes," John answered. "I was at Gettysburg."

"Me, too. Wrote the missus an' told her how lucky she was to have ol' Amos comin' back to her after that little fracas. Lotsa good boys stayed up there."

"On both sides," John said. He dipped water from a puddle to fill the coffee pot. Then he brought it back and made a circle of rocks on which to set it.

"You own any niggers, John?"

"Beg pardon?" Gleason was surprised by the question.

"I asked, do you own any niggers?"

"No. No, I don't."

"Me neither. I'm beginnin' to wonder why folks like me 'n' you is even fightin' in this war in the first place. So the rich folks can hang on to their niggers? Hell, that ain't no good reason. You got 'nything to eat?"

"Couple of biscuits with bacon," John answered. "If they're dried out yet. Got pretty soaked last night."

"You got biscuits? Where you get biscuits?"

"My . . . wife made 'em."

"Your wife? You mean you was home?"

"Yeah, for a couple of days."

"An' you left?"

"Yes."

"You're one patriotic man, John Gleason. Tell you the truth, if'n I was to get home 'n' see my wife 'n' kids now . . . why, I don't know as I'd ever come back."

"Here," Gleason said, handing one of the biscuits to Amos.

Amos held the biscuit under his nose and sniffed. "Man, oh man, does that smell good. Bet she's a good cook." He took a bite of the biscuit. "Umm, tastes as good as it smells. She *is* a good cook. What's her name?"

"Claudia."

"Good cook, purty name. Bet she's a purty woman too."

"She's beautiful."

"Well, sir, my wife, Norma Jean, ain't exactly what you call beautiful. Don't rightly know as you'd even call her purty. But she's a good woman with a heart of gold, and she sure dotes on me 'n' the kids. An' it's like I told her. Hell, ain't no women purty on the outside oncet they get old. Then the only thing that counts is what's on the inside. And when you're talkin' inside-purty, Norma Jean done got most women beat by a country mile. Course, if'n anythin' was to happen to me, I don't know as Norma Jean'd be able to get herself another man. Most men likes their women purty, you know, 'n' they don't look at nothin' else."

"She sounds like a good woman."

"Yes, sir, she is," Amos said, taking the last bite of the biscuit, then licking his fingers. "Say, John, do you mind if I take off my clothes 'n' spread 'em out by the fire alongside your'n? Love to get 'em dry."

"Sure, go ahead." Gleason pointed toward the rocks where his clothes were.

Amos was almost to the rocks before Gleason realized the danger. As soon as Amos saw the uniform, he would know Gleason was not who he claimed to be.

"Your clothes look dry. You want me to toss 'em

over . . ." Amos stopped in mid-sentence, then turned and looked at Gleason. The men stared at each other for a long moment, then Amos made a break for his rifle. Gleason started toward it, too, and they reached it at the same time, grabbing it simultaneously.

"You're a goddam Yankee!" Amos shouted.

"Listen to me!" Gleason yelled, as the two men struggled over the musket. "Amos, listen to me! It doesn't have to be this way!"

"Yankee bastard! What was you goin' to do? Kill me when my back was turned?"

"No! We could walk away from this! We don't have to—"

Gleason's plea was cut off by a loud bang as the rifle fired. He felt the concussion of the blast, and his face was burned with heat from the muzzle flash. He also felt something wet and sticky, just as he saw Amos going down with a big hole in his forehead.

"Amos!"

Amos fell back onto the ground, his arms thrown out to either side. His eyes were open and sightless; and they, his nose, mouth, and hair were red with blood. Gleason put his hand to his face, felt the wetness, then pulled it away and looked at it with horror. His face was covered with Amos' blood.

"Son of a bitch!" Gleason shouted in anger and frustration. He knelt beside Amos and put his hand on his neck to feel for a pulse, though he knew there would be none.

"Why did you do that?" he asked Amos' silent body. "It didn't have to be this way! Goddamn it! It didn't have to be this way!"

His eyes brimming with tears, and his throat choked, Gleason stood up and looked down at the body. Amos' words came back to him.

"Course, if'n anythin' was to happen to me, I don't know as Norma Jean'd be able to get her another man."

Gleason went over to the rock to pick up his clothes. He

started to put them on, then looked back at Amos's body. In that moment he made his decision.

"Amos," he said quietly, "I'm going to have to borrow your uniform. Hope you don't mind."

Gleason pulled the trousers off first, then the tunic. He saw that Amos was wearing a locket, and he bent down to look at it, then turned away quickly, tears stinging his eyes.

"Stay safe in the arms of the Lord. Norma Jean."

"God, why?" John asked, his voice breaking. "Why did you let this happen?"

Gleason waited until he had fully regained his composure, then put on the Confederate uniform. His own uniform he folded and stuffed into the haversack. He looked at the coffee pot. The coffee smelled good, but its having been fixed to share with Amos spoiled any appetite he might have had for it. Angrily, he poured the coffee onto the fire, then put the pot into the haversack. With one last look at Amos's nearly nude body, Gleason left the shelter to continue his journey north.

Chapter 15

Star fort, outside the south gate at Andersonville:

Two guards accompanied Jared Hopkins from the south gate of the prison to the star fort, where the six leaders of the Raiders were being held. This would be Hopkins' first interview with his clients.

"Wait there, Yankee," one of the guards said.

"Is there a place I can sit and speak with my clients?" Hopkins asked.

"I don't know about that. I'll have to ask Sergeant Martindale."

"Please do."

The guard disappeared for a moment, then came back with Sergeant Martindale. Unlike Captain Wirz, and even Lieutenant Barrett, Sergeant Martindale was not universally hated. He had even been observed, on a few occasions, showing some compassion for the prisoners. Consequently, Hopkins was glad he was talking to him.

"The guard said you're looking for a place where you can interview the prisoners. What do you need?"

"Nothing much. A chair or a stool to sit on. Maybe a table to write on."

"There's an old school desk in the back. What if I had that brought up?"

"That would be fine."

"Get the desk in here," Martindale ordered one of the guards.

"Are my clients here?"

"Yeah, they're here. Don't know why you'd want to defend them, though. They're the dregs of the earth. Especially when you consider that it was among your own people that they were causin' all the trouble."

"I'm defending them because it's my job. No," Hopkins corrected, "it's more than a job. It's a sacred obligation."

The desk was brought in and set down.

"Will that do?"

"Yes, it will do nicely, thank you. Would you have the prisoners brought in now?"

"Bring 'em in," Martindale ordered.

A moment later, six men came shuffling in, the length of their footsteps restricted by shackles and the fact that they were chained together. Their hands were cuffed in front of them and connected to another chain around their waist.

"May I?" Hopkins asked, pointing to the desk. One of the guards nodded, and Hopkins sat down. He put a tablet he had been holding on the desktop.

"How do you do?" Hopkins said.

"Who the hell are you?" Collins growled.

"I'm your attorney."

"You're our attorney? What do we need an attorney for?"

"You need one because you six are charged with murder."

Collins laughed. "Who the hell is charging us? The Rebel

government? Let 'em charge all they want. I don't recognize the Rebel government."

"It isn't the Rebel government that filed the complaint. You are being charged by the provisional government of the prisoners of Andersonville."

"That's a pretty high-falutin' name for nothin' but a bunch of prisoners," Collins said. "What the hell can they do to us?"

"They can hang you."

Collins gave another scoffing laugh. "That bunch of chickenhearted, yellow-livered bastards can't do anything to us. They got no authority over us."

"Oh, but they do, Collins. They have the same authority over you that you exercised over so many for so long."

"Authority? I had no authority. All I had was the power to do whatever I wanted to do."

Hopkins smiled at him. "My point, precisely. Now, I suggest we begin exploring ways to construct a defense."

"You're the lawyer, you do it."

"I can't do it without your help."

"You the best they could come up with?" Collins scoffed.

"As far as you're concerned, Collins, I'm the *only* thing they could come up with."

"Well, you ain't much. What're we supposed to do? Get down on our knees and thank the good Lord for sendin' you to us?"

Hopkins sighed, then laid his pencil alongside the tablet. "Quite frankly, Mr. Collins, I don't care whether you're thankful for having me or not. What's more, I don't really give a shit what happens to you. But I'm the only hope you have, and that isn't much."

"Collins, listen to him!" Munn pleaded.

Collins looked over at Munn with distaste. "Don't whine." He turned back to Hopkins. "If you feel that way about it, how do I know you'll do the best job you can?"

"Because what I feel about a person—and I'll tell you right now, Collins, that I think you're a sorry piece of shit—has nothing to do with how I defend them. You're entitled by law, and by moral code, to the best defense possible."

"Moral code?" Collins laughed. "That's a good one."

"Yes, Collins, moral code. And it means something to me, whether it means anything to you or not. That moral code decrees that I give you the best defense I'm capable of providing. And, by God, I intend to do just that, if you cooperate with me. If you don't, then my best bet would probably be to plead you guilty and throw you on the mercy of the court."

"What mercy?"

"Good question, Mr. Collins."

"All right, Mr. Lawyer. You got my attention," Collins said. "Tell me what you want us to do, and we'll do it."

"Fortunately, the defense I intend to use doesn't depend upon you doing anything. If it did, you truly wouldn't have a chance."

"But, you do have a plan, don't you?" Munn asked anxiously.

"Yes, I have a plan, though it will pain me to use it, for it means that I must attack the very system that has nurtured me."

"I don't understand," Collins said.

"Don't worry about it. You don't need to understand. All you need to do is follow instructions. "

With Horace Trimble, inside Andersonville Prison:

"We can't draw up a bill of particulars on every one of them," Trimble was telling Josie, McSpadden, Blackburn, and at least a dozen other interested parties. "We're going to have to concentrate on the six leaders."

"I hate to see those other sons of bitches get away," Limber Jim said.

"Yes, especially Georgie. He's a mean bastard," Samson added.

"Have you ever seen Georgie kill anyone?" Trimble asked. "Or anyone else, for that matter, except for the six leaders?"

"No, but you know they have," Limber Jim insisted. "They must have."

"I don't intend to let this court get dragged down by trying to prove capital crimes against everyone who ever called himself a Raider. If we're going to make this thing work, if it's really going to be effective, we're going to have to concentrate our efforts where they will produce the greatest return. In this case, it means going after the leaders."

Josie nodded. "I agree. And the truth is, no matter what the others did, they wouldn't have done it without their leaders' influence."

One of the others voiced his support. "If it's good enough for Josie, it's good enough for me."

"All right," McSpadden said to Trimble. "So we'll only go after the main six, and let the others go."

Trimble shook his head. "No. I didn't say that. I don't believe they should get off scot-free just because we can't prove murder against them. They're guilty of lesser crimes, and they should have to pay for that."

"Hear, hear," Samson shouted.

"So what do we do?"

"The first thing we do is round up as many witnesses as possible. But"—Trimble held up a finger to emphasize his point—"you have to make absolutely certain that they were eyewitnesses. We don't want anyone who 'heard' about an atrocity. They're effective witnesses only if they actually saw it with their own eyes."

"I saw them kill Dick Potter," Josie said. He pointed at his eyes. "And I saw it with my own eyes."

"Very good. You'll be one of the witnesses," Hopkins said. "Now, those of you who want to help, spread out, start

225

asking around, find people who're willing to bear witness to the crimes committed by these men."

Inside Wirz's headquarters:

"How long more will it be before the Yankee's hold their damn trial?" Wirz asked Sergeant Martindale.

"I think it will be soon now, sir."

"Nothing have they come to say to me. If I do not find out soon *was ist los*, the prisoners I will turn back in to the prison."

"I think they're moving it along as quickly as they can, Cap'n Wirz. You, yourself, set the rules. You said you wanted it to be a legitimate trial, with lawyers representing both sides. I think they're taking their time to prepare the case."

"Why do they need time? They are going to hang them. This we all know."

"Yes, sir, I expect they will hang at least some of them. That's why they asked for wood, planks, timbers, and a goodly supply of rope."

"For what do they want such things?"

"To build a gallows, I suppose."

"A gallows we do not need. Let them use the cross tee on top of the gate. Would be more better anyway. We can leave the bodies hanging until they rot and fall apart, to show others why is more better to have order in prison."

"Yes, sir. But the gallows is a symbol that might well have the same effect on the prisoners."

"*Ja.* Very well, Sergeant. Tell the prisoners the gallows they shall have."

"Thank you, Captain."

Wirz watched Martindale go, carrying the promise of material for the gallows. Was he doing the right thing by letting the prisoners take matters into their own hands? This whole business had come up too quickly for him to get specific orders on what he should do. Orders he could follow, and follow without question. If they gave him more prisoners, but did not increase the ration allowance, then he could decrease the amount of food each prisoner was allocated. That was a simple decision to make, based upon the orders he received.

But where were the orders that would help him in this case? Would a court investigate the hanging of these prisoners, and then find him guilty? That was entirely possible, he knew, for he had turned total authority over to the prisoners when, in fact, they had no authority. It was difficult to be a soldier when there were no orders to follow. Orders were the armor protecting the soldier from all blame. As Christ assumed the sins of the world when He died upon the cross, so were commanding officers the propitiation for those under them. Just as the orders he received from his superiors left him without blame for all the ills of Andersonville, so were the guards on the parapet blameless for anything they did while carrying out his orders.

At the Massachusetts shebang:

Josie sat in his usual writing position, composing another letter that he knew might never be delivered:

> *Death continues to be our main subject of concern. The grim angel stalks the prison grounds, sometimes taking one who has lingered for many weeks in agony, at other times striking swiftly at those whom we thought were faring quite well. I have visited acquaintances in other shebangs and left them, apparently strong, only to return the next morning to find they had died during the night. I have said my final goodbyes to some weeks ago, though they yet linger at death's door.*
>
> *I do not know if, in all history, anyone has suffered as we have suffered. We have no clothes to replace those we*

were wearing when we arrived, and the clothes we do
have are becoming thinner and thinner. Now many in our
number are totally naked, and I worry about what will
happen to them when winter comes.

We are affected by sores, scurvy, and dropsy. Mad
Matthew lost his mind months ago, and that affliction is
beginning to reach many others now, so that, with each
passing day, the number of those who are mad grows
within our ranks.

All appears to be in readiness for the trial. We have
secured the services of two lawyers, one to act as
prosecutor and one to act as lawyer for the defense. We
have said that we want the trial to be fair, but already
lumber and other material have been acquired for the
gallows. I wish we could get lumber as easily for the
building of shelters.

It is good that the Raiders have been put out of
business, for their crimes against their fellow prisoners
were foul indeed. Life will have to improve somewhat
now, for at least we need no longer fear that what meager
possessions we still cling to will be suddenly and brutally
taken from us.

It is also good that the men are looking forward to the
trial. It is the subject of many conversations, and talking
about it has provided an escape from the day-to-day
horrors we all must face.

"Josie, Josie!" Billy called excitedly. "The trial! It's about
to begin! Come! You're to be a witness, remember?"

Josie put away his pencil and paper, then stood up. Like
sand slowly shifting in an hourglass, nearly all who could
walk were now starting toward the area where the trial was
to be held.

Tension and excitement were high as prisoners from all
over the compound began gathering. The south gate was
chosen as the site because a natural bowl there would allow
them to sit in rows on the sides of the hill, the better to see

what was going on. The banks were steadily filling with new arrivals as the sea of humanity swelled larger and larger.

Those with the better places were selling them to the latecomers for tobacco, pocket knives, even shoes.

Because they were among the principal witnesses who would be called during the trial, Josie, McSpadden, Blackburn, and the others from the Massachusetts and Pennsylvania shebangs had a place reserved for them. As they arrived, a few minutes before the trial was to begin, they picked their way through the crowd to reach their appointed position. Some of the prisoners grumbled at being pushed aside, but many recognized Josie and the others as being principals in bringing about the trial, so they gave way willingly. Some stood and applauded as they passed.

When everyone was settled, Sergeant Cavanaugh stood up to face the prisoners. Everyone knew that neither the jury foreman nor any of the members of the jury had been here during the activities of the Raiders. Thus, the jury's decision, when it was rendered, would come from testimony and evidence presented during the trial, uninfluenced by personal experiences.

"Who's speaking first?" the foreman asked.

The six ringleaders and their lawyer, Jared Hopkins, were sitting about twenty feet from the other Raiders. All were under strong guard. Collins started to say something, but Hopkins shushed him, then nodded toward the man who had been appointed prosecutor.

"I'm speaking first, Your Honor," the appointed prosecutor said. "I'm Sergeant Horace Trimble, 9th Indiana Volunteers, duly licensed to practice law in the state of Indiana, appearing for the prosecution. I introduce to this court the Honorable Jared Hopkins, Esquire, 102nd New York Volunteers, a member of the bar of that state, appearing for the defense."

A roar of rage and thousands of catcalls came cascading down from the sides of the bowl. Hopkins walked over to address the court. The stenographer waited, his pencil poised, but when Hopkins tried to speak, the prisoners began howling him down with catcalls and booing.

"Shyster!"

"Liar!"

"What you want to defend them for?"

"Save your breath!"

"Sit down! You're just wastin' our time! Get on with the hangin'!"

"Your Honor, if it please the court . . . ," Hopkins said.

"Boo!"

"You try an' defend them, you're as bad as they are!"

The boos and catcalls continued unabated, despite Hopkins' efforts to speak. Finally, in disgust, he waved his hand angrily and sat down.

Most of the Raiders were terrified. It was all Munn could do to hold himself together. Only Collins continued to show defiance, glaring at the crowd as if issuing a personal challenge to them.

Trimble stood up again and raised his hand for quiet. After a few minutes people in the crowd began shushing the others. When at last it was quiet enough, he began to speak.

"It's my job to prove to these men," he said, taking in the jurors with a wave of his hand, "who arrived here but recently, that the men on trial have behaved like savages . . . barbarians . . . and worse in this camp. The rest of you are soldiers in the Federal Army who conducted, and will conduct, yourselves accordingly."

Two faraway voices called: "And sailors!"

"And marines!"

When Trimble saw that he still had everyone's attention, he continued. "I know you want revenge. I know you want justice. But how much more satisfying will be revenge, how much sweeter will be justice, if these concepts are legally and fairly applied? Now, I hope we have no more such outbursts." He stared at the crowd, challenging anyone to defy him, then turned toward the defense attorney. "Mr.

Hopkins, I beg your pardon for the interruption. Please say what you have to say, sir."

Josie, McSpadden, and Blackburn were thankful for, and impressed by, Horace Trimble. So, too, were most of the prisoners on the hill, for after only a few more catcalls, which were quickly put down, the crowd grew quiet and strained to hear as the defense attorney again took his position to plead his case.

Before he began, Hopkins nodded his thanks to Trimble, then turned to the jury. "I do not envy you men at all," he began. "For yesterday, you arrived in hell."

"You got that right!" someone said. Most listened quietly, for he had been effective in getting their attention.

"I do not speak lightly," Hopkins continued. "This prison . . . this prison called Andersonville is not just a place without food to eat, or water to drink, or even without a place to give a body shelter from the rain. It's not just a place where guards murder for sport. It is much more than that. It is a place without civilization."

Hopkins paused for a moment, then leaned toward the jury to emphasize his next statement.

"It is *a place without law!*" Hopkins boomed out the last four words.

Josie frowned at that statement. To say that there was no law here would be to undermine what they were trying to do now. Which, he suddenly realized, might be exactly what Hopkins was trying to do. Josie remembered a remark Hopkins made when he recruited him.

"Where there's law . . . ," Hopkins mused. *"Hmmm, an interesting point."*

Josie had wondered then why Hopkins made such an observation. Now, he believed, he knew. Hopkins might be assuming the position that no matter what kind of face they put on it, there *was* no law. What was taking place here, now, despite all the trappings, would in fact be nothing more than a lynching.

"Andersonville is hell," Hopkins continued. "And you will hear how men . . . good Union men, good Federal soldiers . . . and sailors were driven mad."

The prisoners on the hill renewed their boos and catcalls.

"Those men never were soldiers!" someone called.

"Never were any good!"

"They were bounty jumpers!"

"Cutthroats!"

"Murderers!"

"Thievin' bastards!"

Hopkins tried to continue his opening remarks, but the prisoners on the hill wouldn't let him speak. "I will not be silenced!" he shouted at the top of his voice. He pointed to the defendants. "These men were *driven* by these circumstances, not of their own making, to commit, *understandably*, acts of desperation they never would otherwise have committed!"

"We stood it!" Limber Jim shouted.

"Without resortin' to murder!" another cried.

"And I will be heard, sir!" Hopkins screamed.

"Liar!"

"Shyster!"

"Somebody ought to string this son of a bitch up along with those bastards he's defendin'!"

Josie stood up and raised his hand toward the crowd, pleading with them to be quiet. Billy followed his example.

Horace Trimble waved for quiet. Finally, with everyone calling for quiet, the boos and catcalls settled down enough for Hopkins to continue his opening remarks.

"The second reason I don't envy you, gentlemen, is that you're being asked to sit in judgment on soldiers in your own Federal Army. Soldiers who are themselves victims of Ander . . ."

"We stood it!" Samson shouted, raising himself to full height on his one crutch.

"Victims of Andersonville," Hopkins continued, forcing his comments over the crowd reaction, "whose conduct must be understood as being *caused* by. . . ."

"Hogwash!"

"What a load of shit!"

"That the best you can do?"

"You're wastin' our time, here!

"Sit down, so we can get on with hangin' the bastards!"

". . . as being caused by the Rebels," Hopkins went on. "The Rebels who run this camp, the commandant, his lieutenants." Hopkins pointed to the guards in the nearest turkey roosts. "The guards who shoot every time one of us crosses the Deadline . . . *they* are the ones who ought to be on trial before you! Not the men of your own army.

"In closing, let me suggest to you that in order for anyone to be guilty of anything, there must be rules and regulations that are violated. Gentlemen of the jury, no such rules and regulations were broken, because no such rules and regulations exist!"

Hopkins boomed out his last comment, but by the time he finished his statement there was so much noise that Josie doubted the jury could hear him.

Sergeant Cavanaugh, as foreman of the jury, stood, then turned to Trimble. "It's your time to speak."

Trimble got up to address the jury, as well as the more than one thousand who were close enough to hear his remarks.

"The United States of America is a nation of men. And because men make laws, it is therefore, by extension, a nation of laws. We are citizens of that great country. We, here, represent all the states of the Union. We did not abandon our home states, nor did we abandon our country. We joined in the great crusade to defend our people, and to defend our nation's laws. Therefore, the rights we enjoyed as free citizens, we still enjoy.

"We are met here to conduct a trial to determine what disposition will be made of men who have violated the laws

233

of God and man. The transgressions of some of these defendants are so severe that we will seek the ultimate penalty, death by hanging.

"Let no one tell you that we do not have the authority to hold this trial. Let no one tell you that we do not have the authority to carry out the sentence. We have the authority because, even in here, we are still a nation of men and of laws. Let no one tell you that it isn't right to do this, for with authority comes obligation, and we have the sacred obligation to see to it that the laws which govern us all are followed by us all. These thoughts I want you to bear in mind as we conduct this trial."

He turned to Sergeant Cavanaugh. "And now, if it please the court, the prosecution is ready to begin its case."

Cavanaugh nodded. "You may begin."

Trimble walked over to stand in front of the rank-and-file Raiders, including Georgie. He pointed toward them. "We charge these men with being thieves who stole from their fellow prisoners: food, clothing, and possessions of every kind, always brutally, always without mercy, and frequently under cover of night." He looked toward the jury. "You will have all the witnesses to this charge that you want." He turned toward the prisoners in the hills. "And I ask now, as an officer of the court, is there anyone here who can say these men did more? Who saw one of these men . . . ." He pointed to the rank and file. "I'm exempting the six ringleaders from this charge. Is there any among you who saw one of *these* men commit murder, or order another to commit murder? If so, and if he will swear to it, let him now come forward!"

There was a murmur among the prisoners on the hillsides, and Trimble waited patiently for someone to respond. When no one came forth, he nodded, then walked away from the rank-and-file members.

"Never did no murder!" one of the rank and file said, and the others, relieved that they were not being so charged, nodded and babbled in agreement. Trimble, without looking back toward them, held his hand up to quiet them. Quickly, they fell silent.

Now Trimble was standing in front of the six ringleaders, pointing to them as he addressed the crowd a second time.

"Is there any man here who saw any of these six commit murder, or order another to commit murder of another Federal soldier, to steal his goods or for any other reason? If so, and if he will swear to it, let him come forward now, or forever hold his peace."

Josie got to his feet. Unlike the other soldiers who had been booing and catcalling, there was no triumph in his action. He was a soldier performing his duty.

Other men began to rise from their positions on the hill, scores of men, hundreds of men. They started moving through the crowd, working their way down the hill to give their testimony before this court.

Trimble waited patiently as multitudes of men began coming forward. Hopkins, seeing the overwhelming load of witnesses against his clients, shook his head slowly, then stared at the ground. His task, which had been practically impossible to begin with, had just grown infinitely more difficult.

Trimble guided the first man into what was serving as the witness box.

Josie stood to one side, watching as, one by one, the witnesses were called into the box. He was unable to hear them, but from the expressions on their faces and on the faces of the defendants, he could gauge the impact of their testimony.

The process was the same in every case. Trimble asked a few questions, the witness answered, sometimes pointing to a particular person among the six. Then Trimble said a few words to the jury. He was followed by Hopkins, who tried to dilute the testimony the jury had just heard.

With each new witness, Munn, and now Curtis, deteriorated more and more, their fear palpable. Collins, on the other hand, became more and more defiant until he seemed to have become the accuser rather than the accused.

"And who will be the next witness?" Trimble asked. When no one else made a move, Josie stepped forward. Someone held a Bible out, and he put his left hand on it, then raised his right hand.

"Do you swear to tell the truth, the whole truth, and nothing but the truth, so help you God?"

"I do."

"State your name."

"My name is Josiah Day. I'm a corporal in I Company of the 19th Massachusetts."

"How long have you been a prisoner in Andersonville, Corporal Day?"

"I was captured at Cold Harbor in June of this year."

"And you were brought directly to Andersonville?"

"I was."

"Corporal Day, tell the jury what you have seen with your own eyes."

"Yes, sir. I . . . ah . . . before I do . . ." Josie looked toward the foreman. "May I ask a question of the defense attorney?"

The foreman nodded.

Josie turned to Hopkins. "Did I understand you to say, sir, that no law applies here?

Seizing the opportunity, Hopkins jumped up quickly, and nearly ran to the center of the court. "You did indeed hear me say that, Corporal. That is the very point!" Hopkins turned to the jury. "I thank my young friend for his understanding. There *is* no law here. There *are* things here. There is starvation here, there is thirst here, roasting heat, freezing cold. There is disease, acts of barbarism and cruelty on all sides. But law?" Hopkins shook his head. "What law? Whose law?" He made a sweeping gesture that took in the walls, the turkey roosts, and the Confederate guards. "Rebel law? We do not obey Rebel law! The fact is, there is no law here for my clients to have broken. Therefore, they cannot

236

be guilty." He turned to Josie. "And I thank you, sir, for your observation. You are wise beyond your years."

Hopkins sat down triumphantly, and there was a widespread mumble of discontent among the prisoners on the hill.

No! Josie thought. *That's not what I mean at all!* He felt a moment of panic. Had he, somehow, just lost the case for the prosecution? He looked toward McSpadden and Blackburn, and saw by their expressions that they, too, were worried. Quickly, Josie turned back to Hopkins.

"But that cannot be, sir. We *do* live by laws in here."

"The law of survival, Corporal," Hopkins said, resolutely.

"No, sir. We do not stop belonging to the Federal Army just because we are here."

Out of the corner of his eye, Josie saw Billy nodding, and the fact that Billy was following his reasoning reassured him.

"We have our sergeants . . . we do what they command. We maintain order and discipline."

Hopkins moved his arm in another sweeping gesture, this time taking in the entire prison compound. "Order and discipline? In here?" he bellowed.

"Yes, as best we can. We stand in line to get what little food they give us. We do not steal from each other. We do not betray each other to the Rebels."

Hopkins turned to the jury and began speaking, cutting Josie off. "And I am saying that men can be excused if they do extreme things . . . necessary things . . . in order to stay alive in a place like this."

"The things they did," Josie rebutted, "they *knew* were wrong. Everyone knows they are wrong. They're against every man's law and understanding. None of the rest of us did these things!"

"They did them to live, Corporal! To live!"

"All men want to live, Sergeant," Josie shouted, so intense in his rebuttal that the veins were standing out on his neck. "But there are some things men won't do *just* to live!"

"What things?" the foreman shouted. "Don't forget, gentlemen, that we have just come in here. That is what we must hear. What was done here?"

"Murder was done here!" Trimble shouted, jumping up to make his voice heard.

"We'll hear about that!" the foreman insisted.

"Ask me about Dick Potter," Josie said to Trimble. Josie looked at McSpadden and Blackburn, and saw them smiling at him. He was relieved that they now understood where he was going. He had recovered the ground they thought he'd lost, and more.

"The court wants to hear about murder, does it?" Trimble said to the foreman. "All right, let's get to it, shall we?"

He walked back to stand beside Josie. "Corporal Day, tell us about Dick Potter."

Josie had been waiting for this moment, but there was so much to say, and so little time in which to say it, that it wouldn't be nearly as easy as he thought. He paused for a moment, trying to organize his thoughts.

"Dick Potter," he began, then paused. "Dick Potter . . . ." He cleared his throat. "Dick Potter and his father were the best fishermen in New Bedford, Massachusetts. He joined up the first summer of the war because he wanted to, and because he thought he should. He was a good soldier, brave and dependable. And then he was shot in both legs at Antietam, taken prisoner by the Rebels, and brought here."

Josie went on with his statement, his testimony more a celebration of Dick's life than an attack on the way he was killed. He shared with the others the story of Tucker catching the flower and declaring that he was in love.

"Dick was there," he said. "And he didn't tease Tucker the way the other boys did."

He told about sneaking into a henhouse to get eggs, and being chased out by a chicken and a duck, who had joined forces to guard their combined broods.

As he talked, the old prisoners appeared to be listening. But in truth, their memories were revisiting such battlefields as Shiloh, Antietam, Gettysburg, Cold Harbor, and countless others. And the jury, though having just arrived at Andersonville, had nearly four years of war behind them; they, too, connected in a deeply personal way to Josie's testimony about a friend.

And in the group of Raiders, those who were not being charged with murder but had been tarred by the brush of association, looked at the ground in shame and contrition.

In the turkey roosts the Confederate guards were struck with the vision of thousands of silent and reflective faces. And they, who also had lost friends in this war, found themselves remembering, and sharing the sorrow of this Yankee soldier.

Chapter 16

Twilight, the same day:

Lieutenant Barrett was standing at the railing at the nearest turkey roost, looking down on the court. By now both sides had rested their cases and the foreman was in a tight circle of jurors, conferring quietly with them.

Josie had returned to McSpadden and the others; they, like Lieutenant Barrett, the Confederate guards, and all the prisoners on the hill, were watching and waiting.

Twilight faded into night, and a circle of torches was lit so that the court could continue its deliberation. The foreman and the jury, the Raiders and their ringleaders, the prosecutor and the defense attorney all were bathed in orange light. They were being watched closely by the prisoners on the hill.

The prisoners could not understand was why it was taking so long to reach a verdict. The guilt of the accused was glaringly obvious to them. How could the jury be so thick as not to see it?

What the prisoners did not know was that the verdict of guilty had been reached almost instantly, and for the six ringleaders a sentence of death by hanging had been assessed. It was what to do with the others—those whose guilt was, in many cases, just as great as the ringleaders' but whose redemption came in the fact that they were dull men, without ambition or any leadership ability.

"I think we should hang the lot of 'em," one of the jurors said.

"That would be a spectacle, wouldn't it?" Cavanaugh asked. "Fifty or more Union men hangin' in a Rebel prison, with us the reason."

"They don't deserve to be called Union men. Not the way they behaved."

"But the evidence isn't strong enough for all of them. Perhaps some deserve to be hanged, but what of those who don't? Are we to hang them as well, just to get the ones who are more guilty?"

"What do you think, Sergeant?"

"We could put them on ball and chain," Cavanaugh suggested.

"I have an idea," one of the other jurors said. He had been silent until now, and the fact that he was speaking for the first time caught everyone's attention.

"All right, lad," Cavanaugh said. "What's your idea?"

"I think they're about finished, don't you, Josie?" McSpadden asked. "They're all nodding. It looks like they've come to some sort of decision."

"I think you're right," Josie said. "Here comes Sergeant Cavanaugh now."

"Wonder what they decided?" Blackburn asked.

"I think we're about to find out," Josie replied.

"We've heard enough," Sergeant Cavanaugh said to those who gathered around to hear the decision. "Those men," he jerked his head toward the rank and file of the Raiders, "are guilty of theft and low, cowardly assault on their fellow soldiers. Make 'em run the gauntlet. Every man here who wants, gets a swing at 'em, with fists, sticks, anything you can get your hands on."

The prisoners on the hill, led by Limber Jim and Samson, roared their satisfaction at the verdict.

On balance, Georgie and the rest of the rank-and-file Raiders were relieved. It could have been a lot worse.

Now Cavanaugh looked at the six ringleaders, and he could not hide the disgust on his face, nor could he keep out the derision in his voice. "Those six," he said, then paused. "Hang 'em."

This time, the roar of approval was deafening. It echoed back from the hills and reverberated across the compound. It was a sustained cheer, led by Limber Jim and Samson.

Munn was trembling so much now that he seemed to have gone into convulsions. Collins, on the other hand, acted totally unconcerned. "Hah!" he said, trying to give the impression that the verdict meant nothing to him.

Still sustaining the cheer, the prisoners on the hill began dancing for joy, yelling and screaming until they started to lose their voices.

Josie felt a profound sense of awe at what had just taken place. It was a manifestation of law in a place that Hopkins would have all believe was lawless. And yet, for all his satisfaction at justice finally being done, he did not feel like celebrating.

"Form up!" Limber Jim shouted. "Form up for the gauntlet!"

There was a loud shout of excitement as the men hurried to form two rows, creating a long passage through which the rank-and-file Raiders would run to fulfill their punishment. Many of the men had clubs, some were holding belts or straps, while the rest were perfectly willing to use their bare hands.

Billy started to join the gauntlet, and Josie was about to

call him back. Then, to Josie's surprise, Tyce put his hand on Billy's shoulder.

"No, Billy," Tyce said gently. "We don't want to do this."

Neither the Massachusetts nor the Pennsylvania men joined in the gauntlet. Instead, they held their position on the side of the hill and watched as the prisoners were unchained, then taken to the end of the long double line.

Georgie was first. The biggest and strongest of all the Raiders, and glad that he wasn't going to be hanged, he started down the gauntlet with a broad, defiant smile on his face.

The first blow missed, but someone punched him hard in the ear and another hit him in the side. Like a pack of wolves, the men forming the gauntlet shouted and taunted and punched and swung. A third of the way down the line the smile had left Georgie's face. His nose was bleeding, and one eye was swelling shut; he raised his arms to ward off the blows that continued to rain down on him. Hacked, kicked, punched, and bloodied, Georgie, completely subdued, made it to the end of the line, then fell face down, thanking the God he had abandoned long ago for deliverance.

Those who followed Georgie learned from his mistake. They realized that if they went through one at a time, they would be subjected to as terrible a beating as he had received. After a brief consultation and agreement, several of them dashed into the gauntlet at the same time. Angered at this final trick played on them by the Raiders, the men of the gauntlet yelled in rage and excitement, hitting harder but with less coordination. Weaker than the Raiders, whose regular feeding had allowed them to maintain their strength, the blows delivered were not nearly as severe as they would have been under ordinary circumstances. As a result, the rest of the rank-and-file Raiders managed to make it through with no serious injuries.

Then, when the final man was through and the last blow had fallen, the bloodied and injured former Raiders were granted asylum, with the unspoken warning that the slightest transgression on their part would result in instant and severe punishment.

Now all that remained to close the chapter on the Raiders was the final, terrible act, scheduled for the following morning.

With Sergeant Gleason:

Gleason stood on top of the hill, looking down at the little town on both sides of the railroad. There were half a dozen boxcars on a side track, but he saw no engines. There was a great deal of activity around the depot, however; boxes were being stacked and artillery pieces were being rolled into position.

A Confederate flag fluttered from a pole in front of the depot, and another flag flew from a staff in front of a rather large tent. At the end of the loading platform, a field kitchen had been set up, and even from here, Gleason could smell meat cooking. His stomach rumbled in anticipation.

Gleason sat down on a rock, then pulled a telescope from Amos' haversack. Through the telescope he spotted at least two generals. Seeing them gave him a sense of security, for that meant the army there would be too large for everyone to know everyone else. He could mingle with little fear of being recognized as an outsider.

Gleason started down the hill toward the little town. As he got closer, he could see the name on the end of the depot building: Allatoona Pass.

"Soldier," someone called. Startled, Gleason looked around and saw someone approaching him. The single star on his collar identified him as a major. He saluted, and the major returned the salute.

"Yes, sir?" Gleason said, starting toward him, forcing himself to keep calm.

"What did you see up there?"

"Beg your pardon, sir?"

"I saw you looking through your spyglass. Did you see anything?"

"No, sir."

The major stroked his chin. "Sherman's got his calvary poking around near here, sure as a gun's iron. We've got to get loaded and out of here before they discover us. Otherwise, they'll be waiting for us when we get there. You sure you didn't see anything?"

"I'm positive, sir."

"Well, so far, so good." The major nodded toward the field kitchen. "We came on a bit of luck. Captured some Yankee beef. General Hood ordered it cooked and passed out to the whole army. Better get over there and get some before you go back up the hill."

"Yes, sir. Thank you, sir."

"And the moment you see the first sign of Federal cavalry, you hightail it down here. You hear me, soldier?"

"Yes, sir."

By the time Gleason reached the field kitchen, twenty or more men were in line. He took his place at the rear, pulling Amos' mess skillet out of the haversack.

"Umm, umm, don't that smell good?" someone said.

"Beats the shit out of the mess clubs," someone else answered.

"Beadie, that's jus' 'cause you ain't in a good mess club. You should be in ours. Ol' Gordie over there can cook up the finest mess of poke and possum you ever put in your mouth."

"Shit. Don't have to be too good to be the finest poke and possum I ever ate," Beadie grumbled.

The soldier in front of Gleason turned toward him. "Seen you over there talkin' to Major Lewis a while ago. You with him?"

"Yes."

"Thought so. Don't 'member seein' you aroun' before.

What's Hood got in mind for us? You don't ever seen Major Lewis showin' up, 'less Hood has somethin' planned."

Gleason shook his head. "Don't ask me. I just go where they send me."

Gleason reached the head of the line then, and a serving of steaming, aromatic beef stew was slapped onto his mess skillet. He moved to the edge of the depot platform, then sat down and started eating. It was his first real food since he left Claudia's house, and he had to fight to keep from wolfing it down.

The soldier who had been talking to him in line came to sit beside him. "I know you know somethin' 'bout what's goin' on," he said. "You just ain't talkin', that's all. Hell, look at all them cannons over there. What we got them here for? We sure ain't movin' 'em around for a parade."

"No, I guess not."

"You guess not." The soldier laughed. "Man, I know why the major picked you to go with him. You don't give out no more information than he does. The name is Peabody. Gale Peabody, but folks call me Goober."

"Gleason," John said. "Ser . . . uh, John Gleason."

Goober laughed. "Ain't got used to it yet, have you?"

"Used to what?"

"Gettin' busted. You near 'bout said Sergeant Gleason."

"Yeah." John laughed. "Guess I shouldn't have talked back to that lieutenant."

"Ah, lieutenants is all pissants anyway."

In the distance they heard a train whistle, and several men looked south, down the track.

"Here comes the train," Goober said. "Reckon that means we'll be goin' for a ride."

"One thing is for certain, boys. We'll be goin' north," someone said. "Leastwise, that's the way the engine is pointin', and there ain't no roundhouse here."

"It's about damn time. It's time to fight the damn Yankees in their own territory," another offered.

247

"I doubt we're goin' that far north," Goober said. "More'n likely it'll be up aroun' Resaca, or some such place."

"Wisht we could go all the way to Tennessee."

By now the engine, pulling a string of flatcars, had reached the far end of the platform. It wheezed and clacked and rattled, pumping out smoke and steam as it squealed to a stop. Once stopped, a relief valve was opened, and it began venting excess steam.

"Let's go!" someone shouted. "Get these artillery pieces and this equipment on board! Hurry!"

"Shit, what's the use of hurryin'?" someone griped. "We'll just hurry up, then when we get there, we'll set around and wait."

"Say, John, what's that stickin' outta your haversack? A Yankee uniform?"

Gleason was startled, but he decided the best reaction was to treat the question as if it were nothing.

"Yeah."

"Where'd you get it? Take it off a dead Yank?"

"Hell, Goober, you think he took it off'n a live one?" someone asked. Everyone laughed.

"What're you doin' with it?"

"I don't know. Just thought it might come in handy someday."

"Don't know why anyone would want a Yankee uniform, but I reckon it's none of my business. Come on, John, let's get us a place on one of the cars where we can sit down. Way it's lookin' now, lots of folks is goin' to be standin' for the whole trip."

"Yeah, good idea." Gleason followed Goober to one of the cars. They climbed on, then sat down on the edge, dangling their legs over the side.

"You know, afore I come into the army, I never even rode no train," Goober said. "Used to see 'em ever' now an' then, and I always thought I'd like to ride on one." He spit over the edge. "Been ridin' on 'em so damn much since the war started, I don't care if I never ride one of 'em again."

248

Andersonville Prison, the next morning:

As the sun rose fully above the horizon, the men of Andersonville Prison started waking. They sat up and stretched the soreness from their rail-thin bodies after sleeping on cold, hard ground. Some looked for water or prepared their breakfast from the tiny amount of food saved from the night before.

Others checked on friends, paying particular attention to those who last night had seemed too weak to last another day. Forty-six men had not survived the night, and they were counted out to be taken to the Deadhouse.

One thing, however, made this morning different from all other mornings. From near the main gate, there came the sound of hammering and sawing. At first some of the prisoners were puzzled by this sound. But the bewilderment didn't last long, for quickly they remembered the events of the night before.

Word began passing through the camp, from those whose shebangs were closest, to those who were more than a quarter of a mile away, that construction was under way.

"Scaffold! They're building the scaffold this morning!"

"Scaffold, Perry. You feel like movin' around? Let's go have a look-see."

"Scaffold, fellas. The hangin' is today."

No one had to tell Limber Jim and Samson that the scaffold was being built. Both had gotten up before dawn and gone to volunteer their services on the construction.

"If I can't hang the sons of bitches myself," Limber Jim growled, "I can at least work on the scaffold their miserable carcasses are going to hang from."

As the sun rose higher, prisoners by the hundreds began moving down to watch the scaffold being built. Many offered to help because they, like Limber Jim, wanted to have some small hand in the final accounting of those men who had been responsible for so much of the misery they had suffered in here.

Josie was writing:

Today, six men are going to be hanged by the neck until dead. That was the verdict reached by the special court we held yesterday. The six men are guilty, of that I have no doubt. And justice should, indeed, be served.

But I cannot keep my mind from returning to something Mr. Hopkins, their lawyer, said in their defense. He said that these men became what they are because they are in here. Of course, that is countered by the fact that there are many more of us in here who did not become that way than there are those who did. Nevertheless, the fact remains that their behavior, and their guilt, are a direct result of the brutality of Andersonville Prison.

Many of my fellow prisoners celebrated the verdict when it was handed down yesterday, and they are still celebrating this morning. No doubt, they will continue to celebrate right up until the trap door is sprung and six human beings are hurled into eternity. And though I can find peace of mind with the fact that justice is being served, I find no joy in the death of six of my fellow prisoners.

It's funny. For a while I thought the Raiders were the strongest. I realize now that they are, and always have been, the weakest.

By nine o'clock the scaffold was completed; and when, to test it, a timber was put into place under the trapdoor, then knocked loose, the prisoners cheered mightily.

"Hey, Collins! Watch that first step!" someone shouted. "It's a long one!"

Although Collins was not there to appreciate the joke, the

prisoners within hearing of that piece of black humor laughed uproariously.

There were, of course, hundreds, perhaps thousands, of prisoners in the camp who were not part of the celebration. A significant number of them, whose lives had never been touched by any of the Raiders, didn't have the sense of visceral hatred for them. None of them attempted to take up for the Raiders, nor did they try to change the verdict or the sentence. It was just that they had absolutely no personal interest in it.

There were also those who were closer to death than to life. They lay in ragged shebangs on the far side of the prison camp, or in the open alongside the Swamp, or near the Deadline. Some were so weak that their clothes had already been stolen from them, and they lay nude and dying on the ground. Death was but minutes or, at the very most, hours away for them, and their senses had already ceased to operate. The sun beat down on them, but they didn't know it. Their tongues swelled with thirst, but they were not aware. Flies, gnats, and ants crawled over their suppurating sores, and in and out of every opening of their blistered, nude bodies, but they did not feel them. They were, perhaps, the lucky ones.

Others, though dying, too, were not quite as close to death, and could still feel the gnawing hunger, the burning thirst, and the pain of unprotected bodies exposed to the elements. Their suffering was such that there was no room in their fevered minds for anything except the misery of their own condition. They were totally unaware that this day justice would be done to six men who had victimized many of them.

And then there were those who had not advanced so far in their deliriums as to be unaware of what was going on around them. They knew that six men were being hanged today, and some of them secretly envied the Raiders their quick exit from this misery.

But the prisoners who were gathered for the hanging either didn't know, or didn't care, about this pitiful part of their society. They cared only that six evil men were about to pay the supreme price for their brutality. They were here to watch the show.

Josie, McSpadden, Blackburn, and the others had taken a position close enough to the scaffold to see what was going on. The Massachusetts and Pennsylvania men were much more solemn than most of the others.

It was as Josie told Sergeant McSpadden: "I don't believe that the death of any man should be cause for a celebration."

News of the upcoming hanging had spread to the civilians in and around the town of Andersonville, and they, too, had come to watch the spectacle. They gathered by the hundreds on the side of a hill so that they could look over the top of the palisade, into the prison ground, at the completed gallows. All the guards and the reserves lined the parapets, not only from curiosity but also for security; Wirz was concerned that the prisoners might use the hanging as a diversion for a mass breakout attempt.

"If only the prisoners knew how vulnerable we really are," Wirz had told Barrett on several occasions. "Think about it. Over thirty thousand of them, a few hundred only of us, and that few hundred poorly armed boys and old men."

Barrett listened to Wirz express his fears, but said nothing. He could have told Wirz that less than one-third of the prisoners would be able to stay on their feet long enough for any kind of escape attempt. As far as Barrett was concerned, they were following the best security policy there could possibly be right now. They were keeping the prisoners weak and sick from malnourishment and dehydration.

Nevertheless, Wirz made no complaint about the extra soldiers who had found places from which to watch the hanging. He asked only that they be certain that the civilians be kept back, out of the line of fire directly in front of the cannon.

"If the damn Yankees want to try something today, I will open up on them with cannon," Wirz said. "So many of them together in one place, I think very effective the cannon fire will be."

One of the prisoners walked over to the Deadline, then called up to the guard nearest the gate.

"Hey, you! Reb guard! Where at's Cap'n Wirz? Is he bringin' them prisoners in yet, or what?"

The guard looked behind him, then turned back toward the prison yard.

"He's a-comin' with 'em now."

"They're a-comin' in, boys!" the prisoner shouted to the others. "Cap'n Wirz is a-bringin' 'em in now!"

There was a general shifting of the crowd as people turned toward the gate, anxious for their first look at the condemned men.

The gate opened, and the prisoners, their hands bound behind them and walking between a double line of guards, came through. They had spent their time, since the sentencing, locked in the stocks. They were showing the effects of their treatment.

Captain Wirz came in, dressed in white and mounted on a white horse.

"And I looked, and behold a pale horse: and his name that sat on him was Death, and Hell followed with him," Tyce said quietly.

"What's that?" Billy asked. "Is that something from the Bible?"

"The Book of Revelations, chapter six, verse eight," Tyce said. Those near him stared, shocked that he was able to quote chapter and verse of the Bible.

"How'd you know that?" Billy asked.

"Once studied it."

"Thought you didn't believe, Tyce," Blackburn said in surprise.

"I didn't. Now I do."

Josie studied Tyce. The change in the young man over the last several days had been dramatic. No longer moody and belligerent, he had actually been helping people. Tyce, helping others—that was proof to Josie, if he needed it, that miracles did happen.

The group of guards and the condemned men moved to the center of an open square formed by the prisoners standing around the gallows. Once in the square, they halted.

For a moment there was absolute silence as the spectators, prisoners, guards, and civilians looked into the men's faces and tried to imagine what each one must be thinking in these, their last few moments on earth.

Wirz did not dismount, but put his good hand on the saddle pommel and leaned forward. He looked directly at Josie, McSpadden, and Blackburn.

"Prisoners, I return these men to you as good as I got them. You have tried them yourselves, and guilty you have found them. Nothing have I had to do with it. Of everything connected with them, I wash my hands. Do with them as you like, and may God have mercy on you, and on them."

The condemned men looked at Wirz anxiously, as if pleading with him not to release them to the prisoners. Wirz ignored them.

"Squad, about face!" Wirz said to his guards. "Forward march!"

The armed detail flanking Wirz marched out of the prison, leaving the six condemned men standing behind them.

The six looked around, their eyes darting like the eyes of trapped animals. They looked into the faces of the thousands of prisoners there for the execution, trying to find some among them who might offer some compassion. Then they looked at the scaffold, standing stark against the blue sky. Six nooses dangled from the cross beam.

Seeing the nooses, Curtis gasped. "My God, men! You don't mean to really hang us up there?"

Samson nodded. "That seems to be about the size of it."

Suddenly Munn, then Curtis, then one of the others, bolted toward the gate.

"Stop 'em!" Limber Jim shouted, and scores of prisoners swarmed after them. They were caught quickly and easily, then dragged back to the shadow of the gallows.

"No!" Munn screamed. "No! You can't do this! It ain't right! We're good Union men just like you! We been prisoners in here, just like you!"

"Please!" Curtis screamed. "Have mercy on us! I beg of you!"

"Help! Someone out there, help us! You can't do this! It ain't right!"

As Collins watched and listened to his fellow prisoners, the expression of disgust on his face deepened. He made it a point to stand tall, bold, and unflinching.

"Don't you want to run, too, Collins?" someone jeered from the crowd.

"Go to hell," Collins snapped back.

"Funny you should say that, seein' as that's where you'll be findin' yourself in just a few minutes."

"Give me a week and I'll be runnin' things in hell just the way I ran things in here," Collins boasted. He smiled at his tormentors. "And I'll have the place all nice and ready for you boys when you get there," he added with a demented laugh.

"Let's go, boys," Limber Jim said, prodding them into motion. "Up the steps."

"No, for God's sake! You can't do this!" Munn shouted.

"We're from New York, f'God's sake. Look at what you're doin'!" Curtis added.

"Please, fellas, please. Spare our lives!" one of the others pleaded.

"There's nothing to worry about!" Collins yelled, shouting so loud that it quieted everyone else. "Keep your peckers up, boys! We'll have no weakness here! What the hell? Did you boys think you were goin' to live forever?"

"Get 'em up there!" someone shouted, obviously irritated that Collins wasn't showing more fear. "Shut him up!"

"Yeah! The son of a bitch won't be talking when his neck's stretched!"

A chant began. At first it was only a few voices down front, then it was picked up by more voices and more still, until the entire prison reverberated:

"Hang 'em!"

"Hang 'em!"

"Hang 'em!"

The six condemned men passed Josie, McSpadden, Blackburn, Benton, and Tobias, none of whom were chanting. Josie looked into the faces of each man, then looked away. Of the Massachusetts and Pennsylvania groups, only Tyce seemed to be participating in the deathwatch. He was walking with the condemned toward the gallows.

In view of the recent changes in Tyce's personality, Josie found that unusual, and a bit disturbing. Did it mean he was reverting to his old self?

Mad Matthew jumped out of the crowd in front of the six manacled men, and began dancing and clowning. Many in the crowd, especially those who did not know him, laughed. Josie reached out and gently took Matthew by the arm.

"You don't want to do that, Matthew."

"Oh? I don't?"

"You don't."

"All right. If you say so, Josie." Mad Matthew stopped his dancing and stepped back into the crowd, standing alongside Josie.

The route the prisoners were taking to the gallows was a circuitous one, designed to let as many of the prisoners get a close look at the condemned as might want to. They were led down to the Swamp, then up the hill, then through several of the closer shebangs so that some of those who were too weak to attend the hanging could participate. Then they were taken over to the Deadline, as if to allow the guards and civilians a close look, and finally they were turned toward the gallows.

All the while, they were subjected to the verbal abuse of those who were waiting to see justice fulfilled, and all the while, Tyce was walking alongside them, matching them stride for stride.

"Say your prayers, boys!" someone shouted to them.

"If you know any!" another added.

"What you reckon they'll have for supper in hell?" someone called.

"Whatever it is, it's prob'ly better than here," another answered. Again the camp reverberated with laughter.

"Not so brave this mornin', are you, boys?"

"Hang 'em!"

"Hang 'em!"

"Hang 'em!"

Josie looked at some of the chanting men, and at the hate reflected in their faces. He wondered if, years from now, they would recall these moments in shame.

"Hang 'em!"

"Hang 'em!"

"Hang 'em!"

Samson was one of those yelling the loudest. So was 2nd Wisconsin.

"Up the steps with you now," Limber Jim said.

The six moved up onto the gallows. Tyce walked up with them. Then, to the shock of Josie and everyone else who knew him, Tyce raised his hand and made the sign of the cross.

"Kyrie eleison.

"Christe eleison.

"Kyrie eleison."

Then, speaking loud enough to be heard, not only by

the condemned but also by the first few rows, he began saying the prayer for those who are to be executed.

"Oh God, who declarest Thy almighty power chiefly in showing mercy and pity: We beseech Thee to have mercy upon these Thy servants, who for their transgressions are appointed to die. That they may take Thy judgments patiently, and repent them truly of their sins; that they, recovering Thy favor, the fearful reward of their actions may end with this life; and whensoever their souls shall depart from the body, they will be without spot presented unto Thee. Through Jesus Christ our Lord. Amen."

"My God, Josie," McSpadden gasped. "Is Tyce a priest?"

"I don't know," Josie said, shaking his head at the wonder of it all. "I truly don't know."

Limber Jim and Samson had also climbed the steps, and had put themselves in charge of the blindfolds and ropes. Limber Jim put hoods, made of meal sacks, over each man's head. Samson followed Limber Jim, putting the nooses around their necks, starting with Curtis.

"No, God, please!" Curtis whimpered.

Then on to Munn. "God in heaven, boys, you're not really going to go through with this," Munn whimpered.

Then Collins. Collins was grinning broadly, defiantly, as Limber Jim approached him.

"Let's get this done right, now, Jim," Collins said brightly. "Don't mess it up."

"Don't you worry about that."

Next was Delaney, then Sarsfield, and finally Rickson. Then all the men were hooded, and all the ropes were in place.

"You've a few minutes now," Limber Jim said. "Make your peace."

"Get it over with," Collins growled. "Don't take all day about it."

Josie watched in continued awe and surprise as Tyce moved the length of the gallows, stopping by each condemned man and speaking so quietly that what passed between them was known only to them and to God. Everyone responded to him except Collins, who so pointedly turned his head away that the movement could be seen, even under the hood.

Finally Tyce stepped to the rear of the platform. Once again he raised his hand and made the sign of the cross.

"Holy Mary, Mother of God, pray for us sinners, now and at the hour of our death. Amen." Tyce turned and walked down the thirteen steps.

Now only the six remained up there, standing in clear view of tens of thousands of onlookers. Josie could hear one of them repeating Tyce's last prayer, but, muffled as the voice was by the hood, he didn't know which one it was.

"Holy Mary, Mother of God, pray for us sinners, now and at the hour of our death."

Josie could see that the legs of one of them were shaking. As he looked closer, he realized that it was Munn. He got a quick image of Munn's face, spread in the fixed grin he always wore as he greeted all the new arrivals. *"Hey, fresh fish!"*

"Holy Mary, Mother of God, pray for us sinners, now and at the hour of our death."

By now the chanting of the crowd had stopped, and a great stillness moved over the camp. The sun was nearly straight overhead, and Josie could feel it warming his skin. He wondered if the six men on the scaffold could feel the sun as he did. Were they aware that they would never feel the sun again? Were they frightened? Resigned?

"Holy Mary, Mother of God, pray for us sinners, now and at the hour of our death."

A crow called from the distant woods, the same woods Josie and McSpadden had run through when they tried to escape.

"Holy Mary, Mother of God, pray for us sinners, now and at the hour of our death."

In the towers, on the parapets, and at various vantage points along the wall, Confederate guards and Andersonville civilians watched, transfixed by the drama being played out in front of them.

Josie looked for Lieutenant Barrett. He was leaning against the wall of the nearest turkey roost, his arms folded across his chest. Barrett was just a few feet from, and slightly above, the gallows, and thus had an excellent view. In fact, the only ones with a better perspective were the ones who were getting hanged.

"Holy Mary, Mother of God, pray for us sinners, now and at the hour of our death."

Then realizing that he didn't want to watch the actual hanging, Josie looked away. Finding the distant crow, he watched it circle high in the bright blue sky, concentrating hard on that bird.

On the scaffold, Willie Collins waited. Let the others whimper and whine. By God, he wasn't going to give these bastards the satisfaction.

"Willie, if ever anyone was born to hang, it was you," his mother used to tell him.

Under his hood, Willie laughed.

"You're laughing?" Munn asked, his voice breaking in fear. "You're laughing? What are you laughing at, you son of a bitch?" It was the first time in his life that Munn had ever been anything but totally obsequious to Willie Collins.

"I'm laughing at something my mother said," Collins replied. "Turns out the old bitch was right after all."

Below him, Collins heard Limber Jim and Samson get into position at each end of the board upon which the six men were standing. The board was held in place by two four-by-four timber supports, one at each end. Limber Jim took hold of one of the supports, and Samson took the other.

"Holy Mary, Mother of God, pray for us sinners, now and at the hour of our death."

A long moment of silence followed. There was nothing now between Collins and eternity but the removal of those support timbers. It would be but a brief moment for those watching, but for Willie Collins and the others with him, it would be a lifetime. He used it to fix upon his mind the vision of himself holding court with the Raiders, so that if any impression survived this transition, it would be one of him in control.

"Holy Mary, Mother of God, pray . . ."

The support timbers were yanked out, and the board fell away. Collins fell . . . stopped . . . then fell again, hitting the ground hard. The rope broke!

"Shit!" someone said. "What happened?"

Quickly, Limber Jim ran over to Collins and jerked the hood off, then pulled him to his feet. Collins looked up and saw the other five hanging, slowly twisting, from the scaffold.

"I'm alive!" Collins said.

"Not for long," Limber Jim growled. "You're going back up there."

"No!" Collins said, now losing the bravado that had served him so well. "No! Don't you see? It's a message from God! I'm not supposed to die! God doesn't want me to die!"

"God had nothing to do with it," Samson said, looking at the rope. "It was the cheap Confederate rope."

Protesting every step of the way, his courage and self-control completely gone, Collins was herded back up the thirteen steps, then put on the trapdoor that had been repositioned. Once again a rope was placed around his neck.

"No!" Collins shouted. "Don't you see? I'm not supposed to . . . ."

The trapdoor fell open, and for the second time in less than five minutes, Collins made the plunge. This time the rope held, and he felt a sharp pain, like a blow to the back of his neck and head.

In the prison yard there was absolute silence, except for the creaking of the ropes as the six bodies twisted slowly.

Chapter 17

"John. John, wake up," Goober said, shaking Gleason gently. "We're here."

It was dark, but already there was activity alongside the track as the soldiers began climbing down, and the artillery and equipment was being off-loaded.

"Where is *here*?" John asked.

"Way I hear it, we're just south of Resaca."

"Men," someone's voice called from the darkness, "gather round. General Bate is going to say a few words to us."

"Come on," Goober said, taking Gleason by the arm. "Let's see what the old buzzard has to say."

Gleason's first thought was to hang back, then find an opportunity to slip away. But upon further consideration, he decided that it might be wise to find out what was going on. Not only would it help him find his own lines, but it might also provide some helpful information for General Sherman, once he did return. He moved through the darkness with Goober and the others.

General Bate was standing on a little rise, his arms folded across his chest. A lantern gleamed from a rock just beside him, so that he was fully visible in the little circle of light. He had a full, rather long beard that he pulled at nervously as he waited for all the men to get into position to hear him speak.

"Boys," he said, "we've fought long and hard during these past four years. We've buried many of our brothers, often in battles that later proved to be of no real consequence. So when the opportunity arises to strike a blow against the enemy that will have some real effect, then we should seize it without fail.

"We now have such an opportunity. As you know, Sherman has surrounded Atlanta. What we do here in the next few days might well provide some relief for the women and children of that city."

"General, how many Yankees we goin' to fight this time?" someone asked.

"I won't lie to you, boys. Looks like there may be as many as fifteen to twenty thousand in front of us." General Bate smiled broadly. "But there are five thousand of us, and seeing as one Southerner is worth ten Yankees, I'd say that puts the odds in our favor, wouldn't you?"

"Yeeehaaaa!" someone shouted, and that shout was immediately picked up by the others. It was the first time Gleason had heard the Rebel yell from inside the ranks.

"All right, boys, get back to your companies now. Listen to your officers and sergeants, do your duty as I know you can, and pray to the Lord for a victory."

"Yeeehaaaa!" the men shouted again.

They started moving up and down the track to find others from their own companies, so as to be able to form into units.

"I'll see you later, Goober," Gleason said. "Good luck to you."

"Yeah, to you too. Hey, what company's your'n, anyway?"

Gleason was stuck for a moment, then he remembered that he had told Goober he arrived with Major Lewis.

"Don't really have a company. I'm a courier for Major Lewis."

"Hey, that's great! You can come with us."

"Better not. Best get back in case the major needs me."

"Too late now," one of the other men said.

"What do you mean?"

"Major Lewis stayed back in Allatoona. Surprised you didn't know that."

"Well, then, guess that means you can stay with us," Goober said. "Come on, I'll introduce you to the rest of the boys."

With no opportunity to slip away, Gleason had to go with Goober. A few minutes later, he was standing with the other men of Goober's company, listening to the captain explain what they were going to do.

"We're leavin' the track here," Captain Ellis told them. "And we're goin' that way"—he pointed—"due east for three or four miles. Then we'll go north for five miles, then we'll come back in this direction. According to our spies, all the Yankees up there is facin' the railroad. They won't be expectin' anyone to come up on 'em from the rear, and if we're lucky, most of their fortifications will be facin' in the other direction, too."

"Them Yankees won't know what hit 'em," someone said.

"Feel sorry for them poor boys, only outnumberin' us three to one. Don't hardly seem like a fair fight."

"Gleason," the captain said.

"Yes, sir?"

"I understand you just joined us?"

"Yes, sir."

"Don't have time to find a place for you now, so I'm goin' to have you stick with Goober. He's been in his share of fights. Reckon he'll get you through this one all right. Don't like to lose anyone their first time out."

"Yes, sir."

"All right, boys, keep your muskets on half cock. Don't want none of 'em to go off by accident while we're on our way. Let's go."

The company started east. Gleason looked around at the other men, heard them crack the same jokes and register the same complaints he had heard many times before.

"Dear God," he prayed, "I've gotten myself into some kind of a fix here. Please help me find a way out of it."

In the hills near Resaca:

The night passed slowly, almost reluctantly. When the darkness lifted, the morning sunlight revealed an army of gray spread out in a long line stretching from the top of one hill, down the slope, across a rather narrow valley, then up the opposite slope to the top of the next hill.

Gleason had thought to slip out during the night but had decided against it, thinking that nervous pickets from either side might not give him an opportunity to explain what was going on. It would be much better to cross over in the light of day. That way, the Union soldiers could see that he represented no threat to them as he approached their lines.

"You scared, John?" Goober asked.

"A little."

"Me, too. I know that when your time's up, it's up. But seems to me like the more times you do this, the more chances you have of gettin' yourself kilt. And I've been sorta of hopin' I could get through all this without gettin' myself kilt." Goober took a chew of tobacco, then handed the twist to Gleason. "Want a chaw?"

"Thanks." Gleason took a chew, then handed it back. The

266

tobacco made him dizzy—it was the first time he had used it in nearly two years.

"All right, listen to me, men," a senior officer said, marching back and forth behind the line. "When you aim, aim low. You don't do any good by discharging your weapons into the trees."

"And you green 'uns, be sure'n prime the pan," one veteran called. The other veterans guffawed. Gleason laughed, too, for he had seen the same thing happen when, in the heat of battle and pitch of excitement, a soldier poured in powder, wad, and ball, then snapped the trigger uselessly against a firing pan that was not primed, and thus would not discharge.

"Don't be afraid," the senior officer went on. "Just keep in mind that you're defending your homes, your families, and your sweethearts. There's no army in the world that can prevail against you when you have truth, right, justice, and God on your side."

Gleason was beginning to get anxious. When, and where, would he get the opportunity to leave? He wasn't the only one growing restless, however. All up and down the line, the soldiers were beginning to get nervous.

"Why don't we attack?" someone asked. "We been in line since before sunup."

"We're supposed to attack at eight o'clock," another said. "I heard the officers talkin' about it."

"Eight o'clock? It's nearly that now."

The rumor about attacking at eight spread through the line. As the seconds ticked off toward eight, nervous hands began to squeeze the muskets, and itching fingers started to caress the triggers, waiting for the word to move out.

Eight o'clock came and went, and no orders were issued.

"Why doesn't it come?" the soldiers asked over and over again. "Don't them damn generals know the hardest thing is the waitin'?"

"Yeah," another would answer. And then, as if he had

made the observation for the first time: "Don't they know that the hardest part is the waitin'?"

Slowly, relentlessly, the sun climbed higher in the sky. Still, the long gray lines waited, and now it was nearly nine. No order to attack came, and no opportunity to escape presented itself.

Word came down the line that they had delayed the attack until the artillery was in position. As soon as the guns were brought up, they would begin.

Shortly afterward, Gleason heard the thunder of cannon fire. However it wasn't Rebel cannon fire; it was coming from the Union lines.

"Boys, the Yankees have discovered us!" one of the officers shouted. "We can't wait. Form up! We're going across!"

"Form up! Form up!"

"Come on, John, you can come with me," Goober called.

By now the artillery shells were coming in from Federal guns, rushing through the air with a whistling sound, then bursting loudly in the trees just behind them.

The officer who had been pacing up and down all morning now moved to the front and, drawing his saber, signaled the men to move forward. Flag and guidon joined him, and the gray army started down the sides of the hills, toward the Federal positions, two thousand yards away.

Gleason had never participated in a massive frontal attack before, but he had been on the receiving end of Rebel attacks against his position. And though it was frightening to see a wave of gray coming inexorably forward, he had thought then how much more difficult it must be to be one of the attackers than one of the attacked. The attackers were exposed for the entire way, whereas the defenders had the protection of their earthenwork fortifications.

Now, not only was Gleason one of the attackers, he was participating in an attack as a Rebel! He knew that there was every possibility he would be killed by his own men before he could get away.

The first thousand yards was traversed with little difficulty, the bursting artillery fire now far behind them.

They covered another five hundred yards before the Union gunners found the range, and started dropping artillery fire on them. Now it became more frightening, for the shells were coming close enough that he could hear the whine of the pieces of shrapnel from the bursting shells.

"Guide on the center, boys. Guide on . . ." That was as far as their captain got before he was cut down by a cannonball. Quickly a young lieutenant hurried forward to take the captain's position.

"Guide on the center, boys!" the lieutenant shouted without missing a beat. "Keep the lines straight!"

The air overhead was rent with the screech and scream of cannonballs and mortar shells, now going in both directions as the Rebel guns opened fire.

Federal shells were exploding within the ranks of the attackers, and Rebel artillerymen had found the range for the defenders, some five hundred yards ahead. Gleason realized that the one advantage the attackers did have was that once the artillery found its range, it would not have to be reaimed, for, unlike the attackers, the defenders' position was stationary.

They had come more than three-quarters of the way across the open meadow and were close enough now for John to clearly see not only the United States flag but also the guidons and flags of the various Union regiments. After another hundred yards, individual soldiers began to emerge from the solid mass of blue.

"Watch yourselves, boys, watch yourselves," the lieutenant called. "We're coming into musket range."

As if to illustrate the lieutenant's point, there was a massive, rippling flash of light, followed by a billowing cloud of smoke, all up and down the Federal lines. The order had obviously been given to fire in volley. That volley had a devastating effect, for dozens of men on either side of him went down, including Gordie, the man who could make a feast of possum and poke.

"Hold your fire, men! Hold your fire!" the lieutenant called.

They closed to within two hundred yards of the Federal breastworks, and a second volley loosed by the Union soldiers had as terrible an effect on the Confederates as the first. Gleason looked up and down the Rebel line. Though they had not yet fired a shot, one-third of their number had been taken out by enemy fire.

When they reached one hundred yards, the order was given to halt.

"First rank, kneel!" the regimental commander ordered, and the company commanders issued the supplemental orders. Half the long gray line dropped to one knee.

"By volley . . . ," the regimental commander shouted. That was as far as he got, for he was cut down by musket fire from the Federal lines.

"Fire!" a Rebel captain shouted, picking up the order and hurrying out front to take command.

Those who had knelt, fired. Staring through the billow of smoke, Gleason could see that the Rebel volley had been effective, for several Union soldiers fell.

The rank that had just fired now began reloading as the second rank continued forward. Gleason and Goober were in the second rank, and they moved until they were only fifty yards from the Federal lines. A bullet took off Gleason's hat, and another clipped his earlobe. Then Goober was hit in the side. The force of the bullet spun him around, causing him to drop his weapon.

"Second rank, kneel, fire!"

This was the rank Gleason was in, and though he knelt, he didn't fire. Instead, he looked at Goober, who was still standing upright, holding his hand over his side. He was staring, surprised, at the blood spilling through his fingers.

Suddenly all the Union troops in front of them lay on the ground, and Gleason saw that the Federal cannons had been moved into the line to fire in a flat trajectory. He knew what that meant.

"Goober, get down!" he called. Dropping his own weapon, he lunged toward Goober, knocking him down.

"What the hell are you do . . . ?" Goober was interrupted by the deep-throated roar of a dozen artillery pieces firing as one.

The Union volley consisted of grape, canister, and double-shot cannon, and its effect was terrible. Fully half of the attackers who were standing when the volley was loosed were cut down. Now less than one-third of the original attacking force remained.

The Union losses had been minimal, and the troops were in well-entrenched positions. Gleason knew that to continue the attack would be suicide. Mercifully, the Rebel commanders in the field realized it as well, for they ordered a general retreat.

"We're goin' back," Goober said. "The sons of bitches have beaten us."

"You're out of here," Gleason said, trying to pick him up.

Goober stood up, then staggered and fell. "Can't make it. Can't walk that far. You go without me."

It had not been Gleason's intention to go back. Now that he was this close to his own lines, his plan was to hold up his hands in surrender, then go toward the Union lines.

"Go on," Goober said. "Don't stay back here an' get caught 'cause of me."

Gleason looked toward the retreating Rebels and saw that they had already covered several hundred yards. There was no way Goober would be able to catch up with them. Mercifully, the Union soldiers were now cheering their victory rather than firing on the retreating army.

Gleason sat down on the ground beside Goober.

"What're you doin'? I told you to go on," Goober said. "You can still make it. They ain't shootin' now."

"I'm not going anywhere, Goober," Gleason said. He took off his tunic and tossed it aside, then reached into his haversack and pulled out his blue coat and began to put it on.

"What're you doin'?" Goober asked. "You're crazy. They'll never believe that."

"Yes, they will believe it," Gleason said quietly, "because it's true. I really am a Yankee."

Goober's face registered surprise, then anger. "You mean you're a goddamned spy?" He tried to get to his rifle, but Gleason picked it up, then tossed it away.

"Goober, it's not like that. I'm not a spy."

"Then what the hell were you doin' in our lines?"

"I'm an escaped prisoner of war. From Andersonville."

Almost as suddenly as it appeared, the anger left Goober's face, replaced by an expression of awe. "You was in Andersonville?"

Gleason nodded.

"Heard it was hell." Goober's face was washed with pain, and he had to close his eyes and bite his lips to keep from calling out. He took several deep breaths, then opened his eyes again. He took Gleason's hand in his, and squeezed hard. "Glad you escaped from there."

By now soldiers from the Union lines were coming out from behind their works to investigate the Rebels who were left behind, separating the wounded from the dead. Seeing them, Gleason stood up and beckoned to two of them.

"We need a medical orderly over here."

"You let us worry about the medical orderly, Reb," a private said, covering them with his musket.

"I'm not a Rebel. My name is Sergeant John Gleason. I escaped from Andersonville Prison, and I would like to be taken to see General Sherman."

Startled, the private turned to his corporal, who was close enough to hear what Gleason said.

"What should I do, Corporal?"

"Do what the sergeant says. Get a medical orderly for the Reb. Sergeant, you come with me. I'll take you to the Cap'n. If you can convince him you are who you say you are, why I reckon he can get you through to see Uncle Billy."

Andersonville Prison:

It started raining before dawn, and was still raining far into the day. It wasn't a thunderous downpour, but a steady rain that turned the camp into a quagmire. It poured through the shebangs and drenched the men, who had no way to get out of it and no way to find some dry warmth.

The main gate opened, and a new batch of Union prisoners was brought in under guard. Only a few days removed from the battlefield, these men were still in top physical condition. When they saw the poor wretches who made up the prison population, they turned white in shock and fear. It was a reaction the old prisoners had seen so many times that they barely noticed it.

Josie and the others from his group were gathered at the Massachusetts and Pennsylvania shebangs. They were miserable in the cold rain, and dirtier, more emaciated, and more bug-infested than ever.

Second Wisconsin and Tyce were sitting together, shivering and in rags. They looked toward the main gate and at the batch of new prisoners.

"Fresh fish," 2nd Wisconsin said. "Lots of 'em. Means Uncle Billy's army is close by. We could be rescued soon."

"Don't get your hopes too high," Tyce cautioned. "Rebs have to keep ferryin' new boys in, just to keep the population even. So many of us are dyin' in here."

A few feet from Tyce and 2nd Wisconsin, Josie was trying to help Martin Blackburn drink. Blackburn was shivering so hard that he was nearly in convulsions, and he trembled violently as Josie held the battered cup to his lips.

"D-d-don't w-w-want it," he stammered, pushing it away.

"It's rainwater, Martin. It'll be good for you," Josie said, holding the cup to his lips again. "Try."

At Josie's urging, Blackburn tried to drink, but he couldn't keep it down. He began coughing, and regurgitated the water. Then he reached into his mouth, tugged on a tooth, pulled it out, looked at it for a moment, then threw it away.

"S-s-scurvy," Blackburn said. He ran his fingers around inside his mouth, feeling his gums. "My gums are all rotten now. C-c-can't even chew the mush anymore."

"Try some more water." When Josie held up the cup, Blackburn shook his head and waved it away.

"I miss Thomas," he said after a moment or two. "D-d-don't you?"

"Yes." Josie put the cup down. "Sergeant McSpadden and I were talking about him just this morning."

"Did you know him before the army?"

"No, I didn't, even though we didn't live but ten miles apart. Sergeant McSpadden was saying, for a man so strong, we never saw him use his strength in anger."

Blackburn smiled. "Except to get my banjo back," he said proudly.

Josie returned his smile. "Yes. He would use it for a just cause. He lived on a farm with all his brothers and sisters. He had a big family."

Blackburn was silent for another moment. "I have six children," he said.

"Six? Really? That's a nice-sized family, Martin. You must be very proud of them."

Blackburn nodded. "I am. Had eight, but two d-d-died."

"Come on, Martin. You want to see your children again, don't you? You've got to get some of this good water down."

Once more Blackburn tried to drink the water, and once more it came back up almost as quickly as it went down.

Ten feet from Josie and Blackburn, Tobias and Benton, also filthy, disheveled, and shivering in the rain, were sharing their fantasies as McSpadden was trying to ignore them.

"She'll start us out with some nice, plump chickens from our own stock," Benton was saying.

"Yeah," Tobias said.

"We breed 'em ourselves," Benton added. "Rhode Island reds. They're the best, you know. Tenderest meat you ever ate. She fries 'em . . ." Benton paused for a minute, then held his fingers under his nose and sniffed, as if catching the aroma of frying chicken. "We'll have it with mashed potatoes and gravy."

Tobias shook his head. "I like my mashed potatoes with butter. We make butter in our springhouse. You never had butter like we churn."

"You bring the butter," Benton said. "We'll put it on the biscuits. My mother makes the best biscuits in the world. You just open 'em up. Lift the top off real easy."

"You got honey?" Tobias asked.

"Course we got honey," Benton replied with a snort, as if the answer was too obvious for the question.

"I like honey and butter on my biscuits."

"Honey and butter is good," Benton said. "Like gravy on 'em too."

"What'll we have after?"

"Pie."

"Apple pie?"

Benton nodded. "Apple or cherry. You can take your pick. My mother makes 'em both better'n any you've ever tasted."

Tobias shook his head. "Not apple *or* cherry." He grinned. "Apple *and* cherry."

"I like apple, with a piece of cheese melted on top."

"Yeah, yeah, that's good too."

By now Sergeant McSpadden had heard about as much of it as he could stand. He called to them, "Oh, for God Almighty's sake, you want to drive us all to the lunatic asylum with that kind of talk? Put a plug in it, for the love of . . ."

At that moment a handful of the new prisoners walked by, and McSpadden interrupted his tirade to call to one of them. "Hey, friend, give us the news. Who were you with?"

A corporal answered. "I was with the 10th Kentucky. So was he." He pointed to one of the others. "These two were with the 17th Maine."

"Seventeenth Maine? You don't say! I'm a sergeant in the 19th Massachusetts. Nice to see some more New England boys. Where were you?"

"Well, we were with Uncle Billy Sherman here in Georgia," the 10th Kentucky corporal answered.

"And we were with Grant in Virginia," the 17th Maine corporal added.

"Yeah. All over Virginia," said one of the privates from the 17th Maine.

"Makin' it warm for 'em, were ya?" McSpadden asked.

"Warm? Warm? We burned Atlanta to the ground! That warm enough for you?" The Kentucky corporal laughed. "Now we're headin' to Savannah, and we'll give them some of the same, you can bet."

None of the older prisoners had known that, and they nodded happily to each other. That had to mean that the Rebels were on their last legs.

"Tell us more," McSpadden said.

"Well, sir, we're movin' through Reb country pretty good now," one of the new prisoners said. He was looking around, and growing visibly sicker with each new sight.

"This is Andersonville, huh?" one of the Maine privates asked. "Is it as bad as they say?"

"Nope," 2nd Wisconsin replied. All the old prisoners looked at him, waiting for the joke. "It's worse!" He and the rest of the old prisoners laughed.

"You boys want to stay with us?" Tyce asked.

The Kentucky corporal looked around at his friends.

They nodded. The corporal turned to McSpadden and the others. "Is it all right with you?"

"Sure," McSpadden said.

The Kentucky corporal nodded. "Don't see why not, then."

"You boys hear anything about an exchange?" Benton asked.

"Won't be any exchange, and that's a fact," the Kentucky corporal said.

It was a definite statement, and the old prisoners looked at each other in shock and despair.

"You seem awful sure of yourself," 2nd Wisconsin growled.

The Kentucky corporal's face showed instant anger at being challenged.

Josie laughed.

"What the hell're you laughin' at?" 2nd Wisconsin asked.

"Look at you, Wisconsin. You're so damned weak you can barely stand," Josie said. He took in the new prisoners with a wave of his hand. "There's not one man among them who couldn't handle you with both hands tied behind his back, yet here you are, damn near challenging them to a fight."

Josie's words disarmed the Kentucky corporal and he laughed; then the others, and finally, reluctantly, even 2nd Wisconsin joined in. "Well, you did seem pretty sure of yourself," he said.

"I should be. I was at Sherman's headquarters the day Grant issued the policy."

"Policy? What policy? We never heard nothin' about a policy," Benton said.

The Kentucky corporal shook his head. He didn't appreciate having his word constantly challenged.

"You fellas seem to have a hard time listenin' to the truth," he growled.

McSpadden held up his hand. "We've been out of touch

a while, friend. That's all. Now, what policy you talkin' about?"

"Well, sir, it seems like any Reb soldiers we let go just bust their paroles and get right back into the line fightin' us ag'in the next week. So Grant's not goin' to do it anymore. He says his only job is to win the war.

"Also, the Rebs are sayin', as part of an exchange, they wouldn't send back our colored soldiers. Grant says they're part of us, and without 'em there's no deal."

"Colored soldiers?" 2nd Wisconsin erupted in a fury. "We're supposed to die in here for colored soldiers?"

"Yeah, what kind of policy is that?" Benton asked. "The folks back home know that?"

"What do you say, Josie?" Tobias asked.

"I say good for Ulysses S. Grant." Some of the others nodded in agreement.

"Damn right," someone said.

"Well, I don't like it!" 2nd Wisconsin growled. "Does Grant know what it's like in here?"

The Kentucky corporal nodded. "He does for a fact. Someone who got out told General Sherman, and Sherman told Grant."

There was a sharp inhalation of breath among all the old prisoners, and they looked at each other.

"Really? Someone got out?"

"Yep."

"Who?"

"Yes, who got out? Who could it be?"

McSpadden looked over at Wisnovsky, who was so excited that he could scarcely breathe. He cocked his head sharply, anxious to hear more.

"His name, man? What was his name?" Benton demanded.

The Kentucky corporal shook his head. "Sorry, don't remember the name exactly." He looked toward the other Kentucky men. "Any of you boys remember?" The other Kentucky prisoners shook their heads.

278

"Tell you this, though, he had a hell of a story to tell," one of them said. "Know how he reached our lines? He jumped onto a Reb train and rode north with them, then, when they attacked us, he come across the field with 'em and walked right into our lines. He had a hell of a lot more guts than he did sense, if you ask me."

"Well, what'd he look like?" Tobias asked.

"He was sorta tall. Thin. Hair has some yellow in it. Older'n me, I reckon."

The description fit Gleason, and the Pennsylvania and Massachusetts groups, who had already been through so much together, prayed now that it was true.

"Could his name have been Gleason?" Benton asked hopefully.

The Kentucky corporal hit his fist into the palm of his hand. "Yeah, Gleason, that's it. Sergeant John Gleason. Coal miner fella, from Pennyslvania, he told Uncle Billy."

"Sherman! John got through to Billy Sherman!" Josie shouted.

"He made it! He made it!" Tobias screamed.

All the men of the Massachusetts group stood up then, even Blackburn, and they began laughing and crying, and dancing, and hugging each other in the rain.

"What is it?" someone called from the neighboring shebangs.

"Sergeant Gleason!" Benton answered. "He made it! He made it all the way back to General Sherman!"

"Gleason made it?"

"Yes!"

"Gleason made it! John Gleason made it," the neighboring shebangs called, passing the word to the next group, and the next, and the next, until nearly everyone in the prison was aware that John Gleason, one of their very own, had defied all the odds and escaped from Andersonville Prison.

McSpadden, moved even more than the others, went over to Wisnovsky. Shaking his head in silent wonder, he put his hand on Wisnovsky's shoulder. "He did it," McSpadden said, reverently. "By God, he did it!"

"Martin! Martin!" Tobias and Benton shouted, running toward him, carrying his banjo. "Play us some music, Martin! We have to celebrate!"

Both men paused when they saw Martin Blackburn lying on the ground . . . asleep, or unconscious, or dead.

Later the same day:

Josie took out his writing materials and began another letter. He still called them letters, and he still told himself that he was writing them with the intention of trying to mail them. But, in truth, he had long ago given up hope of ever sending any of them out. They had become, therefore, his journal. So far, he had managed to write, if not every day, at least on a regular basis.

> *We know, now, that we are coming to the end of our time here. Wars do end, and there are signs all around us that this war, too, will end someday soon. The rebellion will be crushed and our great cause shall emerge victorious, though until that day, it still will go very hard on the men.*

Josie saw a few prisoners nibbling tiny pieces of dough. Most, however, had nothing, nor did they appear to have any interest in food.

> *The rations have been cut, and cut again, to scarcely four ounces of rough cornmeal . . . including cob and husk, each day. The cob tears a man's bowels all to pieces, and some choose to die rather than eat it. This may be mere meanness on the Rebels' part or, though none of the boys think so, it may simply be that there is*

not enough food for the Rebels to feed themselves and feed us too.

Josie looked toward the guard towers, manned with the very young and the very old. Though not slowly starving to death like most of the Union prisoners, the guards were just barely getting enough to eat. And the tents that provided the guards with their shelter were only marginally better than the shebangs that sheltered the prisoners.

Limber Jim and Patrick passed between Josie and the guards. Patrick was on Limber Jim's shoulder, flailing a stick at low-flying birds, trying to knock one of them out of the sky as Limber Jim staggered around.

Josie laughed. "Would you fellas mind tellin' me just what in the sam hill you're doing?"

"You ever tasted one of these blackbirds?" Patrick asked, swinging again and missing.

"Can't say as I have."

"Taste just like chicken." Another swing and another miss.

"Oh? And you know that because you've eaten so many?"

"You got to keep me up here, Jim," Patrick said, reaching down to grab hold in order not to fall off.

"I'm trying," Limber Jim replied. "But if you don't get one soon, I'm goin' to have to put you down. Not as strong as I once was. Must be gettin' old."

"I never tasted one," Patrick said, answering Josie's question. "But I've talked to them as has."

"Hey, wait a minute, what's going on down there?" Josie suddenly asked.

"What do you mean?"

"Something's going on at the gate," Josie said.

"What is it, more prisoners?"

"No. Something different."

Limber Jim turned toward the gate, and Patrick, giving up his attack on the birds as a lost cause, jumped down.

They saw a flatbed cart, wheeled in by slaves under the direction of Lieutenant Barrett. Captain Wirz and a Confederate colonel came into the compound just inside the gate, and waited for it to be put into position. When it was, Wirz and the colonel climbed onto the cart.

"Now what is all that about, do you suppose?" McSpadden asked.

"Don't know. But it *is* different," Limber Jim said.

Lieutenant Barrett moved alongside the cart, then called out loudly. "You Yankees, you listen now! Colonel O'Niel's got somethin' real important to tell you all. Sergeants, get your men down here double quick."

Josie looked over at McSpadden, who was still weak. "Want me to go down there for you, Sergeant?"

"Nah. God love you, Josie, it's about time I started feeling like a sergeant again. Give me your arm. I can listen to their nonsense well as you can."

Josie helped McSpadden to his feet, and they started toward the cart. Then they saw 2nd Wisconsin lying curled up in the mud. Tobias was sitting next to him.

"You all right, Wisconsin?" McSpadden asked.

"Lost his last two days' rations in that keno game the 33rd New Jersey runs," Tobias explained.

"Those robbers," McSpadden growled.

"My own fault," 2nd Wisconsin moaned.

"Sorry we don't have anything," Josie said. "Won't, till the food cart comes tomorrow."

"Own fault," 2nd Wisconsin repeated.

"C'mon," McSpadden said, "walk with us. Can you?"

Painfully, 2nd Wisconsin struggled to his feet and joined the others, including Martin Blackburn, whose condition was fully as bad as Wisconsin's. Limping, they followed McSpadden and Josie to the cart where Wirz and the Rebel colonel were waiting for them.

Men were coming from all over the prison grounds. Finally, it was the largest single gathering of prisoners since the hanging of the Raiders. The sergeants moved out front, making a military formation of the assembly. Josie was holding Blackburn upright, and Tobias was supporting 2nd Wisconsin.

"What the hell's goin' on here?" someone growled.

"What they bring us here for?"

"Why the hell can't they just let us die in peace?"

"You Yankees," Wirz called out to the men when he was convinced that enough were gathered, "the colonel comes with an important message for all of you." Wirz turned toward the colonel. "Colonel O'Niel," he said, then stepped back.

"You men, you prisoners," O'Niel began, "I want to speak to you about your situation. It must be clear to you now that your government has cruelly abandoned you. As you know, they have turned down all our efforts to exchange you. They know of your suffering, which, though terrible, is no worse than our men are suffering in Northern prisons."

Josie was no longer listening. He had spotted a flock of geese heading south, and he tried to project himself up there with them, high over the prison.

Neither Limber Jim nor young Patrick was listening either. They stood there, biding their time until this was all over and they could go back to their shebangs and be left alone.

"And they know," O'Niel continued, "as we all do, that you have already endured far more than should be expected of anyone. Your government has no more use for you. You are being thrown aside to starve and die. That being so, and with the Southern Confederacy certain to succeed and gain its independence in only a few more months . . . ."

"Fat chance of that happening," Tyce said, rolling his eyes. Most of the others around him were so uninterested that they didn't even react to the statement.

"I make you all this offer," O'Niel continued. "If you will join our army, and if you serve it faithfully to the end, you will receive the same rewards as the rest of our soldiers. You will be taken out of here at once, today, this very minute, clothed and fed, given a good cash bounty, and, at the conclusion of the war, receive a land warrant for a nice farm."

Although no one had been paying attention to Colonel O'Niel when he started, by now everyone was. The men were listening attentively, looking at each other to see if they were hearing what they thought they were hearing.

"That is our offer," O'Niel concluded. "What is your answer?"

For a long moment there was absolute silence, save for the honking of the geese Josie had been watching.

"Colonel, *sir!*" McSpadden said, booming out *sir* in a command voice that had all but disappeared since he'd come in here.

"Yes, Sergeant?"

"Sergeant James Dudley McSpadden, 19th Massachusetts Volunteers, *sir!* I have the honor to speak for my detachment, *sir!*"

Coming to attention, McSpadden called over his shoulder. "First Detachment, attention!"

To a man, the detachment came to attention.

"About face!" McSpadden commanded.

In a precise military maneuver, the men turned, as one, on their heels. Josie did it perfectly. Martin Blackburn stumbled badly, but made it with Josie's help. Tobias helped 2nd Wisconsin, and once more they were soldiers. They were rabble no longer.

"Forward, march!" McSpadden commanded.

They marched back into camp, their heads held high. As they passed in front of the next column where Samson was standing, he called out, "Three cheers for Sergeant McSpadden!"

A mighty roar rose from all those within sound of Samson's voice.

"Hip, hip . . . Hooray!"
"Hip, hip . . . Hooray!"
"Hip, hip . . . Hooray!"

When McSpadden's detachment was clear, the sergeant in charge of the detachment that included Limber Jim and Patrick came to attention. "Second Detachment, attention!" he called.

The ragged, emaciated, dying prisoners came to attention.

"About face!"

As if they were on a parade field in their home town, the soldiers turned proudly, crisply.

"Forward, march!"

The second detachment joined the first in exiting.

The maneuver started by McSpadden was picked up by every sergeant present. Each, in turn, brought his detachment to attention, then marched them away.

Wirz and Colonel O'Niel stood on the cart, watching the impromptu parade in increasing anger. Before their very eyes, thousands of men who this very morning had been dying prisoners, were miraculously reborn as soldiers.

Josie looked into the smiling, proud faces of Billy, Tyce, and Martin Blackburn, of Tobias and Benton, and, most of all, of McSpadden. It had been a long time since Josie had seen that look. McSpadden was limping, battered, and a mere scarecrow of a man. But he was a sergeant again.

Chapter 18

Winter, in Andersonville Prison:

Josie was sitting outside his shebang, blowing on his fingers to keep them from freezing. It was hard work, trying to write on a day like today, but he was convinced that the ritual of writing something every day had kept him alive so far. He blew on his fingers one more time, rubbed them briskly, then resumed writing:

> *I truly thought we would be out of here by now. I had no idea the Rebels would be able to keep the war going, and yet, somehow they do. Why do they continue to fight? They no longer have any hope of winning, nor even of gaining favorable terms to end the war. Surely the Rebel government knows the hardships its people are undergoing.*

Hearing a commotion, Josie looked up. He saw a corpse frozen in a sitting position, a position many in the camp called "the attitude of death." His eyes were open, flat, and dead. The commotion was from a couple of nearly naked prisoners who were fighting for the dead man's shirt and pants. It was ludicrous, Josie thought. They were too weak to fight . . . yet they were doing so.

Martin Blackburn was lying beside Josie, looking up at the dull, slate-gray sky. He was still alive, but only barely. Benton and Tobias were nearby.

About twenty yards away, a dozen scrawny men were running around, obviously chasing something . . . now going here, now there, veering off again until finally they stopped, and someone stamped the ground. That was followed by a loud cheer, then the one who stamped reached down to pick something up. He displayed it to the others, a tiny ball of gray something, dangling from the end of a string.

"Caught 'em a rat," Benton said matter-of-factly.

"Too small," Tobias replied. "Won't feed that whole bunch."

Looking over at Blackburn, Josie saw that his friend was slipping away. He put down the pencil and gently began to rub Blackburn's bare feet, and to breathe on them. Blackburn was too weak to do anything more than blink his thanks.

Picking up his pencil again, Josie resumed his writing:

I have tried to keep my hopes up all these months, but now I know there is no hope. I pray only that whoever finds these letters will take them to you as a keepsake of your son, Josiah Day. You will know I do not mind dying, for I know the Union must be preserved, and one man's life is no great price to pay for so great a cause as that.

But if whoever finds these letters needs to burn them to keep warm . . . then I will have no quarrel with him.

"Main gate's opening," Tobias said.

Josie looked up, then put down his pencil. "Food cart's here, Martin," he said. "I'll bring you something."

Again, Blackburn could only blink in reply.

Josie got up and stumbled the few yards toward the food cart. He saw Limber Jim coming toward him. He was shocked at how much gaunter Limber Jim looked now than even a few weeks ago . . . but he knew he must look just as bad.

"Some of the boys . . ." Limber Jim started, then stopped. Clearly, he was very angry about something. "Some of the boys sneaked out last night. Took the Rebs' offer and joined up with 'em. Walked right out the gate."

Josie knew it was true. Still, he no longer had it in him to be angry. He put a consoling hand on Limber Jim's shoulder. He was about to say something when his attention was diverted by Captain Wirz. On foot, Wirz came in at the head of his guard, then climbed onto the food cart. The prisoners who were coming for their rations gathered around to hear what he had to say.

"So," Wirz said. "Gather 'round. I have good news for you. It will make you very happy. You are being exchanged, starting today."

Josie wasn't sure he heard correctly, and he looked at the others to see if they heard what he thought he had just heard.

"Every one of you, starting right now, this morning. You see? All this time I was right. Go tell the rest. Everyone is exchanged. The train leaves in two hours." Wirz pointed to the gate, which had been left standing open. "The gate is open. You see?"

By now the men were beginning to understand what he was saying, but very few had the strength to do anything about it. One who did was Limber Jim, who started shouting to the heavens before he ran back to his shebang to gather his things.

Josie also understood, and, limping as quickly as he could, he hurried back. "Martin! Martin! We're exchanged!" he shouted. "We're free! We can go home, Martin! You'll see your wife and kids again!"

But Blackburn was dead. His flat, lifeless eyes and toothless mouth were open to the sky.

Tobias and Benton, hearing the news, embraced each other and began to dance. From all over the camp cheers could be heard as the news reached the farthest corners.

Limber Jack threw Patrick up in the air, then caught him as he came down. Tyce knelt, crossed himself, and began to pray.

"Oh, Martin," Josie said. "Oh, why couldn't you have hung on just a little longer? Just a little longer?"

Josie sat down beside Blackburn and folded Martin's hands across his chest. "We're free, Martin," he said. "We're free."

Josie picked up his pencil and a scrap of paper; on it he wrote: Martin Blackburn, 184 Pa. Then he took a loose thread from his shirt and used it to tie the death tag around Martin's big toe.

The celebration was in full swing now, but Josie did not join in the revelry. Instead, he sat there, trying to take it all in, to fix it in his heart and mind in order to understand it.

He saw McSpadden limp out of the shebang, and Billy, Tyce, Limber Jim, Patrick, and Samson: hundreds, then thousands, of prisoners blinking in the sun. They began stumbling and dancing around. Unable to turn off the memories of all that had happened, Josie could not join them. He felt apart from the others, living not in freedom but in memory.

Finally Josie stood with McSpadden and watched as everyone headed for the main gate. For a long moment he just stood there, not moving when McSpadden suggested that they go. Instead, he took a last look around. Again, his gaze fell upon Martin Blackburn.

"Sergeant," Josie said, "take his arms."

Josie took Blackburn's feet and, carrying their burden between them, they started to the gate.

Others, quicker and happier, passed them.

At the main gate, Lieutenant Barrett and a few armed

guards were watching the men file past them. They were looking closely at the prisoners, as if seeing them as individuals for the first time, and many of the prisoners were returning their gaze. Some, like Billy, Samson, and Limber Jim, glared back in anger. Some, like Tobias and Benton, looked at them triumphantly. And a few were even cheerful, like Patrick and Mad Matthew.

After delivering Martin's body to the Deadhouse, Josie turned to look back over the prison. It was completely deserted, not one living soul to be seen. There was nothing but the battered shebangs, the empty towers, the waste . . . and loss . . . and emptiness . . . and hollowness.

A low, thin, ground fog began creeping up from the Swamp, so that Josie's final vision of Andersonville was like a vision from hell.

With Sergeant Gleason, three days later:

Gleason was standing in the warehouse at the Andersonville depot, looking at the canvas, wood, nails, and tools. He shook his head sadly. So much equipment, so many shelters that could have been built.

Though Gleason had been unable to talk the generals into changing their policy of no exchange, he had been promised the privilege of being with the first Federal troops to reach Andersonville Prison. Yesterday, when General Sherman decided it was time to rescue the prisoners, he notified Sergeant John Gleason, and Gleason gave up his other duties in order to do this. They arrived this morning, only to discover that the prison camp was absolutely empty.

"Sergeant, all the civilians say the prisoners were taken out by train a week ago," Corporal Kincaid said to him.

Gleason turned away from the warehouse. "Did they say where?"

"They didn't know."

"What about them?" Gleason asked, pointing toward the Rebel prisoners they had captured.

"Them? What would they know, Sergeant? They're nothin' but a bunch of boys and old men. They prob'ly didn't even get here until after the prisoners were gone."

"Not true. I know *that one* was here," Gleason said, pointing to Private Allen. He walked over and stood in front of him. "How many did you wind up killing, you little pissant?" he demanded angrily.

Allen said nothing. His bottom lip began to tremble, and his eyes brimmed with tears.

"Him?" Corporal Kincaid said. He snorted. "Why, he's just a pup. If he heard a gun go off, he'd prob'ly pee in his pants."

"Yeah, a deadly pup. I know he shot at least one man for crossing the Deadline. Probably a few more."

"I was just followin' orders."

Gleason grabbed his collar and twisted it into a knot. Putting his face about one inch from the boy's face, he shouted at the top of his voice. "How many did you kill, you runty little son of a bitch!"

"Four!" the boy answered. "I killed four." By now he was sobbing. "Don't kill me. Please don't kill me."

John shoved him into the wall. "I'm not going to kill you, you chicken-shit little bastard. I'm going to have enough nightmares over the men I killed. But at least I killed them in battle. The men you killed—husbands, fathers, sons, and brothers—were innocent men. Innocent men—and you killed them for sport! I hope they haunt you for the rest of your miserable life."

"Sergeant Gleason, Corporal Kincaid," another soldier said, coming up to them. "Several of us are going to go have a look around the prison. You want to come?"

"Yes, I'd like to," Corporal Kincaid replied. "You coming, Sergeant?"

Gleason walked to the end of the depot platform and

looked toward the palisade walls and the towering guard boxes of the prison. Then he shook his head.

"No," he said. "I've seen it."

A final entry from Josie's journal:

It turned out that we weren't really being released. We weren't yet free.

The Rebels had heard Sherman's army was coming to save us, and this was a trick, a ruse to get us to walk to their train. We were taken, under guard, to other prison camps. There we stayed until the war ended.

But none of the ones we were taken to were as bad as Andersonville, and all of us survived them, excepting two of the Indiana boys, and one from Kentucky.

Epilogue

In 1864, more than thirty-two thousand Union soldiers were imprisoned in Andersonville, and almost thirteen thousand died there. Today, a National Cemetery marks their final resting place.

After the war Captain Henry Wirz, the Swiss-born commandant of Andersonville, was arrested. He was taken to Washington, where he was charged with "Conspiring to injure the health and destroy the lives of Union prisoners of war," and with "Murder in violation of the laws and customs of war."

His trial lasted for sixty-three days, and a parade of 148 witnesses gave testimony for the prosecution. Wirz attempted to shift the blame to General Winder, claiming that he had begged for more rations and better living conditions for the men in his charge, only to have Winder refuse his every request.

But Winder had died before the war's end, and the

American public, enraged at what they learned about Andersonville Prison, demanded someone be held accountable. Accountability fell to Wirz, and evidence that his counsel presented on his behalf was given little notice.

In the end, Wirz fell back upon the same excuse that would be used by the Nazi war criminals some eighty years later . . . he was only following orders. And, as with the Nazi war criminals, the excuse of "following orders" was disallowed.

On November 10, 1865, Wirz climbed a scaffold built within the shadow of the U.S. Capitol. After the execution orders were read aloud, he turned to the officer in charge and said, "I know what orders are, Major. I am being hanged for obeying them."

As he went to the gallows, he was surrounded by hundreds of former prisoners, who chanted, "Wirz, Wirz, Wirz," so that the last sound he heard was their angry condemnation of him.

Captain Wirz was the only person to be executed after the Civil War for war crimes, and his conviction and execution helped provide the precedent for the United States' participation in the Nuremberg war crimes trials.